Praise fo[r]
Cackl[e]

"Reading *Cackle* was like stumbling upon a candy cottage in a dark wood: utterly surprising, deceptively delightful, and a little bit scary, too. I gobbled it up in a weekend, cackling all the while."

—emily m. danforth, author of *Plain Bad Heroines* and *The Miseducation of Cameron Post*

"I loved every page of this gripping feminist tale."

—Alexis Henderson, author of *The Year of the Witching*

"*Cackle* is an all-too-relatable story about finding your inner strength even when you're at rock bottom, tackling the realities of post-breakup life with levity and charm. This book is an absolute delight, and everyone needs a friend like Sophie."

—Genevieve Gornichec, author of *The Witch's Heart*

"*Cackle* is that rare book that has it all: a searingly honest portrayal of all-consuming heartbreak, an exploration of the pitfalls of making new friends past thirty, a few revenge fantasies come to life, and a whole lotta witchcraft."

—Molly Pohlig, author of *The Unsuitable*

"It's no surprise that Harrison's . . . latest traffics in witchcraft, but there's nothing predictable about her take. She writes about women's autonomy and how it can be seen as a threat; about heteronormative romance and how it can suppress who women truly are. It's served in a friendship story that showcases Harrison's strength at writing powerful and empowered women with razor-sharp wit and a touch of darkness. This book wonders why this kind of woman is feared; in Harrison's hands, we're totally under their spell."

—*Library Journal* (starred review)

"*Cackle* delivers a lesson that every woman needs to hear: Embrace your inner witch! Sweet, sinister, and 100 percent delightful."

—Alma Katsu, author of *The Hunger* and *The Fervor*

"Weird, disturbing, creepy, and wonderful, *Cackle* is one of my favorite books of the year." —*Mystery & Suspense Magazine*

"As funny as it is frightening, *Cackle* by Rachel Harrison is the perfect book to cuddle up with on a crisp fall evening." —PopSugar

NOVELS BY RACHEL HARRISON

The Return

Cackle

CACKLE

Rachel Harrison

BERKLEY
New York

BERKLEY
An imprint of Penguin Random House LLC
penguinrandomhouse.com

ISBN: 9780593202036

The Library of Congress has cataloged the Berkley hardcover edition of this title as follows:

Names: Harrison, Rachel, 1989– author.
Title: Cackle / Rachel Harrison.
Description: New York : Berkley, [2021]
Identifiers: LCCN 2021008220 (print) | LCCN 2021008221 (ebook) |
ISBN 9780593202029 (hardcover) | ISBN 9780593332726 (ebook)
Classification: LCC PS3608.A78368 C33 2021 (print) | LCC PS3608.A78368 (ebook) |
DDC 813/.6—dc23
LC record available at https://lccn.loc.gov/2021008220
LC ebook record available at https://lccn.loc.gov/2021008221

Berkley hardcover edition / October 2021
Berkley trade paperback edition / August 2022

Printed in the United States of America
7th Printing

Book design by Nancy Resnick

For you! You're real magic.

FORTUNE

The sky is a strange color. Not quite red but too violent to be orange. I search for the sun, imagine it tired and bitter, slouching away after another long shift. I find it hovering over New Jersey. Poor sun.

"Annie," Nadia whines behind me, "you're bumming me out."

"Sorry," I say. I contort my mouth into what I think is a smile, but Nadia winces at the sight of it, so I'm guessing the attempt is unsuccessful.

"Girl," she says, "pull it together! It's your birthday."

I groan.

"All right, all right," she says, roping her arm around me. "Let's get you wasted."

We dodge the bags of trash reclining on every curb, avoid the rogue dog turds swarming with flies, unashamed in the middle of the sidewalk. When I first moved to New York City twelve years ago, starry-eyed and energetic, a college freshman, it didn't seem so dirty. I can't tell if it was because I was young then, charmed by the skyline, always looking up, or if it used to be cleaner.

"Here," Nadia says, putting her hands on my shoulders and ushering me into a random bar. It's almost chic. Draped-bead chandeliers hang from a high ceiling. The place is crowded with couches and mismatched armchairs, stuffing sneaking out through straining seams. Nadia directs me to two stools in the corner where the counter disappears into the wall.

"Perfect," she purrs. She's wearing a low-cut leopard-print jumpsuit, which at first I thought was a smidge much, but now that we've received immediate attention from the bartender, I'm beginning to appreciate her strategic fashion choice.

She orders us vodka lemonades and tequila shots.

I've been out with Nadia only once before, at a karaoke fundraiser for our school that was near torture. She performed an earnest cover of Natalie Imbruglia's "Torn." I sat squirming in the corner, anticipating a flood of secondhand embarrassment, but the crowd was surprisingly into it.

I watch her now, as she sticks her pink acrylics into the bowl of assorted nuts on the bar. She tilts her head to the side, searching for a specific nut, exposing her long, delicate neck. Her hair is dark and thick and falls down past her shoulders, curving like a chain of crescent moons. She's got false lashes that are in a constant flutter.

She teaches biology. She's good at it, too. At school, she doesn't wear a lick of makeup. All the students whisper about how she's the hottest teacher.

It doesn't matter how old you get. A superlative will always be insulting when it's awarded to anyone but you.

The bartender drops the shots in front of us. They're accompanied by a tiny plate with two lime wedges and a crusty saltshaker.

Nadia lifts up one of the shots. "To you. And your new job. Oh, and fuck your ex."

She takes her shot.

I take mine, too. The mention of Sam is like an ice pick to the sternum. I begin to count the bottles of liquor lined up behind the bar. Are there enough? In this bar? In this city? In the tristate area? How much will it take?

"It's all happening," Nadia says, snapping her fingers as our cocktails arrive. "New job. New city."

"It's not a city," I say. "It's a small town no one's ever heard of."

"Yeah," she says, and pauses to aggressively suck the remaining juice from her lime wedge. "But that's how all romance movies start. You're going to move to this, like, small-ass town and meet some brooding lumberjack, and he's going to be named Lucien and have a six-pack even though he's a low-key alcoholic. He'll live in a trailer and have a tragic past. It'll be great."

"Sounds great," I say, my voice flat.

She nudges me. "Oh, come on, Annie. Loosen up! Have some fun. It's your birthday!"

I wish she would stop reminding me of that.

I hadn't planned on spending my thirtieth birthday with a coworker I barely know who just ate a bar cashew out of her cleavage, or drinking a vodka cocktail that's going down smooth as battery acid. Admittedly, it's not the worst. It's just not what I had envisioned.

I saw myself with Sam. On vacation somewhere. Butchering the French language while attempting to order food at a café in Montmartre, in the shadow of the Sacré-Coeur. Or in London contemplating the paintings at the Tate Modern and having cream tea, then smuggling back Cadbury bars in our suitcases. Or a simple weekend trip to the Hudson Valley or Mystic, somewhere we could take the train to and get a nice hotel room with a big tub and laze around in those cozy robes.

"Okay," she says. "What is it? Is it him? Are you thinking about him? Is it thirty? Because thirty is not old, okay?"

She's twenty-seven.

"It's all of it," I say. "I'm sorry. It was nice of you to come out with me."

She raises an expertly shaped eyebrow. "I told you all year we should go out. You were, like, not about it. Look, I don't know you that well. But I know you're not a super-social person. And it's easy not to be social when you, like, have a person at home who's there all the time. What I'm saying is, basically, maybe this is a good thing for you. You can get out there. Meet new people. Live your life."

"I guess," I say. Unfortunately for me, "getting out there" and "meeting new people" are among my least favorite things. I've forgotten how. The years since college have eroded my social skills, and I'm shy to begin with. I prefer the couch. I prefer familiarity.

I prefer Sam.

"Here," she says. She reaches out for a small tea light candle and lifts it up, the yellow flame spasming, the wick decaying. "Make a wish."

"You're serious?" I ask her. In this moment, I do regret not going out with Nadia sooner. I bet she's a good friend. She seems like one of those people who are born knowing exactly who they are. Her entire personality written in the stars, set in concrete.

"Yes," she says. "Quick! Before it burns out!"

I close my eyes and think.

We leave a collection of glasses sweating on the bar, along with a wad of crumpled bills and enough rinds to generously zest a pie. We stagger out into the June night, the air thick, sticky and sweet as syrup. It's going to be a hot summer. For the first time, I'm sincerely relieved to be leaving the city. I won't miss the humidity, thighs sticking to the seats on the subway, everyone grumpy and perspiring, any amount of deodorant rendered inadequate.

Nadia is on a quest for her favorite pizza slice. It's at some hole-in-the-wall place in the West Village she used to frequent during her "partying days." If her partying days are behind her, I'm a little curious what they were like, because right now she's saying hello to strangers in a truly horrendous British accent while somehow balancing on the tallest heels I've ever seen. On a cracked asymmetrical sidewalk. While drunk!

This must be a practiced skill.

I scamper behind her, the bumbling sidekick in a pair of practical flats.

"It used to be right here, I swear," she says as we stand on a side street at the foot of a domestic brownstone. She sighs, and it's interrupted by a single faint hiccup. We're far too drunk for this.

"We should call it," I say.

"It's ten o'clock," she says.

I'm assuming by her horrified expression that she thinks ten o'clock is early. I'm of a different opinion. Ten o'clock is bedtime.

"Okay?"

"We're not giving up on pizza," she says, and hurries down the block, faster than expected, considering her shoes.

I follow her, breaking into a light jog as she disappears around the corner.

"Nadia?"

She's hopping up and down, one set of fingers stuffed in her mouth, while another finger points down the street.

"What is it?" I ask her.

"Look!" she squeals. "We're going."

I turn my murky drunken gaze in the direction she's pointing. It takes a few seconds for my eyes to focus on what's there. A neon sign floating in a glass window. A crystal ball.

"No," I say.

She seizes my wrist. "We're getting our palms read."

"Nope."

She's laughing. I'm not quite sure why, but she's got a fun laugh. It's loud and melodic.

"Please, please, please! It's probably extra accurate to get read on your birthday."

"Accurate," I repeat. Now I'm laughing. I'm laughing so hard I can barely stand; I'm hunched like a wilting flower, arms limp.

"It'll be fun," she says.

"Famous last words."

"Annie. Puh-leeeeasssse." In the orangey glow from the streetlamp, her eyes look crazed and inhuman.

"Okay," I say. "But if this goes poorly, I'll do nothing about it and suffer in silence."

"Yay!" she says, clapping and twirling around. The light from the lamp streaks through her black hair, and it looks like lightning threading a dark night sky.

She reaches out for my hand and I give it to her. She swings it back and forth, taking my arm with it. The closer we get, the more I regret agreeing to this. My apprehension quickly mutates into dread. The dread elbows around my chest like a stranger with somewhere to be. By the time we're standing at the door, engulfed in the neon haze from the crystal ball, I'm certain I do not want to do this. Above the crystal ball, there's another neon sign, on but barely functioning, sputtering and pale, that reads PSYCHIC.

It's literally a bad sign.

But it's too late to object. Nadia is already pushing open the door. A bell chimes somewhere above us.

Thick curls of smoke writhe across the room. It smells of incense and antiques, like basement furniture. The smoke stings my eyes and monopolizes my lungs. I try, unsuccessfully, to stifle a series of awkward coughs.

"Hello, hello," says a disembodied voice. A woman emerges from behind a velvet curtain. She's short and covered in scarves. Her hair is in a chaotic bun. She's older. The deep wrinkles on her forehead remind me of the small, illegible script on historical documents. A constitution or peace treaty.

"Hiiiiii," Nadia sings. "We're here for readings."

"Yes," the woman says. "Welcome. My name is Atlas."

She looks more like a Linda to me.

"What kind of readings?" she asks us. "I do a fifteen-minute tarot, half an hour, and a full hour. Ten-minute palm. I could also do birth charts, chakras, numerology."

"Palm," Nadia says. She turns to me for my approval.

"Sure," I say.

"Okay," Atlas says, smiling at us. She's got a gold tooth. I wonder if it's real. "Who's first?"

"She is," I say, pushing Nadia forward.

She doesn't mind. "Me!" she says, swaying her hips back and forth.

"All right, here we go," Atlas says, lifting the curtain for Nadia. They both disappear behind it, leaving me alone.

I wasn't aware that a palm reading was a private affair.

The smoke has dispersed, revealing a room of excess. Congested bookcases. Ceramic figurines perched on crooked shelves. The walls are busy with a variety of charts and maps and the signs of the zodiac, various celestial bodies.

I eye the door. I could leave. I could bail. Nadia might get mad, but that doesn't really matter. We're not close, and I'm about to move hours away. We'll probably never see each other again after tonight.

I shouldn't. If it weren't for her, I'd be sitting at home alone on my birthday. My alternate plan was to cry in the fetal position while listening to "Landslide" on repeat.

I can stick it out.

There's a soft noise, like the hum of an invisible bird. Then a sudden *ding* that sends my shoulders knocking against my ears. I turn around, searching for the source, and find an intricate clock mounted high on the wall. I need to tilt my head back to see its face. Faces. It has two, both enclosed in a tower of carved wood. Despite being pretty tall, I need to stand on my tiptoes to examine further.

The bottom face tells time, but I can't read the top. It's strange and complex, with multiple cogs and golden hands moving in all different directions over a kaleidoscope of colors. Green, orange, yellow, blue, pink. The longer I stare, the more the colors blend together, like in a mood ring. It's purple now. There must be some kind of liquid inside. Mercury? As it morphs, I can almost make out a shape. What's maybe a flower.

"Oooh, cool clock!" Nadia says, popping up behind me. "Your turn."

"What'd she say?" I ask her.

"That I'm going to be filthy rich!" she says. "Just kidding. I'll tell you after."

"Through there?" I point to the curtain.

"Yup!"

I lift the curtain back and duck underneath it. There's a short hallway that widens into a circular room. In the center is a round table draped in layers of silky fabric. It's slightly askew on a stack of Persian rugs. Two mismatched wooden chairs are tucked underneath. One of them is occupied by Atlas, who is shuffling a deck of tarot cards.

"Please, have a seat," she says, gesturing to the other chair.

I'm ready to get this over with. I step onto the rugs and seat myself in the chair. I wonder how many people have sat in it before me and what brought them here. A pushy friend. Spontaneity. Curiosity. Desperation.

Maybe I'm letting my cynicism deprive me of a positive experience. Even if this is nonsense, won't it be a comfort to hear about a future, any future, that could possibly be mine? To temporarily escape the pain of the present and be reminded that one day this will be behind me? That I won't wake up every day feeling like my chest is full of stones. That I won't be constantly thinking about Sam or about everything I might have done to prevent myself from ending up where I am now.

Maybe there's someone or something in my future worth moving toward. A dangling carrot.

Atlas sets the deck of cards aside. She reaches for my hand and I give it to her. She takes a deep breath, her heavily lined eyes closing. They stay closed for a long time. Too long.

Should I be closing my eyes?

Her eyes open. I wish they were still closed. They're gloomy and awful. She's grimacing.

"You have dark energy," she says.

"Sorry," I say, because what else?

She unfolds my hand. She squints. She shakes her head.

She pulls my hand closer. Since my hand is connected to my arm, which is connected to the rest of me, something she doesn't seem to realize, my entire body jerks forward, my ribs slamming against the table.

She leans over and turns on a table lamp. I recognize it. It's from IKEA. I imagine Atlas roaming around IKEA in all of her scarves, letting the spirits guide her. It takes the edge off of my current situation.

Atlas is examining my palm like it's an unexpected medical bill. Like the insurance actually isn't going to cover it.

I did not anticipate this. I'm too afraid to ask her what the problem is, so I sit silently, studying the cuticles on my free hand.

She's shaking her head and making a noise like she's chastising me. *Tsk, tsk, tsk.*

I can't believe this is happening, but at the same time, of course this is happening. I relent.

I ask, "What is it?"

Her brow is furrowed so deeply I can no longer see her eyes. She's making no effort to look at me. She's too busy with my hand.

"It is your birthday?" she asks me.

Nadia must have told her.

"Yeah," I say.

She sighs, then folds my hand and returns it to me, pushing it back across the table.

"Happy birthday," she says. She looks up at me finally, and her eyes are bulging. She's clearly upset about something.

"What's wrong?" I ask her.

She hesitates. Swallows. Adjusts her choker, a series of stars on a thin silver chain.

"Your life, your future, your fate . . . it's shrouded in uncertainty. I sense a darkness. It's all I can see," she says. "I'm sorry."

"Oh," I say. I wipe my hand on my jeans. It grew sweaty during its time in her too-firm grasp. "That's okay. It's fine."

I wait for her to wish me well or offer me an aura cleanse or specifics about a short life line, something. But she doesn't say anything, doesn't move. She remains in her chair with a look that's equal parts sour and distressed. I can't tell if she feels sorry for me, or if she's about to chase me out of here with a vial of holy water and a crucifix.

I nod at her, muttering a quick thanks as I hurry away, out through the velvet curtain. On the other side, Nadia stands in front of one of the bookshelves with her hands on her hips.

She's surprised to see me.

"That was fast," she says. "What happened?"

"I don't know. I'm shrouded in darkness."

"What did she say?"

"Nothing. Can we go?"

Nadia is fun, sweet and bubbly as Coca-Cola, but she's not so happy-go-lucky she can't tell when something's wrong. She says, "Yeah, let's go."

As we turn to leave, I catch Atlas poking her head through the curtains. Her face is drained of color. It floats before the dark velvet like an ominous moon.

I look at Nadia, wide eyes asking, *Are you seeing this?*

She clutches my wrist as confirmation.

We bolt for the door. When we're outside, we don't slow down. We speed up. We don't stop. We run for two blocks, until we're out of breath.

"I mean," she says, "really?"

"She looked at my hand like this," I say, doing my best impression, "and then was like, 'Happy birthday.'"

"So weird," Nadia says.

"Yeah, happy birthday to me and my dark energy."

"She told me I'm going to marry the love of my life at twenty-eight. That's next year! I'm not even dating anyone I'm that into right now. She said his name won't be his name—whatever that means. I'm going to have one son and move somewhere warm, like Florida or California."

"Sounds nice. Except the Florida part."

"What's wrong with Florida?"

"Nothing," I say. "Never mind."

"I'm sorry," she says. "That was supposed to be fun."

"That's okay," I say. "Let's just forget it ever happened."

As we walk, I listen to the sound of her heels click-clacking on the gum-spotted city sidewalk. I listen to drunk strangers in loud conversation. I listen to the distant scream of sirens, the throbbing bass escaping from bars whenever the bouncers open the doors for shrill young girls in skintight dresses flashing their IDs.

The emotional scaffolding that I put up earlier today in preparation for this night out is beginning to come down. I feel old and sad and hopeless. The psychic didn't help, but it's not her fault. My future is dark.

Leaving the city after twelve years, leaving my apartment, the one I shared with Sam, my now ex-boyfriend but still best friend. I can't afford to stay. I can barely afford to leave.

I had no choice but to take the teaching position upstate. I'm going to be living alone in a small town where I don't know anyone. I had never even heard of Rowan before. When that psychic looked into my future, she probably saw a lot of streaming services and microwavable dinners and crying, and I don't know . . . probably cats.

I guess I like cats all right.

"Don't let her get to you," Nadia says.

"It's not that."

"What is it?"

"I'm thirty. Thirty years old. Single . . ."

Nadia clutches her chest. "The scandal."

"There's a stigma. The spinster. I didn't picture . . . I don't know. Never mind."

"It's not like that anymore. Everyone talks about how your thirties are so great. Like, you spend your twenties figuring out who you are, and then you can enjoy your thirties."

"I know," I tell her. "That's what makes it worse. I don't have anything figured out."

"Don't assume everything is going to be bad, Annie. Have some faith."

She spins around and puts her arms up.

She's found it. The pizzeria. We're here.

She leads me inside and we each get greasy slices of pepperoni. We eat them off of flaccid paper plates while sitting on the curb, sipping from the same can of Diet Coke.

When we're done, Nadia calls a car for me. She tells me, "Everything is gonna be great, Annie. You're gonna be great. If life gives you any trouble, punch it in the face. You got this."

She blows me kisses and closes the door.

I cry because I miss her already, because of the friendship we could have had.

The driver turns the music up to drown me out.

When I get home, the futon is pulled out for me, made up with sheets and blankets and two pillows, one with a silk case. Sam is asleep in the bed we used to share. We've been alternating bed and futon, futon and bed. It was hard at first, but I'm used to it now.

That's a lie. It's still hard. I hate it.

I take my shoes off but don't bother to change into the pajamas he laid out for me on the coffee table, along with a glass of water and a lone birthday cupcake. There's a card, too. I open the envelope, swatting aside the false hope that inside it will be a change of heart.

The card has a T. rex wearing a party hat on the front and inside it reads *Hope your birthday is Dino-mite!*

I laugh because it's funny, and because it's 100 percent Sam. I set the card back down on the coffee table, eat the frosting off of the cupcake, close my eyes and fall right asleep.

I wake up to discover a small spray of vomit across my pillow. I remove the case and wash it in the bathroom sink, then hang it over the shower rod to dry. I brush my teeth and take three Advils instead of the recommended dose of two, because I'm hard like that.

I've stumbled into the living room, ready to go back to sleep, when I hear rustling in the kitchen. Sam is in there, standing at the counter making coffee. His hair is crazy, as usual. I always tell him he looks like a mad scientist emerging from the lab after an experiment has gone awry.

He takes it as a compliment.

"Morning," he says. "You were talking in your sleep again."

"What'd I say? Anything interesting?"

"Something about who killed JFK, the identity of the second shooter. Don't know. Wasn't really paying attention. You want coffee?"

"Yes, please."

"How was last night?"

"Pretty fun," I say. "Except she dragged me to a psychic who said I have dark energy."

"Ah," he says. "Well, I guess you're fucked, then."

"Totally fucked."

He pours my coffee first, adds two packets of Stevia and only a splash of half-and-half. Exactly how I like it. He pushes my mug across the counter.

"What'd you do last night?" I ask him. It's a casual question, a standard conversation starter. But there's a brief flicker of suspicion that passes across his face. He thinks I'm fishing. He thinks I'm asking, *Where were you last night? Whom were you with?*

I wasn't, but now his reaction has me wondering.

"Nothing too exciting," he says. "Worked late. Made spaghetti. Then, you know . . . my vigilante stuff. Mask, cape, gadgets, catching bad guys, fighting crime."

"Right, right."

"Then got some bodega snacks, watched the Cooking Channel and went to bed."

"Combos and Oreos?"

"Famous Amos."

"Close. I was close."

"Yeah," he says. He's looking elsewhere. He seems particularly fascinated by a certain point on the ceiling.

"All right," I say. "Well, I'm just going to be hanging today. So . . ."

"I'll be out of your hair," he says. He inhales deeply, squints into his coffee. He's pondering something. "You want eggs? I was going to make eggs."

"Fancy Cooking Channel eggs?"

"No," he says. "Just regular eggs."

"Then okay," I say. "Sure."

I sit at the table and watch him take the eggs out of the fridge, butter the skillet, break the eggs into a bowl, whisk them. We've had so many mornings identical to this one. The same silly banter, the streams of sunlight coming through the window creating the same lattice patterns across the kitchen floor.

I replay the conversation. Us sitting on opposite sides of the couch on a lazy, rainy afternoon in late April, a nineties sitcom muted on the TV, me hugging a pillow, him playing with the fringes on the throw blanket.

"I guess I just don't feel the way I know I should," he'd said. I honestly can't even remember how marriage came up, which, in retrospect, is likely because I'd been bringing it up too much. Working it into conversations where it didn't belong. Dropping hint after not-so-subtle hint. This one just happened to be the one too many.

"Oh," I said. What was most shocking to me about that moment was that it wasn't shocking at all. I didn't know it was coming, so how had I known it was coming?

"I don't want to have this conversation," he said, pinching the skin at the bridge of his nose, like he always does when he's upset. "I really don't. But we can't keep avoiding it."

"Okay," I said.

"I've been feeling, for a while, that we're more like friends," he said. "It's just . . . do . . . do we love each other anymore?"

I couldn't answer the question. Any words I could hope to speak drowned in my throat. Words like "yes" and "of course" and "always."

"That came out wrong," he said. "I meant, are we *in* love? Because I feel like the spark we used to have, it's just fizzled. Over time. It fizzled. And now we're basically roommates. Roommates who have sex, sometimes."

The way he stressed the "sometimes." It was decimating.

"Do you think we could work on it?" I asked, my voice anemic. "We could . . . I could try."

He sighed. "It's on me. I should have brought it up sooner. I was scared. I didn't want to lose you. As a friend. You're my best friend."

Eventually, I said the only thing I could think to say. "You're my best friend, too."

"We're good as friends," he said. "That's our dynamic. That's how it's been, for a long time. And I just think it's for the best. We can't keep pretending our relationship is something it's not. We can't force it anymore."

I stuttered.

"And if we're just friends, if we see what it's like to just be friends, we'll know," he said. "We'll know either way, right?"

I couldn't stand the embarrassment of arguing. I couldn't bring myself to beg for him to want me, to love me the way that I loved him. And I couldn't risk losing him altogether. I had to keep him in my life, even if it was just as a friend. He was my world. I needed him. I still do.

I nodded, and that was the end.

He's currently presenting me with a plate of perfectly fluffy yellow eggs. He sits across from me and raises his mug. I raise mine, and we clink.

"Gesundheit," he says.

"Gesundheit," I say, my insides twisting with ache.

What if I'd said something different? That afternoon in April. Would it have changed anything? Or would we still be here drinking coffee, biding our time before the paths of our lives split?

A few weeks later, I kneel in my closet beside an open suitcase. All of my clothes smell like him. The void goes on and on, like a magician pulling scarves out of a hat.

THE ARRIVAL

It's early morning, and a generous fog sheathes this stretch of highway. I can hear my things bouncing around in the back, the slide of cardboard, the rattle of the zippers on my suitcase. Something clinking. I look forward to unpacking. Should be a fun surprise to see what has leaked, what has broken.

I've been driving around in silence like a serial killer because every song that comes on feels like a bad omen, either too sad or too optimistic.

I make quick eye contact with myself in the rearview mirror. Maybe I should have gotten a facial before leaving the city. Had an aesthetician extract the bad energy from my pores. Exfoliate the past away.

There are some things you can pay for that will greatly improve your appearance, your circumstances. I can't afford most of those things. But I can afford McDonald's.

I pull into a drive-through and get a greasy breakfast sandwich and a coffee that tastes like dessert. I eat in the parking lot, watching the sun rise, the hint of a blue day prodding the soft lavender dawn. I watch as the fog tumbles away, fading between the distant trees and houses, leaving behind an ordinary wet morning.

It's good to drive again. There's something elating about being behind the wheel of your own car. It's an unbridled freedom. Granted, this car is a 2006 Toyota Camry with 130 thousand miles on it, but . . . it drives. And it's brought me here, to this McDonald's somewhere upstate, somewhere closer to where I'm going than to where I came from.

I leave the used, grease-spotted napkins in a pile on the passenger's seat and drive on, listening only to the shift of my things, the sound of my life rearranging itself.

It's a white clapboard house with a steeply pitched roof and a leaning redbrick chimney. The windows are tall and narrow, wedged inside thick white trim, each with its own flower box. The lawn is neat and green.

It's dreamy.

I pull up to the end of the driveway, park and get out of the car. I shake out my legs. They're stiff from the drive or because I'm thirty now. Hard to say.

There's a door toward the back of the house and beside it a squat ceramic frog. As advertised. Lynn, the woman renting me the top-floor apartment, is out of town for work. She told me she'd leave the keys in the frog. I lean down to lift him up. He's oddly lifelike. My mind ribbits just to mess with me.

"You're not real," I tell Mr. Frog. He looks back at me with his painted black eyes, indignant.

I remove his head and reach inside for the keys. They're attached to a gold key ring with a daisy charm. I reassemble the frog and place him gently back on the ground.

"Thank you, sir," I tell him.

I unlock the door. The stairs run parallel to the side of the house.

Three-quarters of the way up, there's a small landing, and the stairs veer right. It's more disorienting than it should be, maybe because of how narrow the stairs are or how stuffy it is without any windows, any circulation of air. It's got that distinct attic smell, like mothballs, like untreated wood.

There's a lone lightbulb glowing weakly above me.

A few steps up from the landing is the door to my apartment, to my new home. I take a deep, nervous breath.

"Here we go."

Inside, it's bright and clean. Even nicer than in the pictures, which is a welcome surprise. There are built-in bookcases. A small fireplace, a comfy-looking couch. In the bedroom, there are a queen-sized bed, a double dresser, a full-length mirror and a petite writing desk with a swivel chair. There's a large window with a built-in bench that faces out to the front yard and, beyond it, the street. Maple Street. According to the map, Maple angles into Main Street a little farther down. Still, I doubt there will be a lot of traffic in front of the house. It's a sleepy place. I crack the window and listen for cars. There's only the soft chorus of nature. Gently rustling leaves, the faint whistle of birdsong.

The air smells so clean. I sit on the naked mattress and breathe it in.

The mattress is pretty comfortable. It's firm, not the memory foam cloud Sam and I shared, but it's better than the pullout. I'm grateful this apartment came furnished. Any furniture I had was actually Sam's, or it was so cheap it was falling apart and wouldn't have survived the journey.

Back in the living room, there's a door sandwiched between the bedroom on the left and the front door on the right. It leads to a tiny bathroom, barely big enough to turn around in. Tub, sink, toilet.

There's a mirror above the sink. I press it and it swings open toward me, revealing an empty medicine cabinet. I leave it open, mirror to the wall. I absolutely do not need to see what I look like right now.

I leave the bathroom and explore the rest of the apartment. At the back, there's a small dining area with a round midcentury table-and-chair set. There are two windows, and between them is a tall reedy plant I apologize to in advance. I've got a poor track record with plants. It's not neglect; if anything, it's overattentiveness. I obsessively water, readjust, ask how they're feeling, if they need anything. Maybe more sunlight? I exhaust them to death.

I've got dirt on my hands.

I wonder if that's what happened to my relationship. Did I exhaust Sam? His love for me?

Or was it the opposite? Did I not give him the same love and attention I give to houseplants?

I sigh, position myself inside the left window and rest my head against the glass. It's cool, and it relaxes me immediately.

I look out to the backyard. It gets lovely shade, surrounded on all sides by dense woods. I watch the leaves gleam in the afternoon sun, shimmy in the breeze.

My phone vibrates in my back pocket.

Sam texted. He wrote, Get there okay?

I reply, Yes. Picked up a few hitchhikers. Seem pretty nice. Making a pit stop at their human farm. Never been to one. Could be fun!

I regret it immediately after I hit SEND. *Human farm?*

I'm trying too hard to maintain our banter, or at least some semblance of normalcy in our relationship. I want to keep it stable, as if it's a volatile chemical. I'm afraid if there's any change too drastic, it'll either disintegrate or explode.

I return my gaze to the woods. They're so lush. I'm not used to being surrounded by this much nature. It's calming, I think. Maybe just a little bit terrifying? I can't shake the feeling the woods are looking back at me, sizing me up just the same as I am them.

I step back from the window.

There's a little kitchen off of the dining space. Pink linoleum flooring, old wooden cabinets with a fresh coat of white paint to match the rest of the apartment. The appliances are old, the fridge snoring in the corner, but I don't mind. On the counter, there's a pretty bouquet of flowers in a mason jar vase. Pink carnations, baby's breath, purple aster and deep burgundy roses. There's another flower, big and purple, but I'm not sure what it is. I lean down to smell it and immediately sneeze.

I apologize to the now snot-covered petals.

Next to the flowers is a note from Lynn.

Welcome, Annie! Call if you need anything!

It's such a sweet gesture, I could cry. I take a slow breath and set my palms flat on the counter.

I see him.

A tiny black spider ambling just beyond my fingertips. He is not hurried. He is small and smooth, his legs are long and he lifts them high as he goes, almost like in a little march.

"Buddy," I say.

I find a glass to catch him under. I slide Lynn's note underneath the spider. I walk over to the window, unlock it and pull it open. It takes some effort, the window stiff and stubborn.

"All right, guy," I tell the spider. I release him, carefully, onto the ledge outside. "You're not afraid of heights, are you?"

He's not. He continues his march toward the siding. I close the window.

I spend the next few hours lugging my stuff up from the car and unpacking. I hang clothes in the closet. I make up the bed with my new bedding, wrestle with the top sheet. I put my books on the shelves, arranging them alphabetically, only to change my mind and rearrange by color and then again by which books I think would be friends. I find another spider on one of the shelves. I catch him under the same glass. I take him downstairs and set him free on the driveway.

"Go find your friends," I tell him as I get my last bag out of the trunk.

I unpack my shampoo and conditioner and bodywash, set them on the ledge of the tub. I put my lotions and potions inside the mirror cabinet. Toothpaste and sunscreen and various moisturizers and a new citrusy perfume I'm trying out. It makes me smell like a new person. The person I'm trying to be. It's aspirational perfume.

I wash my hands, splash some water on my face.

When I look up, there's a spider. Yet another spider. This one is much bigger. He's a different shape. He has a distinct head and body. The same long, spindly legs. He's slinking along the edge of the sink. I think he's attempting to be stealthy. He extends his legs far ahead, staying low.

"I see you," I tell him. "You're coming with me."

I have to fetch the glass from the kitchen, where it's drying facedown on the dish rack after two thorough cleanings.

"This is my house," I tell him as I usher him onto the windowsill. "It's not your house. That's your house."

I point to the woods. He doesn't move. I close the window, leaving him to figure it out on his own.

By the time I finish unpacking, the sun dips below the trees, and I make a lap around the apartment, flipping on every lamp, every light switch. I didn't realize earlier that there are no curtains. No blinds. I'm in a fishbowl.

I check my phone. A response from Sam: Ha ha. Call me later, if you want.

I call him immediately.

"You stop at McDonald's or Wendy's?" he asks.

"McDonald's."

"Left to your own devices. We've been over this. Wendy's is far superior."

"I like McDonald's. I was raised on McDonald's," I say. "Cut me some slack."

"You want that cut thin, thick or cubed?"

Maybe this is hard for him, too. Harder than he anticipated. Not having me home. We've cohabitated for so many years in that space. My not being there must be strange for him.

"How's the place?" he asks.

"Good. Pictures weren't fakes, so that's a relief. It's a nice apartment. Very bright. I'll need to get some curtains, though. It was fine during the day but it's kind of creepy now."

I walk over to the front window and peer outside. A car is coming down the street. The speed limit on Maple is twenty-five, but this car must be going under that. It's crawling.

The car's interior light is on, and I can see people inside. Two in the front, one in the back. They're far away. Blurred by the distance and distorted by the glass. But I think they're looking at me. I squint.

Yeah. They're not in profile, not facing the road ahead. They're turned toward me; their eyes are on me. I feel the hot grip of their stares.

"Annie?" Sam asks. "You there?"

"Yep," I say. I stand back from the window. The car passes, the red glow of its taillights retreating into the silky darkness of the August night.

"Sorry," I say. I shuffle into the bedroom and spread myself across the mattress. "I'm here."

"I'll, uh, actually I'll let you go," he says.

"Oh. Okay."

"Wanted to make sure you got there in one piece."

"Let me double-check," I say. I do. I check. I feel around my body. Is it all here? "Yep. One piece."

He laughs. It's his laugh lite. His *this is amusing but not genuinely funny* laugh.

"Night, Annie."

"Good night, Sam."

He hangs up before me. I hear it. That horrible disconnecting noise.

I roll over onto my stomach. It's strange. Sam and I have been sleeping separately for months, and I'm still not used to it. I want to be, but I'm not. I wonder if I'll ever get used to sleeping alone or if, from now on, I'll go to bed huddled up to one side, waiting in vain for warmth beside me.

It's so easy to adjust when you're newly in love, when you're all gooey, soft and malleable as an infant's skull. You make so much space in your life and in your heart, and when the person you love leaves, you're all stretched out. There's so much room inside me that I don't know what to do with, space I don't know how to fill. I've been waiting for it to shrivel up, for me to take my former shape, to be how I was before I met him, but it's not happening.

It's been so long; I don't even remember who I was before him.

On Main Street in Rowan, there's a sign that reads WELCOME TO ROWAN, AMERICA'S BEST-KEPT SECRET.

I can't even scoff, can't even roll my eyes at the pure Velveeta cheesiness. All I can do is nod in agreement as I drive through town for the first time. It's so quaint it makes my insides warm, and I can feel them churn with instant affection. That new-crush endorphin surge. I bet there are little hearts where my eyes used to be.

The short stretch of Main Street is lined with shops, each one more whimsical than the last. They're all different colors: pale yellow, neon pink, deep teal, muted beige. They vary in style. Some have that classic general store vibe. Colonial boxes, windows with distinct muntin bars, front-sloped roofs and gabled dormers. A few of the shops look like they've been transported from a small village in Europe, like they're made of gingerbread. Others are right out of a Norman Rockwell townscape. Perfect rectangles with vibrant red bricks and decorative cornice molding.

There are petite manicured trees interspersed with flowery bushes along the sidewalks. The lampposts are beautiful Victorian relics. Black cast iron. Flowerpots drape from their arms, all filled with yellow daisies.

I half expect a bunch of adorable children clad in matching outfits to pop out of the bushes and start harmonizing while performing a choreographed dance. Townsfolk in suspenders to emerge from the shops, burst out of the doors and windows to bid me *bonjour.*

I spot a few people out and about. There's a woman in a linen dress and a wide-brimmed sun hat walking her dachshund. There's a tall man in a polo shirt and cargo shorts carrying cups of labelless take-out coffee.

They both seem happy.

Past the rows of shops there are a few lonelier buildings set back from the road. An old geezer of a place with intimidating columns and a gilded eagle on top, probably a bank or municipal something or other. There's a retro train car diner, the most delightful one I've ever seen. A bit farther down the road, there's a small pond, and behind it, secluded in the trees, is a little stone church with an arched door and a steeple.

My phone yells at me to make a right at the stoplight. I do, and that's it. That's Rowan.

There's another sign; this one reads NOW LEAVING ROWAN. KEEP OUR SECRET.

If the town weren't so precious, the sign might be off-putting. But I don't know. It works for me. I get it.

My cheeks ache, trying to resist my giddy smile.

I'm in on the secret!

I roll the windows down. The occasional breeze carries a faint cinnamony smell.

I think about what brought me here. Sam and me breaking up. Not being able to afford to stay in New York City without him. Getting sad and panicky. Crying. In the shower. On the subway. In Starbucks. I was crying into a venti caramel consolation latte when I ran into Matt, an old classmate of mine from NYU. I told him about the breakup, in perhaps more detail than necessary. I said I needed a change of scenery and, more important, a new job. He took pity on me. He knew someone who knew someone who knew about this opening.

I didn't really have any other options. Or I was just too dejected and lazy to go looking for them.

When I did my initial Google search, I didn't look for Rowan. I looked for Aster. Aster neighbors Rowan to the north. It's significantly bigger and—I can see now—entirely less charming. There are strip malls, chain stores. An Applebee's.

I stumbled across Rowan only by chance, on a random housing site during my desperate hunt for a cheap apartment. It's a longer commute, a little over half an hour to Aster High, but I got over it pretty quickly once I put it into perspective. Thirtyish minutes alone in my car versus the horrific, often sticky variables of a subway ride. I told myself it wouldn't be so bad, and I was right. It isn't.

And I'm grateful now that I'm not in Aster. I'm grateful to be in Rowan, despite having to get up earlier and spend more money on gas. The town is so picturesque, so idyllic, it's nudged me somewhere closer to the realm of hope for my future here. Somewhere almost adjacent to excitement.

—

Aster High School is a sweatbox. After a long orientation, an AP English teacher named Roberta escorts me to my classroom in the basement. It's small and windowless and smells of mildew. But I wasn't expecting Xanadu. I have a back closet for books and two big, slick new whiteboards. Exciting stuff.

"Let me know if you need anything," Roberta says, already out the door. I hear her loafers squeak down the hall.

I spend the rest of the day cleaning, gradually getting dustier and dustier until I'm filthy and the classroom is . . . looking about the same. Nothing looks clean under fluorescent lights.

There's not much more I can do. I'm exhausted, and I still have another few days until school actually starts, so I give myself permission to leave. I stop at the TJ Maxx in Aster for some cheap curtains, then drive across the parking lot to the grocery store. It's called Tops Friendly Markets.

I don't find it any friendlier than the average grocery store, which disappoints me more than it should. I buy apples, eggs, guacamole, pita chips, ginger ale and multiple frozen pizzas. I make an impulse purchase of birthday-cake-flavored gum. It doesn't taste even remotely like birthday cake.

Yet another disappointment.

On the drive home, as I chew the bland gum, a negative thought begins to worm around my brain.

Isn't it classic me? To put faith in something implausible, like a grocery store with an exceptionally friendly staff, like birthday-cake-flavored gum, like a storybook happily ever after, like true love. Whenever I'm let down by reality, I'm simultaneously shocked and embarrassed by my lack of ability to anticipate the completely predictable outcome.

I attempt to spit the gum out my window, but it gets stuck on the side of my car.

By the time I get to Main Street in Rowan, there's a sinkhole opening in my chest. All I can think about is how sad I am and how I can't escape the sadness because I *feel* it. It's coursing through my body with the swift ruthlessness of the flu. I can barely hold the steering wheel. I don't have the strength.

I have to pull over.

I park in the first open spot I see. It's in front of a squat cottage. It kind of looks like a mushroom. Brown roof, white stem of building. The door is comically short, and on either side, there are two round windows. There's no sign.

The cottage looks funny next to its neighbor, a neon pink building, the loudest one in town. Luckily, that shop has a sign I can read: SIMPLE SPIRITS, WINE & LIQUOR.

I don't really want to get out of the car, with my halo of frizz, legion of dust mites. I'm wearing my most raggedy jeans, a sweat-stained T-shirt and sunglasses that I thought I could pull off once upon a time, but I now suspect make me look like a ninety-year-old woman. They keep sliding down the greasy bridge of my nose.

I take off my sunglasses and rub my nose with the back of my hand, hoping it absorbs some of the oil or, at least, distributes it more evenly so it's not pooling there. I take a reluctant look in the mirror.

People might shudder as I pass them by, hold their children close while recoiling in horror.

But . . . I could really use some wine.

I grab my wallet and get out of the car. I hurry into the store, hoping no townspeople will spot me and think they've seen some sort of mythical trash monster.

I miss the step down entering the store, and almost fall flat on my face. I catch myself somehow, my arms out in front of me, gripping the air. I look around, ready to be mortified, but there's no one here.

The ceiling is vaulted; there are exposed beams. It's all very rustic. The walls are lined with shelves, and there are two round tables in the center of the store. One has a few bottles of wine on it, the other different types of liquor. There is a little note card in front of each bottle. I walk over to the wine table, ready to pick my poison. As I walk, the thick floor planks squeal beneath my feet.

I pick up a note card. Chianti. It's earthy. Notes of tobacco, of red fruit.

I know nothing about wine except how to drink it.

"You don't want that."

The voice comes from behind me. I'm not startled by it because it's a lovely voice. The tone of it. It's an instant balm.

I turn around.

The floorboards wail under my weight, but when she walks, they make no sound at all.

She's the most beautiful person I've ever seen. Easily.

Dark waves cascade down to her waist. So much hair, thick and shiny. How does it shine like that? It's like her hair is emitting its own light.

She has big almond eyes, an ethereal hazel, like two pools of amber. She has long black lashes and her eyebrows are epic, full and lush, steeply arched. I want to touch them.

Her cheekbones are high, pronounced. Nose delicate and straight. Her lips are extensive, the twin conquerors of her face. They hold a natural color, a rosy pink. I doubt she's wearing any lipstick, or any makeup at all. If she is, whatever it is, I would buy it. Her skin is a new state of matter.

I can't tell how old she is, maybe late thirties? Early forties? She smiles at me, a pleasant, frank smile. Her cheeks round, and soft lines appear at the edges of her eyes.

She reaches out and runs an elegant manicured hand along my forearm, then takes the card out of my hand and places it back on the table.

"Come," she says. She leads me over to the back wall. "The Bordeaux. You want the Bordeaux."

She scans the shelves until she spots the bottle she's looking for. She materializes a ladder and begins to climb up the bottom rungs to reach the bottle.

She's wearing a long, silky black dress. It's got a low-cut sweetheart neckline and she has it cinched tight at the waist with a braided black leather belt. I peel my eyes away. If I let them linger any longer, I don't think I'll ever be able to stop staring. How is she possible? Is she famous? Why is she here?

She passes the bottle down to me.

"Here," she says. Her voice is like smoke. "Drink this."

She climbs down the ladder.

"If you don't like it, you can bring it back," she says. "But you'll like it."

"Yes," I say. "I mean, I'm sure I will."

She looks at me for a moment, her eyes bright and full of affection.

We just met a minute ago, but I swear she's looking at me like we're best friends, like I'm her favorite person.

"You wouldn't tell me, would you?"

"Sorry?"

She circles behind me as she speaks. "If you didn't care for the wine. You wouldn't bring it back. You wouldn't pour it down the drain. You would drink it anyway. Have one glass. Give it another chance. Have another."

A strange, prickly chill travels up my back.

Am I that transparent?

"I don't mean this as a bad thing," she says. "You seem so open.

So polite. I appreciate it. These are rare qualities, especially these days."

She walks behind a counter at the back and begins to write something down in a leather-bound ledger. I assume this store is hers. She seems too glamorous to work anywhere. She should be draped across a chaise longue underneath a large palm.

She has some kind of accent. It's vaguely European, a little haughty. I can't identify it.

"Feel free to tell me to fuck off," she says. "I like to think I've got good instincts about people. That I'm intuitive. But what do I know, really?"

"No," I say. "You're not wrong. I'd drink the wine. Even if I didn't like it."

"Close your wallet, darling. I'm not going to charge you for it. Just marking for inventory."

"Oh, wow. Thank you," I say. "Are you sure?"

"Quite," she says. "You're new, yes?"

"No, I'm thirty," I say, losing the battle with my reflex to make everything weird, to tell bad jokes when I'm feeling uncomfortable or overwhelmed.

She laughs, and the relief is euphoric.

"Almost new," she says.

"I did just move here. Yesterday, actually."

"Welcome," she says. "I'm Sophie."

She reaches out her hand. She wears gold and silver rings. Thin, delicate bands on all of her fingers. On her right index, she wears an enormous garnet. It looks medieval.

I shake her hand, ashamed that mine is clammy, that my nails are short, dirty and broken, the cuticles out of control. I wear no rings.

Her grip is firm, and she puts her other hand over mine, like my hand is something precious or fragile, something that requires extra care. Like a gem or a sick bird.

"I'm Annie," I say. "Annie Crane."

"Annie," she says. My name has never sounded so beautiful. "Lovely to meet you, Ms. Crane."

Should I curtsy?

"Have you met anyone else in town?" she asks.

"No, not yet. You're the first."

She smiles like she takes some satisfaction in this. "What brings you here?"

"I'm teaching at Aster High. I teach English and ASL."

"Mm," she says. "Teaching is a very noble profession. Requires quite a bit of patience."

"I think it's the same as any job," I say. "Can be hard sometimes. But that's why there's wine."

Why did I say that? That was so corny. I wish I could melt into the floor.

"Annie," she says, "we should get coffee sometime. Won't you come to the farmers market this weekend? It's on Saturday. Every Saturday, Memorial Day through the end of October."

"Sure," I say. Is this small-town life? Inviting strangers to coffee? But are we strangers? It doesn't feel like we're strangers.

"Wonderful," she says with a single clap. "I'll introduce you to everyone in town. They'll be so excited to meet you."

"Really?" I ask, my skepticism slipping out of my mouth like excess sauce.

"Of course." She laughs. "We don't get many new faces here."

"Oh," I say. "Um, where is the market?"

"Just down the road, there's a little path. You won't be able to miss it," she says. She's standing so close to me that I can smell her perfume. It's lavishly floral.

I'm taller than her by a few inches, which is not unusual. I'm five foot nine and typically taller than my friends. But I don't *feel* taller than she is. She carries an air of authority.

It could be because she's so beautiful. It elevates her. Puts her on another plane of existence. Or maybe it's the accent.

"I'll see you Saturday, then," I say. "Thank you for the wine."

"You're welcome," she says. "Have a good night, pet."

"You, too," I say. I'm careful not to trip on the step on the way out. I don't want to embarrass myself in front of Sophie, this gorgeous, generous wine-store-dwelling goddess.

I get in my car and set the wine down on the passenger seat. I consider fastening the seat belt around it. It's a straight three-minute drive back to my apartment. Back home.

I drive slowly. Bottle on board.

I park at the end of the driveway, in my spot, back wheel lined up with Mr. Frog.

"Mr. Frog," I say, tipping my imaginary hat to him.

I load my bags onto my wrists. I carefully hold my wine in one hand as I unlock the door with the other. I climb the stairs. My feet land in the center of each step; my knees lift the exact right height. My body knows them already. It's receptive to this new place.

The hope I felt this morning comes fluttering back. Cute apartment, charming new town, charming new friend.

I should allow myself this moment of optimism. I should give myself permission to feel something other than sad.

You could be happy here.

I open the door to my apartment and choke on my triumphant exhale. There's a spider the size of a silver dollar scuttling across the floor. He vanishes before I can catch him, somehow squeezing into the gap between uneven floorboards.

"Enough!" I tell the spiders.

I'm disturbed by the size of that one, though maybe my mind exaggerated. Maybe it wasn't so big.

I attempt to tap back into that optimism. I play music through the TV speakers, let the sound flood the space.

I set the wine down on the kitchen counter, unpack my groceries and put up my new curtains. I celebrate my privacy by undressing in the middle of my apartment, leaving my jeans on the dining table, my shoes near the window, my shirt over a lamp.

I turn the shower on, dial it as hot as it will go. I disappear inside the steam. I'm going to sanitize myself, scald myself clean. I scrub my scalp like an aggressive hairdresser. The water runs brown at first. I'm horrified.

I'd forgotten just how dirty I was from cleaning my classroom. I'm surprised Sophie wanted anything to do with me.

After my shower, I change into deliciously clean clothes. I cautiously water the plant, then dance around the kitchen while I make myself scrambled eggs for dinner. I eat them with tortilla chips and guacamole, standing at the counter. I look out at the backyard, at the woods, thick and dark and inscrutable. If that's where the spiders are coming from, I guess I can't blame them for wanting out.

I leave my dishes in the sink and open the wine. I pour it into a regular glass because I don't have any wineglasses, which doesn't feel very adult, but oh, well. I settle on the couch.

I'm suddenly hyperaware of my aloneness. Its descent is rapid and heavy as a summer storm. I scan for a spider, almost missing their company.

"If you're hiding somewhere, you can come out," I say.

I give it a minute.

No spiders.

"All right. Suit yourself," I say. "Cheers."

I sip the wine.

It's like velvet on my tongue. My taste buds nod in approval, stand up and applaud.

I polish off one glass. Then another.

I lull myself into a pleasant, loopy state. I drown my better judgment.

I call Sam.

"Hey," he says, "it's the expat."

"I'm upstate, not in Helsinki."

"Where is Helsinki? Finland?"

"Yes."

"Ever been?"

"When would I have ever been to Helsinki?" I ask him. I wonder if I'm slurring.

"As a small child. Maybe you went but don't remember."

"I mean, it's possible," I say. "Highly unlikely, but possible."

"Could always ask Pat," he says.

This conversation is officially not fun anymore.

"Mm."

"Have you talked to Pat recently?"

"Have you?"

Pat is my dad. He likes Sam better than he does me. I'm not sure why. It'd be easier, less painful, to attribute it to the facts that Sam is a guy and that my being a girl was always a great inconvenience to my father, but I know that's not it. At least, not all of it.

My mother died when I was five years old, and my early years of bows and lace dresses, tea parties and dolls, died with her. My dad is a former soldier who worked construction and didn't have the time or patience for a daughter, especially one with such "feminine" interests. No taking me to my beloved ballet lessons. No Barbies. No makeup. It was school, microwave dinners in front of the TV to avoid conversation, chores, sleep. I did the dishes, the laundry, all of the cleaning. I could watch sports with him on the weekends, but I couldn't comment, and if his team lost, I knew to get out of his way.

It sounds worse than it was. He wasn't stern or unfriendly. He mostly didn't know what to do with me or what to say. I'm sure his grief was a contributing factor. My grandparents always spoke about how much he loved my mother, what a beautiful angel she was. But for some reason I could never buy into that story completely. I wanted to, but what else could they say? She was dead. Narratives change when someone dies, especially young and tragically. Their history transforms. It transcends reality, into something more romantic.

Maybe my parents were hopelessly in love. Maybe she was the most incredible woman who ever walked this earth, but I used to wish someone would tell me about all the ways she was human. About her struggles and her suffering. Did she hate losing at board games like I do? Did she always fuck up the laundry? Was she the type to be early or late? Did she break out before big events, put toothpaste on zits and sleep with her fingers crossed?

"I didn't mean to press a button," Sam says.

"No," I say, "it's fine."

The germ of quiet festers into a lingering silence.

When I can no longer stand it, my mouth decides to make the specific and terrible decision to say, "Miss you."

The nothing that follows is devastating.

Eventually, he clears his throat. "When does school start again?"

It's a brutal nonresponse. I would almost rather he said, *You miss me? Really? That's weird. I don't miss you at all. Almost a decade together and nada!*

"Thursday," I say. "But I have to go in for meetings."

"Right," he says.

"I should let you go," I say. The words hang there, slow and bloated as an uncle after Thanksgiving dinner. They don't move, don't dissipate. They're too heavy, too full of meaning.

"All right," he says. "Talk soon."

"Yep," I say. "Bye."

I hang up and throw my phone across the couch. I reach over and cover it with a pillow.

It's a new kind of sadness. Who knew it came in so many varieties? That it had such range? I'd call this one "the anvil of understanding."

Our friendship won't survive. It can't. No more inside jokes. No more long conversations about nothing. No more hanging out. Hating the same movies. Loving the same music. None of that. It's over. It's done.

I was deluding myself into thinking it could be salvaged. I picture those people rummaging through their houses after a natural disaster. A tornado, a hurricane, an earthquake.

I cry into the couch. I use it like a giant tissue.

It's an intense, drunken cry. Theatrical. I exhaust myself, and I must fall asleep, because when I open my eyes, they're crusty and sensitive to the light, and there's a shallow puddle of drool slowly soaking into the couch cushion.

My eyelids are heavy. I have a dull headache. I yawn and go back to sleep.

It's only when I open my eyes the second time that I realize I'm not waking up on my own.

Something is waking me.

There's a sound coming from the staircase. Like footsteps. Like someone is coming up the stairs.

I sit up, ripped from the fog of sleep.

I wait for the sound to come again, to prove itself.

It doesn't.

It was loud enough for me to trust that I actually heard it, that it wasn't imagined. I tiptoe into the kitchen, where I pick up a frying pan to use as a potential weapon, like I'm an old Italian woman. I walk back into the living room.

I press my ear to the door.

I hear nothing but the whistle of my own breathing through clogged nostrils.

"Hello?" I say through the door.

I wait.

Still nothing.

I open the door, pan held high just in case.

I flip on the light. There's the distinct fizz of electricity.

I can see only the first few steps down to the landing. There's no one there, but it's possible that there's someone around the corner, on the bottom half of the steps, waiting.

The bulb sputters. Goes out, comes on again.

I see a strange shape straight ahead of me, hovering above the stairs. At first I think it's my eyes, my vision spotting from the flare of light. Then I realize it must be my shadow.

Only I'm holding a frying pan, and it isn't.

It's not my shadow.

There's a pang of doubt. Am I seeing this? Does it exist outside my vision, in the physical world?

The bulb sputters out again.

There's a faint creaking sound. It's slow, agonizing. And then SLAM!

The door at the bottom of the stairs. It just slammed shut.

The light mercifully returns.

There's no shadow. No shape. I muster enough courage to turn the corner. The bottom half of the staircase is empty.

I go down to lock the outside door. I guess I forgot to do it earlier when I got home. I did have my hands full. The wind must have blown it open. That must have been the noise I heard, the door clattering.

"Right," I say, twisting the dead bolt.

I head back upstairs and close the apartment door. Lock it. I turn around to face the living room, the couch soaked in tears and boogers and drool, the nearly empty bottle of wine on the coffee table.

I sigh, mouth open, and taste a familiar brine.

I don't know if I'm crying because I'm sad or startled or both.

I return the pan to the kitchen and put myself to bed.
You're okay, you're okay, you're okay, I say to myself.
And there's an echo, in a voice not my own.
You're okay, you're okay, you're okay.

Go to sleep now, Annie. Go to sleep.

BIRD NOISES

The next day I nurse a hangover with burned, bitter teachers' lounge coffee. The other teachers all seem to know one another and make little effort to incorporate me into their conversations. They ask each other things like "How's Christine?" and "Did you try the hydrocortisone?"

I don't try to insert myself. Why bother? I don't know Christine. I don't want to know about the hydrocortisone.

I think about Nadia, about how she and I could have been friends if I'd opened myself up to her sooner. But this feels different. These teachers aren't receptive. They don't smile. They don't say "Good morning." It's like how some people walk into a house and know that it's haunted. I know they want nothing to do with me.

Which is fine, I guess, though part of me was expecting to be invited to a book club or margarita Thursdays or whatever. At my old school, I was always invited to teacher things. Trivia nights, karaoke, Frisbee in the park, bottomless brunch. I rarely went, but my coworkers still invited me. There was camaraderie. I didn't realize it was a special thing.

I'd forgotten the difference between choosing not to participate and being excluded.

I spend the rest of orientation keeping to myself. On the first day of school, teenagers descend upon the hallways like a horde of fast zombies. They grunt and paw at one another; they eat one another's faces. As a new teacher, I ready myself for the peculiar cruelty of these hormone-addled, angst-driven evil meat sacks. I'm tested in first-period sophomore English when a kid starts to make fart noises every time I turn to face the whiteboard. At first I ignore him, which only encourages him.

Finally, I try sarcasm.

"You know, whoever is making that noise, you might be the funniest person in the whole world. What a hilarious, original gag. So, so funny."

It silences the class. I'm surprised it works as well as it does.

My two ASL classes are much more pleasant.

But just as I'm feeling the slightest hint of relief, last period is a true nightmare.

A few select students get the idea it'll be hilarious to make bird noises throughout the class. Unlike first period, they don't wait until my back is turned. They do it while I'm facing the classroom, going over the syllabus for the first quarter.

I watch them do it. I watch them make the noises. Move their mouths. Too many of them join in. There's a constant cawing.

Some students look horrified. Others ignore it, too bored to acknowledge.

About halfway through the class, one kid is chirping so loudly and incessantly that I can't get through a sentence. I don't think sarcasm will work, and I'm having a hard time not appearing rattled, because I am.

Because they're making the noises *at* me. Because of me.

Because they think I look like a bird.

It's not the first time someone has thought they were clever by linking my last name, Crane, and the fact that I'm tall and gangly and that, apparently, I have a birdlike face. It's not just my nose. It's my eyes, too. Round and dark. Guessing my cheeks are another contributing factor.

I was bullied for this for the entirety of my youth. Not in the relentless way that required adult intervention, but enough to instill insecurity, to fuse it to my bones so it's part of me I can never be rid of.

I rest on my desk, not quite sitting, not quite standing. I cock an eyebrow up and let them chirp away. I decide to say, "I used to teach in New York City. I used to live in Manhattan. You're suburban kids. You're wasting your time."

This shuts a few of them up. They roll their eyes, slump in their chairs.

Several continue to chirp. It becomes more sporadic.

Finally, a girl wearing an oversized T-shirt and Doc Martens yells, "Will you shut the fuck up? God!"

This only encourages them more.

She looks at me. Her eyes are such a pale blue they're almost transparent. She's got on smudged dark eyeliner, lip gloss and a scowl.

"No homework tonight," I say. "You'll get your first reading assignment tomorrow. You'll have the weekend to do it. All right, I'm just going to take the rest of the class to go around for names again. I want to make sure I know who's who."

This successfully stifles them. I walk desk to desk, asking for names. The first chirper is, naturally, reluctant to tell me who he is. I say, "I'm going to find out eventually."

A classmate rats him out.

"Chris Bersten!"

I put a tiny checkmark next to his name on my attendance sheet. Somehow, this process feels more humiliating for me. The kids are quiet, but they don't seem particularly stressed about potential consequences. The bell rings, and they stomp out into the hall.

The girl in the T-shirt and Doc Martens, Madison Thorpe, hangs back. She says, "They're all animals. I hate this school."

"All schools are like this," I say. "It's fine."

"Did you really live in the city?"

"Yeah," I say.

"I'm dying to go there for college. My top choices are Columbia, NYU and Sarah Lawrence."

"Sarah Lawrence is in Westchester."

She blinks at me.

"It's a good school," I say.

"Yeah," she says. She hoists her backpack higher on her shoulder. It's white, dirty, covered in pins. One reads FEMINISM. I see another that reads SYLVIA PLATH.

"Well," I say, "made it through the first day. Bye, Madison. See you tomorrow."

"Bye, Miss Crane."

When she's gone, I close the door to the classroom and lock it. I gather my papers and shove them into my bag. All I want to do is get out of here. All I want to do is go home.

Home to Manhattan, home to *my* apartment. Home to Sam.

He used to make me an ice cream sundae on the first day of school. Hot fudge, sprinkles, whipped cream from a can, those maraschino cherries that dye everything red. If the day was hard, if the kids were assholes, I knew I had something to look forward to. Someone to look forward to.

I miss him so much I could scream.

The next day is better, but only slightly. There are no fart noises, but there is a lot of texting and side conversation during class. I say, "I'm not going to take your phones away, but I will fail you."

I'm not inspiring respect, but I'm not inspiring resentment, either. They're mainly indifferent to me.

During the final period, there are a few random chirps, but for the most part the class behaves. I assign *The Scarlet Letter.*

Madison lingers after the bell again. She's also in my ASL class. She's more advanced than the other kids in the class, probably because her best friend is Beth, a fellow sophomore who is hard of hearing and signs. Beth wears baby doll dresses and loafers with shiny pennies inside. She has big eyes and a button nose and wears glittery hot pink lipstick. The two of them together look like they're the stars of a network teen drama.

"I've already read *The Scarlet Letter,*" Madison says.

"What did you think?"

She shrugs. "It was fine. What else should I read? Any recommendations?"

"Whatever you want—just make sure you can participate in class and pass the tests."

"I will. Bye, Miss Crane. Have a good weekend."

"Bye, Madison."

I can't tell if she's sucking up for a good grade or if she's the kind of fifteen-year-old who fancies themselves too mature for everyone else their own age. I wonder if she calls her parents by their first names. I wonder if she drinks her coffee black.

Definitely. She definitely drinks her coffee black.

I know it's wrong for me to make snap judgments about students, especially the only one who has gone out of their way to be nice and treat me like a human being. It's a lousy coping mechanism I default to. Being a teacher is hard in ways I can't explain. Being around teenagers is a particular form of torture. I have so many sets of critical young eyes on me. It's a constant barrage of judgment. Sometimes it's too difficult to rise above it.

After school, I stop at the supermarket to buy cartons of ice cream, sugary cereal, a few bags of tortilla chips, hard caramels and a sack of shredded cheese. I go to the self-checkout to avoid the shame of having someone bear witness.

Mr. Frog greets me when I get home.

"Sir," I say.

This is where I'm at: greeting a ceramic frog.

I climb the stairs up to my apartment. It's remarkably humid, and when I get to the landing, I have to pause to wipe a bead of sweat before it drips into my eye. I let my head back so the rest of the sweat will recede.

There's something hanging from the ceiling. It dangles just beyond the lightbulb, over the door.

It's some kind of plant. Branches. Green leaves. Little white buds.

Mistletoe?

It looks like mistletoe. I don't know how I didn't notice it before. Maybe the previous tenant had it up and left it there?

It's too hot to linger on the stairs, staring up at this weird mystery plant. I let myself into my apartment and set my groceries down on the kitchen counter. I open the cabinet to get myself a glass. I'm about to fill it when I notice a dark spot haunting the bottom.

A spider.

I give an exaggerated sigh and ask, "What am I going to do about you?"

I know I must imagine it, but I swear, it really looks like he shrugs.

CHARMING NEW FRIEND

The sun greets me, sweet and yellow. A gentle breeze swims through the open window. I pop out my retainers and set them on the nightstand, a thread of saliva glistening in the morning light.

The weekend looms ahead of me like this. Sunny and pleasant and utterly blank. So many empty, lonely hours. I imagine the time taking human form, standing there at the foot of my bed, a cute but malevolent child, ringlets and overalls, and a knife behind its back. Something that should be good but isn't.

There's nothing for me to do. No one for me to see. I'm relieved not to be at school, but I don't want to be alone.

I think about my last conversation with Sam, about how he couldn't tell me that he missed me. I hear echoes of chirps and cawing. I drop these things on the conveyor belt of embarrassing moments that's consistently cycling inside my head. I wonder if everyone has this, experiences this constant loop of past shame and humiliation, both large and small, replaying over and over again or sometimes popping up randomly when least expected, like in the middle of spin class or while caramelizing onions.

It must be exhausting to be in your head, Sam told me once.

I think what he must have meant was, it was exhausting for him to hear about it. I exhausted him.

When we broke up, he said that our spark had fizzled. I must not be sparkly enough. I must be pretty dull.

I get the idea that doing my hair and makeup will make me feel better about myself. I stand in front of the mirror braiding my hair. If I can get it to grow long enough, I can toss it out the window and whistle for a prince.

I put on some mascara and a berry-colored lipstick. I look marginally more alive. I put music on shuffle, but "Eleanor Rigby" is the first song to come on and I decide silence is best. I start to clean my apartment. Take out the trash and the recycling. When I do, I notice the empty wine bottle and am reminded.

I do have plans this weekend. I have plans today!

I'm going to the farmers market to meet Sophie for coffee.

I dig through my closet for an outfit that might trick Sophie into thinking I'm cool. I pick out a sage eyelet dress with cap sleeves and opalescent buttons. I pair it with black Chelsea boots and a gray knit shawl.

I shove my credit cards and some cash into my small envelope bag and throw the fraying strap over my shoulder.

As I leave, I notice the strange plant hanging from the ceiling in the stairway. A spray of green leaves tied with twine. I really don't remember seeing it before yesterday.

Maybe Lynn put it up? Is she back? I haven't seen another car in the driveway or heard anyone downstairs.

She's the only other person who would have keys, who would be able to get in.

Unless . . .

I remember the other night, when I left the door unlocked, when I thought I heard footsteps, movement. But who would sneak into my stairway in the middle of the night to hang a plant?

No one, that's who.

I shrug it off, like a damp animal shaking the wet from its fur.

I walk out to a perfect day. Early September weather is pure magic.

I resist the urge to take out my phone. I want to drink in this morning. I want to enjoy a leisurely stroll in this charming town. I want to reprogram myself. In the city, everyone is rushing toward the past, trying to get to where they needed to be ten minutes ago.

Things are so different here. The sidewalk is wide and the grass on either side is beautifully green. The trees provide generous shade; the leaves hum above me. I'm able to take a good look at the houses. They're set back from the road so they're hard to see while driving. They're all the same style, Victorian farmhouses. They have porches and shutters and identical landscaping.

There's a man on one of the porches reading and drinking coffee.

"Morning!" he says. He's older, his white hair down to his shoulders. He's got a deep, dusty grandpa voice.

"Morning!" I reply.

It feels nice to be acknowledged. To walk down the street and not be completely invisible.

There are more people on the stretch of Main Street with all of the shops. It's much busier now than on weekdays. There are people out and about holding coffee cups and pastries and loaves of bread and bouquets of flowers and multiple dog leashes attached to multiple dogs trotting ahead or lagging behind. Some people have grocery bags overflowing with greens. As I walk by, they turn to me, smile and say, "Good morning," or "Hello." Every single person.

And every time it happens, it's like a sip of hot tea. It's macaroni and cheese; it's cozy slippers; it's cashmere. It's comfort.

I come across a sign stuck into the grass that reads FARMERS MARKET, with an arrow pointing down a narrow path.

I follow the path, a stream of pale dirt between two rows of tall trees. If I were young, I'd want to climb them. They have those low, sturdy branches. I spot some particularly adorable squirrels scurrying around, all furry and fat cheeked. Eyes big and black and glassy.

Only animals have eyes like that. Innocent voids. I've held a baby before; as soon as we're born, our eyes are filled with want.

The sun reintroduces itself at the end of the path, the shade disappearing at the part of the trees. There's a large field with rows of white tents with peaks like meringue. There's a circle of children playing duck, duck, goose on the grass. There are two teenage boys hovering over open guitar cases, playing a song I've never heard. They're the kind of boys I would have had crushes on in high school, angsty musicians in waffle knits with good bone structure and poor hygiene. Except these boys are actually talented. All the guitar players I ever liked were terrible. I taught myself how to play when I was fourteen, thinking it would impress them. I picked it up fast and was, surprisingly, pretty good. But that ended up being a bad thing. None of those guys wanted to date a girl who was better than them at guitar.

It never bothered Sam. He liked when I played.

I drop a dollar into each of their cases.

Sophie said she would be here, but she didn't say when or where to meet her. She mentioned coffee, so I set off to find coffee.

I walk through an aisle between tents and find vendors selling fresh eggs and milk, selling fish, selling apples and apple cider and apple turnovers, selling jams. I pause in front of the jams. There's apricot. Sam's mom used to make cookies with apricot preserves in the middle. They were my favorite.

"Hello," says a very thin woman with a blunt white-blond bob. She wears giant black sunglasses, the kind that would make anyone else look like an insect, but they make her look chic. She lifts them up to look at me. She wears clumps and clumps of mascara. I'd guess she's in her sixties.

"Hi," I say. "Morning."

"Here, sweetheart. For you," she says, depositing a sample-sized jar of jam in my hand.

"It's raspberry," she says. "Do you like raspberry? You look like a raspberry girl."

"I like raspberry," I say.

"Just a little tart," she says. "Like me."

I must react, because she laughs, holding a hand over her chest. Her hands are older than the rest of her.

"I'm sorry, sweetheart. It's a bad line."

"No," I say, "it's funny."

"I'm Rose," she says. "I sell at Bakery on Main as well. Are you from around here?"

"I just moved."

"Oh," she says. "Welcome!"

"Thank you," I say. "I'm Annie."

"Yes," she says. "Sophie mentioned you."

"You know Sophie?"

She puts her sunglasses back on. Then she says, "Everyone knows Sophie."

"I'm supposed to meet her for coffee," I say.

"She'll be around here somewhere. Look for the flowers."

"Flowers?"

"You'll see," she says. She smiles, but it's weak and fleeting. There's a hint of tension in her face, in her jaw, like she's clenching her teeth.

"Well, Rose, thank you for the jam," I say. "I'm excited to try it."

"You're welcome, sweetheart," she says. "Be sure to tell Sophie I say hello. Tell her I gave you some jam."

"I will."

I turn to walk away and almost trip over a little girl in a white dress. Her hair is in intricate braids. She looks up at me, and she's so cute my body wilts.

"Excuse me," she says. She's holding a daisy.

"That's a pretty flower," I tell her. "Where'd you get it?"

"Miss Sophie," she says. She turns around and points, then pivots and skips off past me.

"Convenient," I say to myself. The universe is leading me to Sophie, leaving me bread crumbs.

I walk down the row of tents and look in both directions.

"Annie!"

Sophie is walking toward me. She's on a slight hill, and the sun is perched directly above her, like it's her own personal sun. She's wearing another long black dress. This one is flowy with dramatic bell sleeves. It's cinched at her impossibly small waist with a silver chain belt. She carries a bouquet of pale daisies and baby's breath.

"I'm so happy you came," she says. "Come, pet. Let's get you some coffee."

She takes my hand and begins leading me somewhere. I don't care where.

"How's your morning so far?" she asks.

"Good," I say. "Everyone is really nice here."

"Ah, yes. That's because we kill anyone who isn't nice." She looks back at me, wearing a smirk like a mink coat. "Don't worry. It's very humane."

"Oh, good," I say. "I was worried about that."

She laughs her sweet, musical laugh.

"Here," she says, stopping in front of a tent. Inside, a tall, handsome man with short silver hair wears an apron and froths milk. Next to him is a much younger version. The kid must be about thirteen or fourteen. He wears some kind of "invisible" braces; I can see the plastic over his teeth as he smiles.

"Good morning, Sophie," he says, bowing his head to her. Is she royalty? I honestly wouldn't be surprised.

Even if she isn't, technically speaking, I think being that gorgeous and owning the only liquor store in town grants her sovereignty.

"Morning, Erik," she says. "This is my new friend, Annie. She just moved here."

"Hi, Annie," he says. He's very *Tiger Beat*, very CW. Striking blue eyes, good hair. He and the older guy, who I assume is his father, wear matching red flannels.

"Sophie," the man says, "the usual?"

"No, Oskar," she says. "Make us something special. Something festive. I want to impress Annie."

"All right," he says. He looks over at us. He's got the same blue eyes as Erik, but his are attached to deep crow's-feet. I bet he smells like coffee grounds and firewood and is a good dad. He and his son work together, passing beans and cups and cartons of milk like it's a choreographed dance.

He's attractive, but I'm not attracted to him. I want him to adopt me. Teach me how to make a solid cappuccino and tell me he's proud of me.

While I'm distracted by my daddy issues, Sophie tucks a daisy behind my ear.

"I don't know yet," she says, "if daisies are your flower."

She slides her bouquet into an empty mason jar resting on the ledge in front of us. I think it's meant for tips.

"My flower?"

"I think everyone has a flower that reflects them. Their personality, their essence."

"What's yours?"

"I fancy myself ranunculus."

"Do you?" I ask. I don't know what a ranunculus is, but I don't want her to know that. She seems very into flowers.

"Yes. A deep purple or burgundy ranunculus. They're my absolute favorite. They don't like the heat and need lots of sunlight, so we're similar in that way."

Oskar sets down two lattes with pretty leaf designs in the foam.

"Maple cinnamon," he says.

"Oh, thank you, Oskar," Sophie says. She picks them both up and then hands one to me. "Sounds lovely."

He bows his head like his son did. "Would hate to disappoint you."

There's something a bit grim about how he says it. Sophie bats her lashes at him. They play a short, silent game. I don't know the rules, but I know Oskar loses. He looks away, wiping his hands on a dirty rag.

"Come," Sophie says to me. "I want to take you somewhere."

"Bye, Sophie!" Erik says.

"Good-bye, Erik. Be good," she calls over her shoulder as we walk away. She leads me to a paved sidewalk that curls around a patch of woods. On the other side is a small park. A playground, a few benches and a beautiful storybook gazebo. It's almost too much. Too perfect. Too picturesque.

I take a sip of my coffee, and it, too, is wonderful.

"You like it?" she asks me. "Oskar owns the Good Mug on Main Street."

"What's his deal?" I ask. This is the kind of thing girlfriends talk about, right? Is this how we bond? Or was that an awkward and intrusive question and maybe I should just leave?

Sophie sighs. "I don't like to share anyone's secrets, but I will say this. He's a very complicated, haunted man."

I follow Sophie up the steps to the gazebo. There are two girls already inside sitting on the ground instead of on the built-in bench. They're close to each other. They might be playing one of those hand-slapping games, or trading secrets, or practicing kissing.

When they see Sophie, they shoot up.

"Hello, Miss Sophie," they say in unison.

"Hello, girls," Sophie says. She pats each of them on the head. When she does this, the girls eye each other. I watch color flood their cheeks.

"We were just leaving," one of them says. "Bye!"

"Bye, now," Sophie says, waving.

The way people react to her . . . is there something I'm missing? Or is she just so beautiful that people don't know what to do with themselves when they're around her?

She sits on the bench and I park myself next to her. She sets her coffee down, removes the sleeve and wraps her hands around the naked cup.

"Did you use to date? Oskar, I mean," I say. I regret it immediately. *I* don't know what to do with myself around her. How to act. "I thought there was a vibe."

"Me and Oskar? Oh, no," she says, laughing. "No, no. I don't bother with men in that way. Or women. Or anyone. I haven't for a long, long time. I've discovered, over the years, that I'm much happier alone."

The words land square in the center of my forehead. *Much. Happier. Alone.*

"Are you all right, Annie?"

"Yeah, sorry," I say. "I just . . . My boyfriend, well, ex-boyfriend . . . We just . . . I'm just going through a recent breakup. We were together for almost ten years. We lived together. I thought we were going to get married. So it's a big . . . It's an adjustment."

I try to retract the tears into my eyes by sheer force of will. I feel one escape.

"Oh, Annie," she says. She reaches for my hand and squeezes it.

"It's okay," I say. "It's just hard."

"I'm sure," she says.

"We're on good terms, which helps. It wasn't contentious. Sometimes things don't work out."

"Mm," she says, sipping her coffee. She gazes out into space, thinking something. Then she says, "I'm inclined to hate him."

"Oh, no," I say. "No, he really didn't do anything wrong. We think we're probably just better as friends."

"This all seems quite diplomatic," she says. "What you're saying. Your words. But your face."

She cradles my face, chin to cheek, in her warm palm.

"Your face, your eyes, they tell me another story," she says, gently removing her hand. "But you can tell me that one another time. Or not at all. It's your story to tell or never to tell."

I shrug. "I'm not sure there is much of a story."

She nods, but it's a skeptical nod. She doesn't believe me. And she shouldn't. There is a story. Of course there is. It's just a bad one. I thought I was settled in a stable, long-term relationship, which led to a complacency on my end that slowly eroded the romance. It's sad and painful and, maybe worst of all, boring. I wouldn't make her sit through it. I can barely stand it myself.

"You may not believe me," she says, lowering her voice to a whisper, "but I am older than I look. And the thing about age is, it gifts you with incredible wisdom. So you must trust me, and all my incredible wisdom, when I tell you that, though you're hurting now and it surely feels like it's a permanent state, like a fog that will never lift, I promise you it will."

I take a deep breath. "Yeah."

"But," she says, pausing to take a sip of her coffee, "you'll discover for yourself soon enough the things that devastate us most in the moment are always the things we look back on with such gratitude."

I wish I could believe her. I want to, but I can't let go of my cynicism. I have to keep it close, tucked under my seat like an inflatable life vest. I'm too afraid of what will happen if I allow myself to become hopeful. What terrible disappointments will attack while I'm stupid happy and unprepared.

She sets down her coffee, and I see it. A spider. It's moseying along the ledge toward Sophie.

"There's a spider," I tell her, pointing. "There are a lot of spiders here."

"There's a lot of nature," she says, turning to look at it. "Hello, little friend."

I let the spider crawl onto the discarded lid of my coffee cup, then tip the lid over the edge of the gazebo. The spider lands in a shrub.

"Beautiful little creatures, aren't they?"

"Eh," I say. "They're creatures. I don't like to kill them."

"It's bad luck," she says. She turns her hand into a spider and creeps it up my forearm. "So, Annie, what are your plans for the rest of the day?"

"Don't have any."

"No plans? Hmm, interesting. No plans," she says. She's plotting something. The corners of her mouth slowly curl into a grin.

"What?" I ask her.

"Now you can't say no to me when I ask you to come over, because I know you have no other plans," she says, laughing. "I'm in the mood to make pie. Would you like to come over and make some pie?"

"Sure," I say. "I've never made pie before."

"I love to make pie. I find it very relaxing," she says. "Let's go pick up some berries, and then we can go to my place, yes?"

"Yeah, sounds good."

She stands up and reaches out for my hand. There's another spider. A smaller one. Brownish. It's crawling along Sophie's finger. I open my mouth to warn her, but she already knows. She leans down, moves toward the ledge, then transforms her finger into a bridge for the spider to cross. I'm amazed that it actually does. It walks in a straight line along Sophie's finger onto the ledge of the gazebo.

"You're the spider whisperer," I say.

"They're uncomplicated," she says. "Humans are complicated."

I follow her out of the gazebo and back to the tents. Everyone we pass smiles at us, bows their head, says, "Good morning. Good morning, Sophie!" or "Sophie! How are you?" I experienced the town's general friendliness earlier, but this is different. Excessive. The people fawn over her. I watch their expressions as they see her, as her presence dawns on their faces.

I look at her. She is stunningly gorgeous. Superhuman. I should be intimidated. I should feel like a hideous troll walking beside someone so insanely beautiful, but I don't. I'm just content to soak in her glow. And she's so nice and open and warm and funny. It's that rumored phenomenon I never believed in; I feel like I've known her my whole life.

So why are these people who know her acting so weird around her?

I turn to her. "Are you famous?"

She laughs. "What?"

"I don't know," I say. "Seems like you're a big deal around here."

She rolls her eyes. "I own a lot of land. Real estate. It's silly."

"You're their landlord?"

She winces. "I don't like that term. 'Lord.'"

She erupts into whole-body shivers, like saying the word was physically painful.

I mime zipping my lips. "I won't say it."

"I hope you won't think of me differently now," she says, "or after you see my house."

We stop in front of a tent where cartons of fresh berries are for sale. Ripe pink strawberries. Chubby blueberries and raspberries. The most beautiful blackberries I've ever seen, clusters of dark bubbles shining like satin. Sophie goes for the blackberries. She plucks one from a pile and slips it into her mouth.

There's an ancient woman sitting in a rocking chair in the corner of the tent.

"These are delicious, Tilda," Sophie says to her. "I'll take four cartons. Do you have a bag?"

The old woman nods and attempts to get up.

"No, no, darling. Just tell me where," Sophie says.

Tilda points and Sophie follows. She sets the berries down to grab a large paper bag. She holds it open, and I put the berries inside.

"Teamwork!" she says, smiling. Her teeth are pearly white and perfect. "Good-bye, Tilda."

Sophie doesn't pay for the berries. She just takes them. I look back at Tilda, who gives a tepid wave.

Sophie leans into me and says, "Tilda and her incessant chatting. Are you all right to walk, pet?"

"Sure," I say.

"It's not too far, but we'll have to cut through the wood."

"That's fine."

"All right, here we go. This way."

She leads me between two large grayish trees. At first I think there might be a path, but I was deceived by pale dirt. There is no path. We're just wandering through the woods.

"I hope you don't mind the forest," she says. "I've always found it peaceful, but I know not everyone shares my view."

"I haven't spent much time outdoors," I say. "My dad took me camping once. It was kind of a disaster. Rained the whole time."

"Camping," she says. "You have to be a true enthusiast to enjoy sleeping on the ground."

"Yeah," I say.

The memory of the camping trip seeps through my whole body. The rain hammering against my poncho. It stuck to me like a second skin. I remember shivering, listening to my teeth chatter. There was no fire; it was too wet. No hot dogs. No s'mores. We ate cold beans out of aluminum cans with plastic spoons. We slept in separate tents. I spent the night waiting for a boogeyman to rip open my tent with a bloody hook. I thought it would be funny, because he would expect to find a scared little girl screaming her head off, but instead it'd be me, sighing, pulling down the collar of my pajama top for easier access to my carotid artery. *Hello, sir. Would you kindly put me out of my misery?*

We pass an old stone well. It's been devoured by moss.

"The well," she says, "is how you know you're getting close."

"Old well in the middle of the woods," I say. "Not creepy at all."

She laughs. "Wait until the headstones."

I assume she's kidding until a minute later, when I see them. A small circle of headstones, chipped and worn and weathered. I can't read what they say; whatever inscriptions were there have been eroded by time.

"Shit," I say. One of them is split, and some kind of green goo oozes from the crack. More moss? Caterpillar guts? Inside the circle rests a mound of dead flowers.

"I like to lay flowers," she says, "or a wreath."

"It's just a random cemetery?" I ask.

She sighs.

"The earth is a giant cemetery," she says. "Not to be morbid, but it's true."

"Right."

"Here we are," she says. "See it?"

Between the trees is a small hut. An assembly of sticks with a thatched roof partially caved in.

"I'm only joking," she says. "If I had better jokes, I would tell them."

"What if I'd been like, 'Oh, wow, so nice, so cute.'"

"I would know you were a dirty liar with a heart of gold."

"I don't know. I've seen some apartments in the city that aren't as nice as that shack and are way more expensive."

"Dreadful," she says. "All right, this is slippery right here, so let me help you."

The ground slopes upward, and Sophie climbs, holding up her dress. I don't know how she manages to look so graceful climbing, but she does. When she's at the top, she reaches back for me.

I accept her hand and use it to steady myself. I fear I'll take us both down, but she's solid. She keeps us upright.

"We're out of the woods!" she says. "I'll reward you with tea and treats and pie."

She threads her arm through mine, so we're linked at our elbows. For a moment, the bright early-afternoon sun burns a hole through my vision. I close my eyes and watch the rust-colored orb float there. When it begins to fade, I open my eyes again and am stopped dead by what's before me.

"Is that your house?" I ask. It's a stupid question, because the structure at the bottom of the hill isn't a house, the same way a T. rex isn't an iguana.

It's basically Versailles.

"Yes," she says, her voice heavy and slow with reluctance, as if she's a child admitting to coloring on the walls. "It would have been torn down if it had stayed empty. I thought it would be such a shame to destroy something so beautiful, with so much promise, just because it was out here alone, having lost some of its former glory."

I'm not sure how it could possibly be more glorious. Parisian limestone with intricate carvings, multiple turrets, dormers, wonderfully ugly gargoyles leering from high above. Two massive wings unfurl from a hulking center tower with a conical roof trimmed with greening ornamental copper.

It looks like a famous museum or a summer palace for royals. It doesn't look like a residential home. For one person. I can't believe she lives here. Château Sophie.

"What do you think?" she asks me. "You're being quiet and I'm nervous."

"It's incredible. Are you kidding?"

Her cheeks go pink, and she claps a hand to her face. "Oh, I don't know. Everyone has their own opinions."

"I don't know if it's a matter of opinion," I say. "It's gorgeous."

Now that I think about it, it suits her. I can't imagine her living anywhere else. Her home is as beautiful and enchanting as she is.

"It's not the coziest," she says as we approach an enormous arched doorway. Sophie pauses, then digs inside her cleavage.

"Forgive me," she says.

For what? I want to ask. *For being impossibly endearing?*

"Got it," she says, pulling out a large iron key.

"That can't be comfortable," I say, "to have that wedged in your bra."

"No more comfortable than the bra itself," she says. "All right, welcome home."

She pushes open the door, its hinges howling in complaint.

We step into a grand foyer. Far, far above me hangs the largest chandelier I've ever seen. Layers of crystals dripping, shimmering in the light, projecting pastels along the limestone walls.

A majestic staircase coils its way up, up, up. There's an ornate gold banister on one side, on the other a series of Gothic wrought iron sconces.

"Don't look at anything for too long," she says. "You'll see cobwebs. Dancing dust mites. This place is terribly difficult to maintain."

"Uh, yeah. I'd imagine. You clean it yourself?"

She nods. "Mm. Sometimes I invite in some woodland creatures. They sweep. I sing."

"Of course."

"I'll give you the tour some other time," she says, "when I know it's clean. Kitchen is this way."

We make a left through one of the many archways. She leads me down a long, bright hallway. A collection of mirrors hangs on the walls, each a different style and shape. Some have thick decorative frames; others are simple, understated. They're all placed in various spots along the walls. There's no discernible pattern, but there is an order about their placement. Everything is where it's meant to be.

"These mirrors are beautiful," I say, trying not to stare at my own reflection. My hair is disheveled from the walk. I pluck a small leaf out of my tangled ends and quickly tuck it into my bag.

"I've accumulated them over the years," she says. "Seems narcissistic to collect mirrors. But I think there's something special about mirrors. Art that frames you. They tell you the truth, if you look hard enough, for long enough. Do I sound completely pretentious?"

"No," I say. "I've never thought of it that way."

"Forgive me. I'm old," she says. "I've had a lot of time to think."

How old could she possibly be? She couldn't be over fifty. Not possible. I need this friendship to work, mostly because she's warm and fun and funny and I love her, but also, I need to know what products she uses.

Probably La Mer.

"The kitchen is right over here," she says. We duck through a low doorway. We walk down two steps and through another hallway, which opens up into a giant kitchen. Literally. A kitchen for giants.

Every piece of equipment, every appliance, every utensil, is gargantuan. There's a stove the size of a Mini Cooper. A fireplace I could walk around inside. Copper pans hang from the ceiling. The floor is alternating black and red tiles.

Sophie glides over to the counter and sets the bag of berries down, then spins around to turn the oven on.

She begins to rummage through the cabinets and procure things. Bowls. Wooden spoons. Sieves. Canisters of flour and sugar. A set of tin measuring cups. A rolling pin.

"Would you like anything? Coffee? Tea? I have some lovely floral teas," she says.

"Sure," I say. "What can I do? Put the water on?"

She shakes her head, and in a swift motion, she turns the stove on, shifts a copper kettle over the flame and returns to setting up on the big butcher-block island.

She makes the dough, talking me through the process as she goes. I'm watching her closely, but I'm not listening to what she's saying. It's too hard to pay attention. She's so mesmerizing. The sound of her voice. The grace and precision of her movements. She presses the dough into a white ceramic pie dish, pinching along the edges.

"Now," she says, sliding the dish into the fridge, "the berries."

"I'm useless," I say as she begins to stir them with sugar and the juice of two lemons. "You're doing everything."

"You're good company, Annie. I'm enjoying your company."

It's such a nice thing to have your presence acknowledged as something of value. For a moment, everything glitters.

"What is it?" she asks. "Something on your mind?"

"I was just thinking that this is nice," I say. "You're fun."

"Really?" she asks, smiling like I just named her Miss America.

"Yeah," I say. "Why are you so surprised? You're a very chic and fun person."

"I don't know," she says, bashful. "Some people find me . . . I don't know. I'm not everyone's cup of tea."

I lift my literal cup of tea to her. We're drinking rose-and-pear tea, a blend she made herself. It's delicious. "You're my cup of tea."

"And you're mine," she says.

She lifts hers. We pretend to clink. The cups are too delicate to risk the damage of an actual clink. Fine bone china adorned with flowers.

Is this how it happens? Is this how you make friends as an adult? You stumble upon someone wonderful, and all of a sudden, you're close?

"I'm sure your friends in the city miss you," she says, examining the blackberry filling.

"Most of my friends left the city a long time ago. They got married and bought houses and had cute babies they send me pictures of. You know that newborn pose," I say. I clasp my hands together and put them to one side of my face, hunch over the counter to demonstrate.

"They can't do much else, you know," she says. "They're limp as noodles. And so *loud*. Tiny, toothless beasts."

"I take it you don't have children?" She samples a small spoonful of the filling. She considers the taste.

"No. I've never had the desire. I suppose it's made me a pariah, especially in my youth. It was expected, and I shunned the expectation. They say things are better now, that society is more accepting if you don't want to become a mother. I'm not sure if I find that to be true. Either you want babies or, if you don't, you must want to eat them."

When I don't say anything, she looks up at me and says, "Never mind me. I'm being dramatic. Bitter, I suppose."

"No," I say. "You have a point. And I think once you have kids, it's such a different life. Maybe it's hard to stay friends with someone who doesn't, because they can't relate. I don't know."

It's easier to think that I lost touch with my friends because they got married and moved away and procreated, but I'm not sure it's the truth. I remember the complaints when Sam and I first got together. *We never see you anymore! We miss you! Come out! Let's have brunch!* I didn't want to. I was too in love. I wanted to spend every spare minute with him. Gallivanting through the grocery store, taking day trips to the Bronx Zoo, to the Brooklyn Museum, having wild new-relationship sex.

When I was a sophomore in high school, my friends cornered me in the bathroom to accuse me of ditching them for my new boyfriend, Josiah. He was my first serious boyfriend, and I was obsessed with him. I remember crying and telling my friends that I was sorry, that I'd be better about making time for them. I promised that I would sit with them at lunch again, go to the movies on weekends. But after they confronted me like that, I really didn't want to. It was mean. So I continued to spend all of my time with Josiah. And after he and I broke up, I started dating Drew. Then Sean, then Griffin and, after a brief intermission, Sam.

I've been accused of being the type of girl who always needs a boyfriend. A "relationship girl." It never bothered me until now, because this lost-at-sea feeling proves the cruel hypothesis.

"I like children," Sophie says, creating a pretty lattice pattern with strips of dough. "Some of them, anyway. And I don't judge anyone for wanting to have them."

"No, I didn't think that."

"Good," she says. "Shall I stick this pie in the oven, then?"

"You mean that oven big enough to fit a few small children?"

She laughs. "Oh, Annie, you're wicked."

"Maybe," I say.

"This will go in for about an hour," she says. "I feel like I've gobbled up your whole day. You're welcome to stay, of course, darling, but I thought I would give you an out."

"I don't have other plans, but I don't want to put you out," I say.

"Annie," she says, "that was just a courtesy. I've actually kidnapped you and you don't know it yet."

"Damn," I say. "I'm locked in a castle and being fed pie. Please, someone help!"

"I am known for my viciousness. Come, let's venture somewhere else. Do you like to read? I'll show you the library."

She takes my hand and leads me back through the mirror hallway and into the foyer. We go through a different archway, down a flight of stairs and then up another flight of stairs to the library.

Oak paneling, coffered ceilings, bronze accents. Everything about the room is rich and dark, steeped in tawny light. There's a marble fireplace that reaches all the way to the ceiling, carved with such incredible detail that I have to fight the urge to rush over and touch it, to run my fingers along each individual swirl, every last groove.

There's so much to drink in, so much room, so much stuff, that when I finally get to the bookcases, I'm not at all surprised by them, despite their grandeur. And there's a sliding ladder! I didn't know people actually had those.

"Look around," she says, "or sit."

She distributes herself across a chaise longue, extending her legs out, letting one arm rest overhead, the other dangle at her side. There are plenty of chairs around, and a set of small uncomfortable-looking couches. That's the downside of antique furniture. Beauty over function.

"After the conservatory, I think I spend the most time in here," she says. "So many stories."

"Yeah," I say, sitting down in a hard armchair. "I don't read as much as I should. Especially for an English teacher. I should read more. Watch less TV."

"I don't own a television," she says.

"Really?"

"Really," she says. She starts to laugh, letting her head fall back. "I use a projector. Please. I love it. Well, I watch films mostly. I like movies. I don't have channels for television. Or what is it now? Streaming? It's all too much for me. But I'll watch a film anytime."

"Me, too," I say.

"I like a good story," she says. She leans forward. "I bet you have a very interesting story."

"Me? No, not really."

"No?"

"I'm boring."

"I don't believe that. Not for a second."

I shrug. "I grew up in a small town in Connecticut. I went to NYU. I teach. That's pretty much it."

"Annie," she says, stretching an arm out to me, "why did you want to become a teacher?"

"My mother was a teacher."

"She's not anymore?"

"Um, no. She died when I was really young, so . . . I don't know. I guess I just wanted to be like her," I say. I feel like this chair is sitting on me, not the other way around. I stand and walk over to the bookcases, begin to browse, feel the spines.

"You pursued teaching as a way to know her experience," Sophie says.

"Yeah, maybe. I guess," I say. I don't talk about my mother often. Ever.

Sophie swings her legs around and pats the area beside her, an invitation for me to sit. I do, and she begins to stroke my hair.

"Is this okay?" she asks me. "You have beautiful hair."

"Yes," I say. She gently lets the strands run across her palm and through her fingers. The show of affection moves me. I picture one of those videos of an iceberg melting, chunks falling away into the dark ocean. I think that's what's happening inside my chest.

I tell her about my mother. I tell her the stories I remember, describe her from the pictures I've seen, the ones I keep in a thin album with pressed flowers in between the pages. I tell her about my dad, about our nonexistent relationship. I tell her about my isolated childhood. I tell her my middle school horror stories and about my high school dramas and college escapades. Then, in spite of myself, I tell her about Sam.

She leads me back into the kitchen and we take the pie out of the oven. She fans it with a cloth as it releases whorls of steam, but she does not stop listening. Not once. Not for a second.

By the time we've each finished a slice of pie, she knows more about me than pretty much anyone aside from Sam.

"I've been talking too much," I say. "You're sick of me."

"Have you learned nothing this afternoon?" she asks me. "You are not boring. You're a very, very interesting person with a very, very interesting story. I was right. That's the thing about me, pet. I'm always right."

"And you make a great pie."

She winks at me.

There's a lull in conversation, and I allow it, fearing I've talked too much. In the absence of my monologuing, I can hear a faint tapping. I look out the window and see fat drops of rain glimmering against the glass. The sky has gone pale. The trees sway, their leaves nodding, collapsing under the weight of water.

"It's raining," I say.

"Is it?" Sophie asks, turning toward the window. A flash of lightning answers her question. It thrills her. "Oh, I love a storm!"

"They make me anxious," I say, interrupted by the boom of thunder. "I don't like loud noises."

She stands up and takes my plate. "Don't worry. You're safe here with me."

She walks over to the sink and sets our plates down on top of all of the other dirty dishes. Mixing bowls, spoons, measuring cups.

"I can help you with those," I offer.

"Nonsense," she says. "You're my guest. Also, darling, I don't want you walking home in this."

"Yeah," I say. I'm assuming she'll be able to drive me back to my apartment. Should I ask?

"Before you think I'm incredibly rude, I can't offer you a ride because I don't have a car. Or a license. Which is ridiculous, I know. But here we are."

"Did you grow up in the city?" I ask. I met a few people at NYU who'd lived in the city their whole lives and never planned on leaving. A license was unnecessary, a car a nuisance.

"No," she says. "I've never been. I don't get out much, really. I lead a very simple life."

"Yeah," I say, gesturing to the room around us. "Simple life. Simple house."

She rolls her eyes. "You judge me."

"I don't!"

"Someone else built this house. A man with too much money and too much ego. He lost it all and left it to rot. I merely saved something beautiful," she says, "though I do have a fondness for beautiful things, especially ones in need of saving."

She begins to fill the kettle. "So, Annie, you should stay here tonight. Imagine the muddy mess it will be out there. To navigate it in a storm or after dark—no. No, no. I'll make up my favorite guest room."

Is she asking me to sleep over?

There's a hesitation, a small anxious creature inside me pulling on my veins, using my stomach as a trampoline. All I've done for the past week is lament being alone, and now I've made a new friend, who's offering for me to spend the night in her mansion. Why am I not more excited? Why am I experiencing this strange trepidation?

"What is it?" she asks.

"Nothing," I say. "It's really nice of you to offer, but I don't want to impose."

"I *invited* you," she says. "It'll be fun. I'll open a bottle of wine. We can eat cheese and bread and read or watch a film. Or I can make up the room and you can sleep. Or take a bath! I made some new soaps and candles."

"Made?"

"Yes. Teas, soaps, candles, salves. Tonics. I grow things. I make things with what I grow," she says. "I told you. Very simple."

"What you think is simple and what is actually simple are two very different things."

She pouts. "What do you say? Will you stay?"

"Sure. Yes," I say, extinguishing my nerves, "if you're sure you want me hanging around."

She claps. "Do you like red or white wine for tonight? I'll get us a bottle, and then we can go somewhere more fun. The ballroom? Music room? Do you play piano?"

"I don't. And red or white. Doesn't matter to me. I trust you. The wine from your store was delicious."

"Oh, it's not my store," she says. "Well, not entirely."

She gave me a bottle of wine and let me take it without paying. Was I wrong to assume she had permission to do that?

"I'll be right back," she says. She opens the door to the pantry and steps inside. There's the unmistakable screech of rusty hinges, then fading footsteps.

Curious, I stand up and look inside the pantry. It's big, and at the back, there's a set of steel cellar hatch doors. They're open, and between them is a dark void.

"Sophie?" I say. "Do you need a light?"

In the gummy darkness, I think I see movement.

"Sophie?" I call out.

There's a quick succession of sounds. Fast stomps getting louder and louder, a rush of volume. It's as if she's running up the stairs, but no one's there. I expect the top of her head to emerge from the dark of the cellar, but it doesn't. Nothing does.

If she's not making that sound, if she's not approaching, who is? It's sudden excruciating confusion. I ready myself to turn, in case I've somehow mistaken the direction of the stomping and it's actually coming from behind me and something is fast approaching my back. But before I can move, a gust of air hits my face. It breaks like an egg, a cold yolk dripping.

The shock of it, the frigid bitterness, robs me of breath. I close my eyes.

"You all right, darling?" Sophie asks. When I open my eyes, she's standing in front of me, right there in the pantry. She follows my eyes behind her.

"I . . . I didn't see you," I say. "I heard . . ."

"What is it?"

How can I explain? Say that I heard stomping and was attacked by a cool breeze? I'd sound crazy.

"Um. Never mind," I say. "I thought I heard something."

"It's a creaky, drafty old house. It likes to complain," she says, closing the cellar doors. "I chose a bottle of rosé. Whenever I can't decide between red and white, I go pink."

I touch my face. My cheeks are freezing, my lips stony.

"Shall I show you the ballroom?"

"Yeah, okay." I can't shake the cold. It's a chill in my marrow.

But then Sophie puts her arm around me, rests her hand on my shoulder, and I feel an overwhelming sense of safety. She smells so good. I need to know how she smells so good. I inhale her. I don't even care if she thinks it's weird. I breathe her in.

Everything else melts away as she walks me out of the kitchen, through the mirror hallway, through the foyer. We go through a different wing, down another long hallway, but instead of mirrors, this one is lined with paintings. Mostly oil paintings, landscapes. A few seascapes. There's the occasional tapestry.

"I feel like I'm in a museum," I tell her.

"I do call this the gallery," she says. "But no museum would hang my paintings."

"*You* painted these?"

She nods, gazing at the paintings with her lips curled in. "I'm not very good."

"What are you talking about? They're amazing!"

She squeezes me. "You're an absolute dove. Pure sunshine."

Every compliment from Sophie is like a straight shot of dopamine.

"All right, here we are," she says. She opens a set of towering French doors. We walk into a dark room, and by the echo of our footsteps, I know it's big. Lights above us begin to glow awake, slowly illuminating our surroundings.

Even considering the truly extraordinary size of the house, it's a struggle to understand how this room could ever fit inside it. It's titanic. A dreamy sea of marble. Ornamental plastering, appliqués, crystal chandeliers. It's somehow even more ornate than the rest of the house. The tall ceiling is painted a rich aqua, and there are delicate gems of constellations strewn across it.

"Wow," I say. "I mean, goddamn!"

She laughs. "I thought you might like it. I never come in here! But it's such a beautiful room."

She releases me and glides onto the dance floor. She does a spin, her dress levitating; then she curtsies to me.

"Really, Sophie?"

"You, my darling, do not take me seriously," she says. She sits on the floor and produces a corkscrew, seemingly out of thin air. She begins to open the wine. "Oh. I forgot glasses."

"We could swig straight from the bottle like degenerates," I say.

She removes the cork with a satisfying *pop!* She waves me over. "You first."

She offers me the bottle and I take it. I lift it to my lips and have a small sip. It's great wine. It slinks across my tongue and down my throat. It leaves a sweetness in its wake.

I give the bottle back to Sophie, before I'm tempted to down the whole thing.

"Annie," she says, "may I ask you a personal question?"

"Sure," I say, seating myself beside her. I've already told her about my dead mother, my aloof father and getting dumped a few weeks shy of my thirtieth birthday. What could she want to know that's more personal than that?

She gives me the wine back. I take a gulp.

"What do you want? Out of life, I mean," she says. She's now lying on her side with her head on her shoulder, arm outstretched.

"I don't know," I say. "Like, my goals?"

"Not goals. Wants. What do you want?"

"I guess I haven't really thought about it. I wanted to be a teacher. I'm a teacher. So there's that."

"Did you want to be a teacher because you wanted to be a teacher, or was it only because you wanted to find a way to be close to your mother?"

Out of the corner of my eye, I see a bolt of lightning slice through a monstrous black cloud. This room is all windows, and they provide a frightening view of the storm outside. It rages over the flat green of the lawn, a series of sculpted hedges, a rose garden.

I wait for the thunder to come, and when it does, it shakes the chandeliers.

"I'm sorry," Sophie says. "We can talk about something else."

"No," I say, "you have a point. I don't know if I want things. I guess I wanted Sam. I wanted for us to get married, be happy. Be together. To have someone."

"Were you happy? With Sam? I mean truly happy. Did you feel fulfilled? Did you wake up excited? Have a sense of contentment, of gratitude?"

I don't know how to answer, so I drink more wine.

"Forgive me," she says. "I thought, perhaps if I knew what you wanted, I could help. You're such a joy, and yet you're sad. It seems an injustice."

"That's nice of you," I say. "Thank you."

"We don't have to talk about anything serious for the rest of the night," she says. "We can finish the wine and I'll get us some food and we can watch something. I keep my thickest, softest blankets down in the theater room."

"Okay, yeah," I say. "Yeah."

There's another flash of lightning, and the lights flicker.

Sophie rolls her eyes. She stands up, marches over to one of the windows and says, "Stop that."

I assume she's talking to the sky. "You tell it," I say.

The clouds mumble.

"There's a limit to my powers," she says, though the clouds have suddenly rolled back, and I no longer hear the rain. "Shall we?"

"You want the rest of the wine?"

She shakes her head. "No, you drink it."

"If you say so." I finish the bottle. It puts a fuzz on everything.

We go back to the kitchen and Sophie prepares a platter of cheese and bread and different spreads. She gets another bottle of wine. It's night now, and the house is so dark I can barely see.

Being a little drunk probably isn't helping.

Sophie helps me down a narrow, winding staircase to a room that's all red velvet drapes and big chairs. There's an elevated stage flanked by gold Corinthian columns. There's a projector screen that Sophie has to pull down.

"What would you like to watch?" she asks me.

"Whatever you want," I say.

She puts on *Gaslight* starring Ingrid Bergman. She opens the wine and this time she's remembered glasses. She pours me one, and by the time I finish it, I can barely keep my eyes open.

The next thing I know, Sophie is pushing my hair out of my face and whispering, "Let's get you to bed."

The house is a maze, especially at night. We go up the main staircase and make a series of turns, and then we're in a frilly bedroom. There's a large canopy bed. The curtains and bedding both have busy floral patterns.

"The bathroom is through there," Sophie says, pointing to a door next to a large armoire. Sophie opens the armoire and takes out a fresh set of sheets. "I'll change these for you."

"I can do it," I say.

"Nonsense," she says. "Why don't you wash up? There should be a spare nightdress in the dresser."

I turn to find a double dresser. I open the top drawer, and there is a single article of clothing folded inside it. A long, formless white cotton dress.

I take it into the bathroom to change. I'm so tired, so tipsy, I feel like I'm being pulled down, like there are invisible creatures hanging off of me, wrapped around my legs like difficult toddlers. I start to undress. It's freezing in the bathroom. It's a windowless room. It's not small, but it feels small compared to the rest of the house. There's a claw-foot tub, an old-fashioned toilet with a chain and a pedestal sink. There's a vanity in the corner with a pretty round mirror, the frame accented with delicate silver butterflies.

I stumble over to peek at my reflection.

I look incredible. Maybe it's the lighting in here, flatteringly dim. My skin looks smooth, glowing, my eyes bright. I linger so long it's shameful, just standing around admiring my reflection. I'm so focused on me, on my face, on how my hair isn't greasy at the roots like it usually is, on how my lips have natural color, that I almost don't notice it.

The other face.

It floats over my shoulder, an orb of pale skin. Two eyes. A nose. A mouth. It's small, far behind me. I gasp, the sound surprising me as I spin around to look.

There's no one there.

I turned too quickly, and an intense dizziness destabilizes me. I collapse onto the vanity stool. I take measured breaths until the room stops spinning.

Clearly, I didn't see what I thought I saw. It wouldn't even be possible for someone to be standing behind me; the space wouldn't allow it.

I wobble over to the sink with all the grace of a baby giraffe taking its first steps. I lean down and drink some water straight from the tap.

This is embarrassing. I had too much to drink. What will Sophie think?

I change into the nightshirt, or whatever it is. It makes me look like a Pilgrim. I fold my clothes and set them on the vanity, avoiding the mirror.

When I open the door, I find Sophie smoothing the covers.

"Ready for you, darling," she says. "Is there anything else I can get you?"

"No," I say. "Thank you."

"I'll see you in the morning. I'll take you to breakfast. Have you been to the diner yet? Tom makes the fluffiest pancakes."

"Haven't been yet," I say. I want her to leave so I can collapse into bed, but I also don't want to be alone. This room is too formal. There's something unsettling about it.

"Good night, Annie. Sweet dreams," she says. "If you need anything else, help yourself. Just don't go into the east wing. That wing is forbidden."

"Okay," I say.

"I'm only joking," she says, laughing. "It was a joke, darling. Anyway, sleep well!"

She leaves, closing the door behind her.

I feel the floor teetering beneath me. I stumble into bed, silently pleading with the room for it to hold still. A single voice cuts through the wine slush in my head.

Go to sleep, go to sleep, go to sleep.

My eyes are open. I'm on my back. The room is dark. I don't remember turning the lights off, but I must have. My mouth is dry, my tongue limp. My limbs are incapable of movement. *Up!* I tell them. *Let's go.* I need water. I need to pee. But my body refuses to move.

I stare at the bed canopy. I try to identify the flowers in the pattern, a challenge in the dark. I see a rose. A peony. My eyes go cross and I blink twice. There's something unusual about the canopy, about the fabric, the way it's draping. There are some places where it sags. I count four. I wonder if it's from the chandelier hanging too low or if maybe there are some rips.

I blink again, and in that brief moment, in the darkness of my own head appears the face I saw in the mirror.

I've never been the type to scare easily. It's one of the few ways in my life I've always been practical. I've never been fazed by slasher movies or ghost stories or urban legends. I was the one at sleepovers rolling her eyes, putting her hands on the planchette. I'm not scared of poltergeists or vampires or Freddy Krueger. I'm scared of real things, like economic recessions and dying alone.

So this kind of fear is unfamiliar to me, and I'm more disturbed by the fear than by the face, or the fact that the impressions in the canopy are now moving, like there's something up there crawling across it.

The fear sends an electric jolt through my body. I catapult out of bed and stare up at the space between the top of the canopy and the ceiling.

I don't see anything unusual, but I keep my eyes locked there. I take a few steps back to get a better view. Another few steps. My back hits the wall.

There's nothing on the canopy. I breathe a long sigh of relief. I turn to walk toward the bathroom, and the wall seems to jump back away from me. My eyes slowly shift to the side, and in my peripheral vision, the distance between where I stand and where the wall is seems significant. A few feet.

So what was I up against? What was at my back?

The relief is sucked from my body with such force that my knees buckle. I listen for something, some noise that would confirm the presence of someone other than myself. The give of the floor. Breathing.

In listening, I discover there's something else at my ear. Not a sound. Well, not really. It's more a sensation. I realize I've been feeling it for a few seconds but have been too flustered to acknowledge it.

It's hot air.

Humidity.

My hand reaches up instinctively.

ShhhhhhSssssss!

Someone is hissing in my ear.

I run.

I run to the bathroom, slam the door shut, lock it. I flip the light switch and look around. I slowly approach the tub and crane my neck to see inside. Empty.

I go back to the door. I wait for the knob to spin or for a set of fingers to appear in the narrow space between the door and the bathroom floor.

I think of what Sophie said earlier. *A creaky, drafty old house.*

I wonder what Sam would say if he were here. He'd probably still be asleep. He's a heavy sleeper.

If Sam were here, I wouldn't be afraid.

It's just because I'm alone.

The realization is sobering. I go pee, wash my hands and splash some cold water on my face. I drink from the tap. I open the door out to the bedroom without any fear or hesitation, just bleak, boring logic. I get back in bed and pull the covers up high over my shoulder.

I close my eyes and pretend I'm back in the city, back in my old apartment. I pretend that Sam and I are still together, that the breakup never happened. I imagine him next to me. His occasional snores. The rise and fall of the sheets. The warmth there beside me.

I can almost feel it.

NEW DAY WITH PANCAKES

I wake up to sunlight nuzzling my face. I roll out of bed, change back into my clothes from yesterday and pull my hair into a sloppy bun.

I didn't sleep well.

At all.

This is made painfully obvious by the dark circles under my eyes. A germ of a hangover floats behind my forehead.

As I step out of the room, I realize I don't know where I'm going. Left, I think? I need to get to the main staircase.

I've never been in a house so big there's a danger of getting lost.

I find the staircase, go down the hall of mirrors and into the kitchen. I find Sophie there, kneading dough. Her hair is in a French braid that snakes down her back. She's wearing one of her signature long black dresses, protected by a burlap apron. She doesn't have a single speck of flour anywhere on her.

"Morning!" she says. "Oh, pet! You look tired. Did you not sleep well?"

"I slept okay," I say. "I have trouble sleeping sometimes."

"Was the bed not comfortable? I'll beat the mattress. Or I can put you in a different room," she says, "if you'll ever want to stay again. Perhaps it was too poor an experience."

"No, no," I say, my voice in its lying pitch. I imagine dogs around the world pausing in unison to consider the sound. "Not poor at all."

"Would you like to go to the diner? It's a lovely day," she says, "though it might still be muddy."

"That's okay. I'll go."

"All right," she says. She sets the dough in a ceramic bowl and puts a damp towel over it. "Let's go."

She leads me back through the woods. She was right about the mud. By the time we get to pavement, my boots are covered in sludge.

When we arrive at the diner, Sophie introduces me to the owner, a tiny bald man named Tom.

He bows to Sophie multiple times as he leads us to a booth in the back corner.

"I'll bring coffee right away," he says, hurrying off.

"Do you own this building?" I ask her.

"I own the land it sits on," she says. "Why?"

I shrug. "Just wondering."

I'm curious to know exactly how much real estate she owns, how much of this town, but I think it'd be rude to ask outright.

"I like to get pancakes with strawberries and a side of bacon," she says. "But you can't go wrong, really."

"All right. Sold on the pancakes."

Tom is back with the coffee, and Sophie orders for both of us.

"Coming right up," he says. He won't make eye contact with her. Or me.

"He's funny," I say.

"Nervous personality," she says. "Annie. What's wrong?"

"What do you mean?"

"You don't seem yourself this morning. Is everything all right? Did I do something?"

"No," I say. "No, I'm fine."

As the words "I'm fine" leave my mouth, I realize how untrue they are. Sophie's right. I'm not myself. I'm hungover, and I'm ashamed to be hungover.

I sigh. "I had too much wine last night."

"My fault," she says. "I'm a bad influence. I'm sorry, pet."

"Don't be sorry. I'm the one who drank it. I guess . . . this is the second time in the past week that I've gotten drunk. I don't want to be this sad, single thirtysomething getting wine drunk multiple times a week. I don't know."

"Do you not like wine?"

"I do."

Sophie takes a slow sip of her coffee. "Annie, why would you say 'sad, single thirtysomething'?"

I've offended her. "I'm sorry. I just meant that's how *I* feel."

"No. No, I don't think you did," she says. She slowly unfolds a grin. "You think being single is a sad state of being. I promise you, it's not."

"No, I know."

"Do you?"

Honestly, I don't. I don't want to end up alone. I don't want to be an old maid. I want to be with someone. Share my life. Have someone love me. Want me.

"But why?" she asks.

"Sorry?"

"Why do you feel you need someone to love you, to want you? Why are you seeking that outside yourself?"

I'm confused. Did I say it out loud? Did I think out loud?

She puts her elbows on the table and leans forward. "You think you need it, but you don't. I'm proof enough of that, don't you think?"

"We're different."

"We're not."

Our pancakes arrive. They're the thickest, fluffiest pancakes I've ever seen in my life. They swim in a garishly pink strawberry compote. A fat dollop of cream sits on top of the pile.

"You want to think we're different, Annie. I'm telling you, we're not."

"Sophie," I say, "you're beautiful. You could have anyone you want. It's not like that for me. I'm not . . . I'm not like you. I want a relationship. I want to love someone and have them love me back."

"You want sex?"

"What? No. Well, I mean . . . that's part of it, I guess. But no."

"Sex is easy," she says. "I, personally, find I can do it better myself. But I understand wanting it from someone else."

She takes a big bite of pancake. A drop of pink strawberry goo oozes out of the side of her mouth. She scoops it up with her tongue.

"It's love," I say. "I want love."

"You want validation." She's not being mean. Her tone is as soft and warm as ever. She's being honest. Only the honesty is just as bad.

"Yeah. Maybe I do."

"You're never going to get it. Not from someone else, darling. Not from Sam."

"He did love me."

"No, pet," she says, "he didn't. Or else you wouldn't be here crying over pancakes."

I bring my hand up to my face. My cheeks are wet. I didn't realize.

"Annie, I only say this because I know you're above what you seek. Meaning, you're . . . What's the word? Lowballing? Is that what it is?"

"I guess." I can't help but laugh a little. It's funny hearing her say it with her haughty accent.

"Your life can be so much more than chasing after some domestic fantasy."

"I don't think that's what I . . . I don't know. I don't know if that's what I'm doing."

She skewers a strawberry with her fork. "All right. I don't presume to know everything."

She winks at me.

I reach with a shaky hand for my coffee. I drink it black.

"I just ask that you hear what I'm saying to you, Annie. Yes?"

"I hear you."

"Good," she says. "Now, onto other things. How's work? How's your class?"

I feel my face fall, my muscles drooping in defeat at the thought of school.

"Oh, dear, I've done it again!"

"No, it's fine. Work is fine. There are a few kids in my afternoon English class who are . . ."

"Fucking assholes?" she asks.

"Yeah, pretty much."

"Want me to curse them for you?"

"Sure," I say.

"Done."

In the morning sun, her skin is flawless. Pearlescent. She doesn't have a single wrinkle, a single pore. She keeps insinuating she's old, older than me, but she doesn't look it.

"I'm sorry you didn't sleep well last night," she says. "I feel like a failure as a host."

She flags down Tom and asks him to refill our coffee mugs.

"You will come back, won't you?" Her eyes go wide and watery.

There's a vulnerability to her. I recognize it clearly because it's so familiar to me. It's like we're wearing the same perfume. It triggers such a profound empathy I want to leap across the table and hug her.

"Of course," I say. "Of course I will."

"Do you like to swim? I can clear out the pool. I don't use it. I don't like water, but if you do, I can clean and fill it. It's indoors, so you can use it in the winter."

"I shouldn't be surprised you have an indoor pool," I say. The tension drains from my body, tension I didn't even realize I was holding. My spine unkinks; my shoulders descend. I'm sitting here eating ridiculously delicious pancakes with my charming new friend, who owns a house with an indoor swimming pool. For all the wallowing I've done in the past few months, leading a one-woman self-pity parade, in this moment I feel nothing but lucky. "I love to swim."

"I'll get on it, then," she says. "If I eat any more, I'll feel sick. I know this and yet . . ."

She takes another bite.

We clean our plates.

"I'm going to be useless the rest of the day," she says, standing.

We haven't received a check, but at this point, I'd be surprised if Tom dared to approach with one. He seems terrified of Sophie. I guess some men from his generation would take issue with having to answer to a woman. With paying rent to a woman.

"When will I see you again, pet?"

"Whenever," I say.

"Maybe Friday? I could come by with dinner?" she asks, holding the door open for me.

"Sure! Do you want my number?"

"Oh, I don't have a mobile. Well, I have one, but I never use it. I think they're dreadful. People walking around hunched over. I'd rather go back to the days of sending ravens. Surprisingly reliable."

She's an unconventional person, so I don't find this particularly shocking. I have a hard time picturing her using an iPhone. Still, I'm not sure how she functions without one.

"Friday. Say six o'clock?"

"Sounds good."

"Darling," she says, giving me a hug, "thank you for a lovely weekend. I'll see you soon."

We walk off in opposite directions, and I make it a few steps before I'm lonely again. Nearly instant separation anxiety.

When I get home to my apartment, it's smaller than I remember. Emptier. I take a shower, do laundry, water my already wilting plant, then prep lessons while eating stale tortilla chips and toast with the free sample of raspberry jam. By the time the sun sets, my loneliness scores against me like rough wool. I want to crawl out of my skin.

I call him.

I want to tell him about Sophie, about her enormous house with a library and ballroom and theater and swimming pool. About how I stayed there last night and in a tired wine fog convinced myself for a minute that it was haunted. I want to tell him about the pancakes, reminisce about the time we got stoned and went to the IHOP in Union Square. We experimented with all of the syrups. Blueberry, strawberry, regular, maple pecan. We tried different flavor combinations, recording our findings on the back of a napkin with a rogue crayon we picked up off of the floor. I want to ask him if he remembers. If he still thinks about it whenever he sees syrup, the way I do.

But he doesn't answer.

A COINCIDENCE

I wake up early, having gone to bed at seven forty-five last night to avoid being conscious. I scroll on my phone for too long, looking at pictures of celebrities out in the wild. An Oscar-winning actress in the parking lot of a Los Angeles grocery store holding a case of trendy seltzer while wearing sweatpants and no makeup. A disheveled former action star in a grubby, sweat-stained T-shirt out walking his dog. A young heartthrob dining alfresco, shoving french fries into his mouth. Something about these photos brings me peace. They help get me out of bed.

I put on a white oxford shirt, navy slacks and loafers. I stare at myself in the mirror, and my celebrity-photo zen dissipates. I have to analyze my outfit, my makeup, my hair. I have to ask myself, *What can they make fun of me for?*

This process involves picking apart my appearance. It involves being mean to myself.

If they're going to make fun of me for being birdlike, there's nothing I can do. I can't change my bone structure, my nose. I can't change my long, scrawny neck. Maybe a scarf? Would they have something to say about that?

I leave my apartment sooner than necessary, just to get away from the mirror. I'd rather not arrive at school super early because I really don't want to be there, so when I see the Good Mug, I pull into the nearest parking space.

I want a latte and to look at that handsome dad.

It's a little pale green building with white shutters. It looks almost like a garden shed. When I walk in, a bell dings overhead. Oskar looks up from behind the counter and smiles politely. He's got a rag over his shoulder. I bet he's always got a rag over his shoulder. I bet he sleeps with it there.

"Good morning, sweetheart." Rose is sitting at a table near the door, reading and drinking coffee out of a comically large mug. She's wearing thick-rimmed round glasses and a beret. "How'd you like the jam?"

"I had some yesterday," I say. "It's great. Thank you."

"You're welcome, Miss Annie," she says. "You'll be back Saturday for more?"

"I will."

"Good, good. Oskar, this girl's a sweetheart."

"Thanks, Rose," I say. My entire face is blushing; I can feel it. My forehead. My chin. I can barely look at Oskar now. "Morning."

"Morning, Annie. What can I get for you?"

"Um . . . can I have a large latte?"

"Any flavor? I can do vanilla, hazelnut, maple, cinnamon, honey, almond. I can do lavender, but that's not for everyone. My son says it tastes like soap."

"I like the taste," I say. "Of lavender, not of soap. Though I haven't tasted a lot of soaps, so who's to say?"

Really, Annie? Really?

"I like lavender, too," he says mercifully. "I usually do it with a little almond. I think it balances."

"I'll do that, then."

"Coming up," he says. He starts working the large fancy espresso machine.

"So, you're a teacher?" he asks.

"Yes. English and ASL." I don't know how he knows. Someone must have told him. I guess it's that small-town thing: News travels fast. Not that my profession is news, but . . .

"Erik goes to Aster. He's a freshman."

"Maybe he'll be in my class next year."

He pours the milk, moving his wrist to create a pattern. His eyebrows pinch together, and a strand of silver hair falls in his face.

He pushes the cup toward me.

"On me," he says. "If you like it, come back again soon."

"You'll be back," Rose says. "Oskar makes the best coffee."

"Are you sure?" I ask. "I feel bad. I lived in the city, so I'm not used to this . . . this . . ."

"Small-town hospitality?" Oskar asks, stroking his scruff. He smiles. "Don't worry about it. Enjoy."

"Thank you so much," I say, taking the cup. "Bye, Rose!"

"Bye, sweetheart. Have a good day."

By the time I'm back in my car driving to school, my mood has done a complete one-eighty. It's all sunshine. The rest of my morning, powered by a latte that tastes like heaven, is pleasant and easy. In my first few classes, everyone behaves.

At lunch, I eat alone in my classroom. I check my phone to see if Sam has reached out at all. He hasn't, but I have a text from Nadia asking how I am.

Good, I say, and it doesn't feel like a lie. Town is precious. People are nice. Met a new friend who is super glamorous and lives in a 🏰. How are you?

> More glamorous than me? Bullshit. I'm good! Hot new history teacher. Mr. Collins. Rawr. I'll send u a pic if I can get one.

Be stealthy, stalker.

She sends me a series of emojis. Detective. Skull and crossbones. Hearts.

It's nice of her to think of me.

The day's going so well that when I hear the first chirp in final period, I get startled and drop the dry-erase marker. But it's not the chirp itself that gets me. It's the fact that I let a good mood delude me into thinking happiness was something I could hold in my hands, that it wouldn't slip through my fingers the moment I stopped fearing it would.

See? my cynicism hisses. *See!*

I pick up the marker and continue like nothing happened. But it's too late. The students sense my weakness. They know they've gotten to me. That I'm emotionally compromised.

"Bacccc-bacccc-baac-caaaa."

I ignore it. The chicken sound is new. It gets a few chuckles.

"Caaa-caaaa."

I can tell it's coming from one direction, from one person. Chris Bersten.

I turn around. He doesn't look conspicuously evil. There are no devil horns poking out of his head, no red pentagrams spinning in his pupils. Maybe it's not his fault. Maybe it's me. Maybe I'm so ugly, so birdlike, such an easy target, it's impossible for him to resist.

He opens his mouth, looks straight at me, and does it again.

"Caaa-caaaa."

Snickers all around the room. A single annoyed sigh from Madison.

"God," I hear her say.

I can feel my heart descend through my chest and land in the pit of my stomach. I can feel it bobbing around in a rough sea of acid. I might throw up. I might cry. Or lie down right here in the classroom, facedown on the floor, waving tiny white flags.

He opens his mouth again, and I've resigned myself to what's coming next. But then the sound catches in his throat. He retches.

Twenty-five heads swivel toward him in unison.

He does it again. This time, he smacks two palms down on the desk, sending a wave of startled jolts through the room.

Chris's face was already rosy from laughing, but now it's red in a way that's unnatural. That's disturbing. Like a fire engine. Like a stop sign. Like all of the blood in his body has collected there behind his cheeks, behind his forehead.

He retches again, his posture contorting, the sharp peaks of his shoulders rising up past his ears. His spine curves; his neck juts forward.

He's making a new noise now. Sam's parents had a calico cat named Cookie who would emerge from the depths of the basement only to cough up hair balls and eat smelly wet food. It's like Chris is about to cough up a hair ball. A terrible dry sound rips through his throat.

The rest of the class watches in horror. *I* watch in horror as he lurches forward. His lips zip together; his cheeks fatten for a moment before he relents. A viscous blob resembling the insides of a rotten black egg slowly emerges from his mouth. The sound it makes when it hits his desk . . . Awful. Like reverse slurp. Eerily wet.

The classroom is silent. Horror is, apparently, an effective tool for silencing a class.

Chris's eyelids flutter and his head rolls back like he's exhausted.

I suspect the ordeal is over and am considering what I should do next; then the blob begins to move. The black yolk of the vomit stirs. Tiny black sticks poke their way out of the gelatinous spit.

It's a spider. A spider the size of a fat baby's fist. And it's alive.

It begins to walk off of Chris's desk, making its way onto the floor.

Someone screams.

Now there's a whole chorus of screaming. Chaos. Kids standing on chairs. Papers flying.

"Kill it!" someone says.

"No!" I yell. I don't know why. The students look at me like I'm insane.

The spider picks up speed. It has a lot of legs. It hurries to the back wall, disappears under a bookshelf.

Kylie Hamilton is shriek-crying. Joe Alvarez is shining his phone flashlight on the floor near the bookshelf. Madison is rolling her eyes.

"Hey!" I say. They ignore me, so I whistle. A proper finger-in-mouth jet-engine whistle.

There are so many eyes on me. Wide and terrified eyes.

"Sit down," I say. "Now."

I take a breath.

"Can someone please escort Mr. Bersten to the nurse?"

They blink at me.

"Anyone?" I ask. "All right. Tyler."

I point to one of the other chirpers. He's well over six feet tall and always looks uncomfortable at his desk. I figure I'm doing him a favor.

"No," he says.

"Why?" I ask.

He can't answer.

"Walk Chris to the nurse. Now. Thank you."

Chris is completely drained of color. A lattice of blue veins emerges on his forehead, also at his temples and on his neck. Tyler groans and makes sure he pushes his desk when he gets up to show he's angry.

"You need help, man?" he asks Chris without looking at him.

Chris gives a slight shake of his head and stands slowly. He shuffles out of the classroom with his whole body bent, like a four-legged animal attempting to walk upright.

As soon as Chris and Tyler are out of the room, the bell rings and spares me from having to salvage the rest of class. If there was any salvaging it.

Probably not, considering a kid vomited up a live spider. That then crawled away.

I watch as a series of faces in varying states of shock and disgust stagger past me.

I lean back against my desk, staring at the glob of spit forming a crust on Chris Bersten's desk.

It's cruel to leave it for the janitor.

I dig a stack of napkins out of the top drawer of my filing cabinet.

I approach cautiously.

There's no bile, no chunks of food. It's not puke. Just thick spit. I fetch the trash can, wipe the desk down, throw the napkins in the trash. I get a Lysol wipe. Another. I go over the desk again and again. After, I go up to the teachers' lounge bathroom and wash my hands until my knuckles are pink and raw.

I do this all without thinking. If I start to think, if I start to question how, or why . . . It's a thread I don't want to pull on.

Isn't there some data about how many bugs we eat when we're asleep?

He probably slept with his mouth open. A true mouth breather.

It's a freak occurrence that the spider survived.

Or maybe he ate the spider on purpose. Maybe he's one of those kids who were dropped on their heads as babies and like to cut the tails off of cats and set things on fire. Maybe he's a psychopath masquerading as a normal teenager in Adidas athleisure wear.

I should go to the nurse to check in. See if Chris is okay. I should ask her, *How could this happen?*

Maybe it does happen. Maybe it's not as strange and sinister as it seems.

I leave the bathroom and plod in the direction of the nurse's office. A few students are milling about, leaning on lockers. Gossiping, kissing, texting. They don't pay any attention to me and that's fine.

I don't want to be seen, to be noticed, because I can feel sweat beginning to drip down. I can feel it wetting the hair behind my ears. I can feel it traveling down my back. I wonder why I'm sweating, why I'm so nervous. My heart is pounding sadistically. Like it's trying to escape.

What do I have to be nervous about? I didn't do anything wrong.

The door to the nurse's office is open. There are two desks up front, and behind them a series of curtains and cots. The room appears to be unoccupied. It smells like hand sanitizer and teen body spray.

"Hello?" I say.

A face appears from behind one of the curtains. It's a student.

"Hey," they say.

"Is the nurse here?" I ask.

"No," they say, like I'm the biggest idiot alive.

"Is Chris Bersten here?"

"No."

"Was he here?"

"Like, when?"

"Within the past hour."

"Nah," they say. They disappear back behind the curtain.

"Cool. Thanks," I say with zero attempt to conceal my sarcasm.

I guess it's not my problem. I did my due diligence.

I go back down to the basement, to my classroom, and get my bag. I leave my papers, my planner, all of the students' homework assignments.

Not tonight, I tell myself. *Tomorrow. Or never.*

As I'm walking out, I run into Madison and Beth. They're sitting in the stairwell eating long ropes of licorice and writing in colorful notebooks with gel pens.

"Hi, Miss Crane," they say.

"I was just telling Beth about what happened in class," Madison says.

"I don't think we should be talking about it," I say, stepping over her backpack to get by.

"All right, but I was just saying, I obviously hope he's okay, but I mean, as someone who appreciates literature, what an incredible example of poetic justice."

"Good night, Madison. Night, Beth."

I stop at Simple Spirits on the way home for a bottle of wine. Or whiskey.

When I step inside, there's a woman there with a pixie cut wearing a large knit sweater and reading glasses.

"Welcome," she says. "How are ya? Can I help you?"

"Just looking," I say.

She smiles at me. She's got on dark purple lipstick. It's mostly on her teeth. "You must be Annie."

"Yes," I say. "Nice to meet you. Do you work with Sophie?"

She flinches when I say Sophie's name. She touches her cheek like I've just smacked her across the face.

"Sorry," I say. "She was here the last time I came in."

What am I missing? I thought Sophie was part owner of the store, involved somehow.

"That's all right," the woman says, her voice squeaky. She shakes her hands at me. "No worries. Sophie's in here all the time. We love Sophie. *Love* Sophie."

There's obviously something else going on here. Is Sophie downplaying the fact that she's actually some überpowerful real estate mogul/investor with a crazy stake in this town? Is she a terrible landlord? What is it? What's the deal?

"We got in a really nice gin," the woman says. "And we have a Malbec I'm partial to. I'm Alex, by the way."

"Malbec sounds good. I'll have that."

"All right," she says. She walks over to the shelf and reaches for a bottle. She's a very small person. I don't think she's wearing shoes. I think they're slippers. If they are, I admire her. I want to wear slippers to work. "It'll be sixteen eighty."

I pick a twenty out of my wallet and hand it to her. From the folds of her sweater, a fanny pack emerges. She stuffs the twenty in and takes out a stack of singles and some coins.

"Here you go," she says, handing me my change and the bottle. "Rough day?"

"Can you tell?"

"Wine on a Monday right around the end of a workday? Easy guess," she says. "You're a teacher? Rose told me. She and I are buds. Longtime."

"Yes, I teach."

"God bless ya," she says. "In my day, probably coulda done it. Kids are different now. Don't need a bag, do ya?"

"No, thanks. All set."

"Hope it helps, doll."

"Thanks, Alex."

"Yep," she says. "Take it easy."

When I get back to my apartment, I waste no time opening the bottle. I sit on the couch drinking and watching a documentary about cults.

It's a valiant attempt, but it does not stop me from thinking about what happened at school with the spider. It does not stop me from thinking about the look on Alex's face when I brought up Sophie.

It does not stop me from thinking about yesterday morning at the diner. The image of her, it's seared into my brain. I can see the light across her cheek, the sprigs of orange sunlight coming in through the slats of open blinds. I can see the stack of half-eaten pancakes, the remaining strawberries steeping in cream, her fork resting on her plate.

I can see her leaning forward, elbows wide, just touching the table.

I can hear her. I can hear her like she's next to me. Like she's speaking directly into my ear. No, like she's speaking from inside my head.

Want me to curse them for you?

A chill climbs my spine.

"No," I say out loud. I put the bottle down on the coffee table and stand up. "One, it's not possible. Two, I'm only psyching myself out because I'm vulnerable and alone. If Sam were around, I wouldn't even entertain the idea."

But he's not, and I am entertaining it.

It would be just my luck, wouldn't it? To move to this charming, picturesque small town and befriend an impossibly cool, glamorous stranger, only to find out that I've wandered into some kind of creepy Halloween town with haunted houses and curses.

Terrible things can happen to women who are alone. And here I am. No family, no friends. No boyfriend.

I'm pacing around my living room, allowing myself to indulge in this ludicrous theory, contemplating my chances of survival if this is an actual real-life horror situation, when my phone goes off.

It's Sam.

I pick up.

"Hey, sorry I missed you yesterday. I just got out of work and am walking to the train, so I thought I'd call. How's it going?"

It's amazing how quickly the rest melts away.

"Good! How are you?"

"Also good," he says. "Probably not as good as you."

"On a scale of good to good, how good are you?"

"Medium good."

"I'm low good."

"Why?" he asks.

I hear a siren going in the background, car horns blaring. For some reason it makes me nostalgic for the city.

"Something weird happened today at school and now I think there's a curse."

"What happened? And from what I know about curses, which is of course a lot, they're not real."

"I know," I say. "Some kid puked up a spider."

"That's disgusting."

"That's not even the worst part."

"How?"

"The spider was . . . still . . . alive! It was still alive!"

"What? That's not possible."

"I swear."

"You're joking."

"I'm not! It was the craziest thing I've ever seen."

"Annie," he says, "I don't believe you."

He's laughing, but it doesn't matter. It's a mean thing to say to someone. An ugly thing.

"Okay," I say. "Don't believe me."

"It was probably a prank," he says.

"Probably." I hadn't considered a prank. If it was a prank, Chris should drop out of school and pursue acting.

"Can't be worse than Peacoat Bob, though, right?"

Peacoat Bob was the nickname I gave to a kid I had my second year of teaching who wore a black peacoat indoors all year. His name was Tanner Robertson. He was a proud contrarian. A big fan of Ayn Rand. His favorite pastime was trying to make teachers feel stupid by proving his superior intellect.

I'd forgotten all about him.

"Peacoat Bob!" I say.

We chuckle for a moment. I savor it. You never realize how special it is to share a random inside joke until something funny happens and you have no one to tell. Then you realize how much of your life fades away without a witness.

"Hey, do you think you can pay the Internet bill another month? I can transfer you the money. Haven't had a chance to switch it over yet."

"Yeah," I say. "Sure."

"Cool," he says. "All right, I just got to the bar. Talk soon?"

"Bar?"

"Yeah."

"I thought you said you were going to the train."

"Oh. I must have misspoken. I'm meeting some coworkers."

"New coworkers?" I know I shouldn't be asking. I know I should keep my mouth shut. But I can't help myself.

"No," he says. "Why?"

"No reason," I say, making my voice flat, unfeeling. "You never used to hang out with your coworkers."

"Yeah, well," he says, "I used to have to be home for dinner."

I almost ask, *What's that supposed to mean?* Except I know what he meant.

"Okay," I say. "Have fun."

"Yeah," he says, sighing. "Bye, Annie. Be good. Jesus loves you."

I hang up.

I set my phone down on the coffee table and pick up the bottle of wine. I drink until the night goes foggy.

I wake up hungover. Late. I don't bother to shower. A few spritzes of perfume, new clothes. I run out the door with enough time to visit the Good Mug for a latte.

"Same as yesterday?" Oskar asks me.

"Yes, please," I say. "It was really good."

"Good enough to be your usual?"

I can't tell if he's flirting or just being nice. Neighborly.

I leave a dollar in the tip jar.

School goes fine, except Chris isn't in class.

"Anyone know what happened to Mr. Bersten?"

"He's dead," someone says.

"That's not funny," Madison says. "God."

I don't ask again. Not the next day. Or the day after that. He's absent the rest of the week, which is fine, because I'm not in the emotional state to handle any more harassment.

On Friday, I drop by the vice principal's office after my last class to express my required concern.

She's a fellow thirtysomething named Jill with straight bangs and a high ponytail. She wears a button-down underneath a sweater. She looks like she could be in a commercial for a wholesome brand. Lactose-free milk. High-fiber cereal.

"I like your sweater," I tell her. I figure the right move here is to open with a compliment.

"The whole outfit is Target!" she says, smiling. "I get all my stuff at Target. Not the Aster Target. You have to go to the Stillman Target. So, Annie, I'm glad you came by. I've been meaning to give you a ring."

My heart does its weird rapid-descending thing.

"I wanted to see how you were doing."

"Oh," I say, relieved. "Good, thank you."

"Good, good," she says. She's got a jar of Werther's Originals and a jar of Jolly Ranchers on her desk. She has framed pictures of herself and a guy I assume is her husband. He's tall, with dark hair and a beard. They look happy together. "So, about Mr. Bersten. That's why you're here, yes?"

"Yeah," I say. "He hasn't been in my class most of this week. There was an . . . Well, I don't know if I'd call it an incident. He got sick in class on Monday."

"I heard," she says. Her expression is overly empathetic. Sad eyes, big frown. I wonder if the kids make fun of her like they make fun of me.

"I had a student escort him to the nurse. I wasn't sure if he was still sick."

"Mm, yeah." She nods a lot, in a way that I think is meant to show me that she's listening but has the reverse effect. "Chris has not been absent. He's in good health, so that's good news. He did request an immediate transfer out of your class."

"Okay." I can't even guess at what reaction I should make, but I can tell she expects one. Her tone indicates this is bad news.

"Now, I think he may be embarrassed about getting sick the way he did. I spoke with Madison, and she gave me a very graphic, detailed description of the incident. It sounded very upsetting."

"He threw up."

"I know," she says. "But you know how it goes. Kids and their imaginations."

"Okay," I say. I'm not going to bring up the spider. *She* can bring up the spider.

"It's typical young-adult behavior. Deferring is very, very common at this age," she says. "It's difficult for them to process their own behavior, their own embarrassment. It's much easier to point the finger at someone else."

"What do you mean?"

She looks solemn for a moment, then shakes her head. "Never mind. I just wanted to make sure you were aware of the transfer and okay with everything."

"I'm fine with him transferring. If I'm honest, he was pretty disruptive," I say.

"Mm," she says, reaching into the Jolly Rancher jar and pulling out a purple one.

I'm baffled by anyone who prefers anything grape flavored. Sam is, too. It was one of the first things we bonded over when we met. Why not go straight for the cherry?

"Every student is different. It's our job as educators to foster a positive environment conducive to growth and learning for *all* of our students. Candy?"

She tips the jar in my direction.

I shake my head.

"I want you to know that my door is always open," she says. "Always."

"Thanks," I say, standing. "Thanks for that."

"You're welcome," she says. "Any fun plans for the weekend?"

"Yeah, actually," I say. "My friend is coming over tonight for dinner."

"Ooh, fun!"

I suppose I should ask her what she's doing, but I don't want to hear about her and her husband going apple picking or kayaking or whatever. Typically, I'd ask anyway because it's the polite thing to do, but there's a little voice in my head that says, *Don't bother. Spare yourself.*

The voice sounds a lot like Sophie's.

"Bye," I say.

"Bye now!"

I let the door slam behind me.

HONESTY

I pull into the driveway, and as I step out of my car, I hear my name being called.

Sophie walks toward me. She wears a long emerald green dress with a square neckline and puffy sleeves. Her hair is down, and it blows back even though the air is completely still. Not even a hint of breeze.

She carries a large wicker picnic basket.

"Am I too early?" she asks. "Perhaps I should let you settle."

"No," I say. "I'm happy to see you."

It's true. I might have my misgivings, but she's been nothing but good to me. I can dismiss my suspicions in exchange for some company.

I mean, they're ridiculous anyway. Curses? Really?

She sets the basket down and reaches for me, giving me the sweet hug that I desperately need.

"Pet," she says, stroking my hair, "you're sad."

"It's been a long, weird week," I say.

"You can tell me all about it," she says. "Or not. We can forget it ever happened. Poof. Gone."

I realize something, and as the words form in my head, they simultaneously blurt out of my mouth. "Wait. How did you know where I live?"

"Oh, I'm here all the time. Watching you while you sleep," she says, picking up the basket. "No, darling. Lynn mentioned she was getting an upstairs neighbor. Have you met her yet?"

"No." I'm beginning to think she doesn't exist.

"She's a photographer, so she travels a lot for work. She's lovely, a bit shy, though I suppose that might be ideal for a neighbor," she says. "Anyway, we don't get many new residents in town. Hardly ever. Ever, ever. But here you are, and here I am."

"Sorry. I just was like 'Wait a second.'" I open the door and we start up the stairs. My footsteps are loud and graceless, *clunk clunk clunk*. Sophie's are orderly, deliberate. Almost musical.

I pause with my key in the door. I haven't cleaned. There are dirty dishes in the sink. Multiple wine bottles empty on the kitchen counter, awaiting recycling.

It's embarrassing.

"What is it?" she asks.

"Nothing," I say, unlocking the door. "It's messy. I'm sorry. Like I said, rough week."

"Please," she says. "No judgment from me."

She sashays into the kitchen and puts the basket down on the counter, then begins to wash dishes.

"You don't have to do that."

"I want to," she says. "You relax. Oh, I brought you a candle, orange blossom and honey. Citrus and sweet. It's in the basket. Here."

She wipes her hands on my grimy dish towel and opens the basket. She takes out the candle. It's in a big glass jar. It's homemade. She made it.

"Thank you," I say, taking a sniff. It smells so good it's absurd. "Wow, Sophie. I love it."

"I made it with you in mind," she says. She pulls a book of matches out of somewhere. A pocket? She tosses it to me.

I put the candle in the center of the kitchen table. After a few failed attempts to light a match, I finally have a lucky strike. I light the candle. But the flame is quick, hungry, and it burns down to my fingers.

"Ow, fuck," I mumble, dropping the match into the candle, and literally lick my wounds.

"Are you all right, pet?" she asks.

"Yep," I lie, my fingers still in my mouth.

I sit myself down before I cause any more damage. I watch her work. She's so fast, so efficient. The dishes are all placed neatly on the drying rack. She begins unpacking the picnic basket. There's a loaf of bread, cheese, some kind of spread. A roasted chicken in a glass Pyrex dish with sprigs of rosemary and thyme. A sack of tiny red potatoes. Green beans.

A bottle of brown liquor.

"I'm going to make rum punch," she says.

"This is really nice, Sophie," I say. "Thank you."

"Annie, I haven't had anything to do on a Friday night in . . . let's just say a very, very long time. It's my pleasure. Truly."

She pulls a pear, an apple, and a container of blackberries out of the basket, which is starting to give off major Mary Poppins vibes. How much stuff is in there? She brought her own cutting board and knife. It's a big knife. She must sense my reaction, because without looking up she says, "Don't worry. The fruit won't feel a thing."

"Well, that's good."

"Do you want to talk about your week? Might feel better to get it off your chest." She begins to chop the apple. The knife makes a crisp slicing sound. It must be very sharp.

"It's nothing."

"It's clearly not nothing, or you wouldn't be upset," she says. She sets the knife down. She approaches me, offering a slice of apple.

"Try it," she says. "They're good this time of year."

It's got pink skin, pale flesh. There's no browning, no bruises.

"What?" she asks. "Don't you like apples?"

The room creeps up on me, walls inching in. There's not enough air.

I take the apple slice and shove it into my mouth. I stand, walk over to the window and crack it open.

"It's stuffy in here," I say, mouth full of apple mush. Delicious mush. Juicy. Sweet.

I notice Sophie is watching me. Not looking at me. Watching. Dissecting.

Something's not right. The feeling is sudden and palpable.

I meet her gaze, and she begins chewing on her thumbnail. Her eyebrows are low. It's an unmistakable expression of concern.

"What?" I ask her.

"You don't trust me," she says.

"What? No. Of course I do. I trust you."

"I understand," she says. "I'm not an easy person to trust. Maybe it's the way I look."

"No, Sophie. Why would you say that?"

"You hesitated. Just now when I gave you the apple. Like you were afraid to eat it."

"No," I say. But I was, wasn't I? Why? Why do I feel like something's off?

"I . . . ," she says. She doesn't finish her thought. She stares out the kitchen window.

I can't let my weird paranoid bullshit ruin this potential friendship. I won't.

"It's not you, Sophie. I'm just preoccupied. I had a bad conversation with Sam. He said something that really bothered me. And then I started drinking. I've been drinking a lot," I say. "I keep thinking, what if I can't do this? What if I can't be alone?"

Her demeanor changes. She softens, returns to cutting fruit.

"I understand why you're asking the question," she says. "But we've talked about this. You will be fine. Who initiated the contact? Him or you?"

I falter. Technically he called me, but he was calling me back. "Um . . ."

"So you?"

I nod.

"We'll have to fix that," she says. "And what prompted the call?"

"I don't remember. General loneliness?"

"Here," she says. She sets a glass down on the table in front of me. "Only if you want."

"Is it just rum in there?"

"Does it matter?" she asks.

I take a sip. It's straight rum. I guess we've abandoned the punch idea. That's fine.

"What did he say that hurt you?"

"He said . . . he said something about how he used to have to be home for dinner. Like, there was an insinuation that I kept him on a short leash, something like that."

Sophie gasps. "What a hideous thing to say!"

"I don't think I had, like, unreasonable expectations when we were together. But I don't know. Maybe. Maybe I did."

"Annie," she says. She pours herself a glass of rum. I notice her hand is shaking. Badly. Something's wrong. Something is very wrong.

The nag of fear is back. The flapping bird of panic.

"Sophie," I say.

She lets the glass fall from her hand. It smashes when it hits the floor. Completely shatters. Glass everywhere.

She steps on the glass without caution. It crunches under her boots. It's a horrible sound.

Outside, the sun bows beneath the trees, a sudden descent that chokes the light from the room. For a moment, in the chaos of the newborn dark, I can't see her at all. She's nowhere. But then she appears beside me, sitting next to me at the table. The only source of light in the room is the candle, the manic dance of an orange flame.

In the candlelight, shadows traverse her face. They climb up her neck, claw at her cheeks. The subtle warmth about her that I've grown accustomed to, the slight upward turn at the corners of her mouth, the fullness in her cheeks, eyelids relaxed to conceal the full whites of her eyes—all of that is gone.

Her mouth is flat, cheeks gaunt, eyeballs bulging out of their sockets.

"Annie," she says, her voice low, hoarse, "are we friends?"

How else am I supposed to answer?

"Yes," I say. "Of course."

"Do you want to be my friend?"

"I already am," I say. "We're friends. I've slept over at your house."

There's a sting on my arm. She's grabbing me. Her hand clutches my wrist. Her nails dig into my skin.

"I need to tell you something," she says. "Something about me. Something I believe you may already suspect."

"Okay," I say. I wriggle my hand and she loosens her grasp, though not enough for me to escape it. She has me.

"I've told you before, I feel real affection for you. A kinship. And I . . . I can sense you pulling away from me. Perhaps I'm imagining it, manifesting my fear. You see, it's very tempting for me to be my whole, true self around people I care for. But whenever I am, I take the chance of scaring them away."

"I don't know what you're talking about, Sophie," I say. "It's fine. We're good."

"I'm so afraid, Annie. I'm afraid if I tell you, it'll ruin everything. It's been so long since I've had a friend. And I could be a good friend to you. I could help you!"

She leans closer to me. "I know what it is not to know your place."

"Sophie," I say, "it's cool. We're cool. We're good."

She sighs, her exhale blowing the candle out.

But only for a second. It reignites itself somehow.

Sophie pushes a closed fist toward me, toward the light. She flips up her forearm. Then she slowly unbends her fingers, revealing her open palm. In it, a giant spider.

It's got a long body, skin like black velvet. Its front legs stretch out, rest on Sophie's index and ring fingers. Its back legs dangle off either side of her wrist.

"Shit," I say, pushing my chair back away from the table, away from her.

"I meant to help," she says as the spider crawls up her arm, settling on her shoulder. "I wanted to make things better for you."

"Sophie," I say. I feel disconnected from my body, weightless in this strange reality. I move to stand.

"No," she says. "Sit down."

There's a pressure on my shoulders, like two strong hands are there wrestling me back down. I collapse into the chair like a rag doll.

"Please," she says. "Do you understand what I'm trying to tell you?"

"Sophie," I say, "I'm sorry, but you're freaking me out."

"Hold on," she says. The spider stirs. It disappears behind her back. A few seconds later, the light above the table comes on. I look over and see the spider on the wall near the switch.

"What the fuck?" I mutter in spite of myself. "What the fuck? What the fuck . . . ?"

"I thought you liked spiders," she says.

I don't know what to say. I don't know what's happening.

"Do you understand?" she asks. "I would never hurt you. Never. I don't like to hurt anyone. Well, unless they deserve it."

"I don't understand," I say. "I don't know what you're trying to tell me."

"I'm not telling you, darling. I'm showing you. This is who I am," she says. "What I am."

"What?"

She shakes her head. "Does it matter to you? If I'm . . . different?"

"Different from what, Sophie? Different how?"

"There are many misconceptions," she says. "I won't say the word."

In the light, I can clearly see her vulnerability, same as the other day in the diner. The way she leans, the wideness of her eyes, the straight line of her mouth—it's all desperation. She's not a threat to me. She's pleading with me.

"The boy is fine," she says. "He won't bother you anymore. Maybe it was a bit theatrical. But he was rotten."

The disconnect returns, the weightlessness. Like I'm on the steep drop of a roller coaster.

"I'm sorry," I say, a nervous laughter escaping from somewhere inside me. "I don't understand what's happening."

"I cursed him," she says. "For you. I cursed them all. They won't bother you anymore. They'll be good students."

"What do you mean, you cursed them?"

She takes a deep breath and smooths her hair. Then she says, "If you keep asking these questions, I will answer them. But before you do, search yourself to see if you already know. Or if you even really want to."

All I want is to be out of this moment, out of this deeply unsettling conversation. I want fun Sophie to come back. I want to eat chicken and drink rum and forget about my problems. The last thing I want is any new ones. I have more than enough already.

I'll concede there is something dark going on here. I wasn't wrong to entertain the idea of the supernatural.

I hear the echo of Sam's voice in my head, his response when I told him about the spider. He said, *That's not possible.*

But it happened. It wasn't just possible; it happened. I saw it. I witnessed it.

Things are possible. All kinds of things.

The spider is in Sophie's lap, and she's stroking its head with her pinkie.

All kinds of strange, crazy, fucked-up, incredible things.

"Now," she says, "are you hungry? Should I put the chicken in?"

"Uh, yeah. Sure."

"I just need to warm him. He's already cooked," she says, turning the oven on. "Don't worry. Won't be dry."

"Yeah," I say. "That's not really worrying me right now. With what just happened. Not worried about dry chicken."

She laughs. A head-back, hearty laugh. It stops abruptly. "You still want to be my friend?"

I don't have to think about it. The answer is already there waiting patiently on my tongue.

"Yes," I say. "Of course."

She hides her face from me, lifting her hands to form a shield. I hear a single loud sniffle. She releases her hands, wipes her cheeks and smiles at me.

"I'm not going to cry," she says. "I haven't cried once in—I don't know—a hundred years?"

A hundred years?!

I know, with what we literally just talked about, with everything

I've observed and experienced, that things I've previously known as fantasy, as pure fiction, can exist within my reality. Still, hearing Sophie casually mention that she's been alive for over a hundred years is jarring.

Jarring and distressing and . . . oddly thrilling? I don't know what I'm feeling. At this exact moment, I'm watching a large, seemingly sentient spider offer Sophie a handkerchief for her to dry her eyes with.

Maybe I should be questioning my sanity, but how can I doubt what's right in front of me?

I start to laugh again, my new default reaction to any information I don't quite know how to process. Because how the hell else am I supposed to process this?

I can't stop laughing. It's cathartic. A strange, exhilarating release.

Sophie glances over at me and joins me in my laughter, though I don't think she understands what we're laughing at. I guess I don't, either.

This makes it all the funnier.

Soon I'm hunched over the table, holding on to it to steady myself so I don't fall to the ground in hysterics.

Sophie clutches her sides, her cheeks turning red.

Finally, she catches her breath for long enough to ask me, "What are we laughing at?"

I shrug.

This is also, apparently, hilarious.

We laugh until we're both on the floor. Sophie's spider and a few other spider friends who've emerged from under furniture and who knows where else congregate by her feet. They vibrate, their bodies bouncing, legs shaking. It's like they're mimicking her movement. Or they're also laughing.

"You know," she says, "I don't really think I'm hungry at all. Are you?"

"No, actually," I say, "I'm not."

She pulls herself to stand. "I'm going to put this all away. You can have it another time."

"Okay. Thank you."

"I'm not hungry," she says. "But I do want a slice of cake. Is that all right?"

She shows me a small iced loaf.

"Yes," I say. "What is it?"

"Lemon cake," she says. "I have some pomegranate seeds we can put on top. Would you like some?"

Ten minutes later we're on the couch eating the lemon loaf with two forks. She has the tray on her lap, and I've got the bottle of rum between my knees.

"So, guessing you're not actually in real estate?" I ask.

"Well, it is my land," she says.

"The town knows?" Their reactions are starting to make a whole lot of sense now.

"Oh, yes," she says. "Everyone in Rowan. No one outside. Well, there are rumors, I'm sure. Were rumors. Long time ago. Occasionally outsiders would show up at my hut. Throw stones."

I laugh. "Yeah, your hut."

"Oh, I'm not being funny," she says. "Remember that hut in the woods? I used to live there! I've been in the house for—I don't know—only about ninety years? The man who built it, a terribly arrogant railroad tycoon, outright stole my land. He did not much care for me bringing this to his attention. He did not much care for me. But as I've said to you before, things have a way of working themselves out."

I decide not to ask how exactly things worked themselves out.

"No one bothers me anymore, really," she says. "They know better."

Not going to ask any follow-ups about that, either.

"Oh, pet! I meant to tell you! The pool is ready for you. You should come over this weekend and have a swim. I was thinking I'd make goulash. Do you like goulash?"

"Never had it," I say.

"Settles it, then. Will you come tomorrow? Are you busy?"

"No," I say. "Not busy."

"Good! It'll be fun," she says. "I can't eat any more of this cake."

She takes another bite.

She's so endearing. So thoughtful and generous and beautiful . . . I mean, so what if she just so happens to be able to control spiders and curse obnoxious teenagers? So what if she dabbles in some dark magic and is over a hundred years old? I like her, and she likes me. She's my friend.

It's hard to make new friends, especially as you get older.

I need her.

"You could sleep over again, of course. If you like."

I flash back to the guest room, to the way the bed canopy sagged under the weight of something. To the face in the mirror.

"Can I ask you something?"

"You can ask me anything," she says. "I'm an open book."

"Is your house haunted?"

She sets the cake down on the coffee table and reaches for the bottle of rum.

"No," she says. "Why do you ask?"

"I don't know," I say. "I don't know what the rules are."

"Rules?"

"Like, if you can make spiders do stuff . . . if you're . . . different, what else is different? What else don't I know about?"

She tilts her head to the side, confused. "I'm not sure what you mean, darling."

"Are there ghosts? Vampires? Werewolves? Like, what else is out there?"

She takes a swig of rum and pats me on the leg. "You have nothing to fear."

"Sophie," I say, "that doesn't answer my question."

"Doesn't it, though?" she asks, passing me the bottle. "Trust me."

"So your house isn't haunted?"

She shakes her head.

"Okay."

"It's just old."

"Okay."

"You believe me?"

"Yeah," I say. "You would know, right?"

"Yes," she says. "Of course."

"Okay. Cool."

"Cool."

I give her back the bottle and pick up the cake. I take two bites in quick succession.

"Is there anything else, pet? Anything else you'd like to ask me?"

"Umm . . . not at the moment," I say.

"You're a very accepting person, Annie," she says. "I appreciate that about you."

"Thank you."

"It's good for me, especially considering . . . But I do worry with other people. I wonder."

"Wonder what?"

"I wonder about how much you've accepted that maybe you shouldn't have. What you may still be accepting."

I finish the cake and slide off of the couch onto the floor. The rum has gone to my head.

I don't feel good.

"More specifically, I mean with Sam," she says. "You told me what he said to you, but what did you say back to him? You should have told him to fuck right off."

"Should I have cursed him?"

She looks wounded. I've hurt her feelings.

"I'm sorry," I say. "That sounded mean. It was meant to be a joke."

She sighs and begins to examine her nails. They're painted black. "You know, that's not a bad idea."

"I'm not going to curse my ex-boyfriend. Sam is fine. Everyone can be a jerk sometimes."

"All right," she says, "I'll leave it alone. For tonight. I've put you through enough, though I did bring cake. And liquor."

"You did."

"Does that even things out?"

"Sure."

She laughs. "I'm convinced!"

Maybe it's the rum, or maybe it's the truth, but right now all I can think about is how much I love her. She's my lifeline. I don't have a single other person whom I can confide in, who cares for me the way that I know she does. She has my back.

I don't know why. Why she wants to be friends with me, hang out with me. I'm not special. I've always been realistic about who I am, about my perfectly average, unexceptional trajectory. I've always been fine with it.

But as she moves her fingers through my hair from behind me on the couch, humming some tune I can't identify, I wonder if maybe I am special, and it only took someone else special to point it out to me.

"I should go, pet. Let you sleep," she says. "Shall we meet at the market tomorrow? Around eleven?"

"Mm. Yeah," I say.

She's carrying me. She's carrying me to bed.

I don't know how. I'm taller than her. I'm all limbs. I'm heavy.

She sets me down gently and pulls up the covers, the way a mother would.

"There we are," she says. "Good night, Annie. Sleep well."

She hovers her hand over my face. My eyes close, and I fall into what will be the best sleep of my life.

CONVENIENT, INCONVENIENT

My apartment is spotless. The dishes are done; my laundry is clean and folded on the couch. There's a bouquet of fresh flowers on the coffee table. Fat-petaled roses and orange chrysanthemums in full bloom.

Resting on the lip of my bathtub is an assortment of bar soaps and jars of thick, buttery lotion. There is a small candle on the top of the toilet in a bronze tin.

Sophie.

I light the candle and take a long, hot shower. I use one of my new bars of soap and it feels like silk, smells like bergamot. After, I slather myself with the lotion. I watch as the persistent scales on my knees and elbows disappear in an instant. I watch in the mirror while I massage the lotion into my face, and my skin glows in its wake.

The marriage of fragrances between the soap and the lotion and the subtle lemony contribution from the candle have relaxed me into a state of complete dopey giddiness. I float around without a thought in my head, without a single fuck to give.

I get my bathing suit out of the bottom drawer of the dresser and pack it along with a pair of pajamas and a sweater in my large purse.

I go to blow out the candle in the bathroom, but it's already been done for me. I go to get a drink of water, and there's a glass on the counter waiting. Cold, with a lemon wedge.

I drink it down.

On the way out, by the door, there's a spider.

I stop to say hello.

I watch as the spider lifts one of his legs and begins to wave it back and forth, back and forth.

I meet Sophie outside of the Good Mug tent at the market.

"My Annie," she says, hugging me tightly, and kisses me on the cheek. "How did you sleep?"

"Great, actually," I say. "I feel amazing. Thank you for the soaps. And the flowers. And for cleaning my apartment."

She puts a hand on my shoulder. "Please. For my Annie? Anything."

"At least let me get you coffee. Are you hungry? What would you like?"

"Yes, coffee," she says. "And yes, food. Maybe something sweet."

I lean in close to her. "You said you *don't* eat children, right?"

She laughs. "Right."

"Just wanted to confirm."

"Common misconception," she says. "I was thinking more along the lines of a donut. Or muffin. We can go to the bakery after we get our coffee. Have you met Deirdre yet? She's a singular talent."

"I haven't."

"We'll fix that."

"What do you want for coffee? Latte?"

"Whatever you're getting. Make things simple for Oskar," she says. "Poor bloke."

He looks up at us. He does have sad eyes. Or maybe they're angry. I can't tell.

"Good morning, Annie," he says. "Good morning, Sophie."

"Morning," Sophie says.

"Two vanilla lattes, please," I say. "Large."

He grunts. He is significantly less friendly when Sophie is around.

To be fair, I think Sophie gets a kick out of making him uncomfortable. As he steams the milk, she begins to twirl her fingers, somehow contorting the steam cloud into a grumpy face. He pretends not to notice, but I know he does.

Sophie presses her lips together, trying not to laugh. I do. I laugh. I can't help it.

"Here you go," he says. "It's eleven."

I pay him, then allow Sophie to lead me away. We walk over to a tent where baked goods are sold. Rose is there talking to a woman wearing an apron over a mustard jumpsuit. She has a shaved head and wears big wooden earrings.

"Deirdre," Sophie says.

Deirdre jumps a little at the sound of Sophie saying her name.

"Sophie!" she says, her voice shrill. "Good morning, Sophie. How are you? What can I get for you?"

"Have you met Annie?" she asks.

"No, I haven't. Rose told me about you."

"Hi. Nice to meet you. Hi, Rose."

Rose is also less friendly with Sophie around. She gives a weak smile, then slips behind Deirdre.

"I made some strawberry-pistachio donuts," Deirdre says. "Here, take some. I can throw in some muffins, too. I've got apple and carrot."

She begins to fill a large box with pastries and donuts and muffins.

"The apple muffins are really scrumptious. We've had a wonderful crop of apples this year, Sophie. Really wonderful."

"Yes," Sophie says, "we have."

Rose holds open a bag for Deirdre to set the box inside. It's difficult for them because their hands are trembling.

"Thank you," Sophie says, taking the bag. "Enjoy your day. Annie, let's go."

"Thank you!" I tell Deirdre.

"You're welcome. Come by the store anytime!" she says. Rose is still cowering behind her.

"Do we need anything else?" Sophie asks me.

"I don't think so," I say. I shrug.

Sophie shrugs. "Let's go home and eat treats and run around like maniacs."

"Let's do it!"

I follow her through the woods. This time, when we get to the well, to the graves, to the hut, Sophie explains them to me.

"I used to get my water from that well," she says. "They were always threatening to throw me down it. And they did a few times! But I could always get back up. That's the thing about me. I'm quite resilient.

"I didn't mind the hut," she says. "Would be hard to go back now, though."

At the circle of headstones, she simply says, "Old friends."

I leave it alone.

When we get to her house, it looks even bigger than I remember. Like there's an extra turret or an extra wing. Sophie holds the door open for me, then leads me into the dining room.

"Let's eat our donuts on fine china," she says, "like proper adults."

The dining room is distinctly medieval. There's a behemoth wooden table surrounded by too many chairs to count. Intricate tapestries hang on the stone walls, and there's a fireplace at the other end of the room. Actually, there are two fireplaces, identical twins, standing side by side. Above the table, chandeliers hang from long chains. Each one is wrought iron with multiple tiers holding what I assume are fake candles. Maybe not. I stand around for a moment bewildered by the room's extravagance.

Sophie sets the table with porcelain plates, linen napkins and large glass goblets etched with roses. She fills the goblets from a decanter that looks like a snake.

"It's cider," she says as she pours. She sets the decanter aside and pulls out a chair for me.

"You sure know how to treat a lady."

She raises an eyebrow. She sits across from me, then offers me the box of baked goods. I select a blueberry donut.

"Our first course," Sophie says, choosing a muffin.

Just as I'm about to take a bite, my phone dings.

Text message.

I take it out of my pocket to check.

"No," Sophie says. The phone is plucked from my grasp by an invisible hand and set screen down on the table. "It'll spoil our fun."

"I want to see who it's from," I say. I flip my phone over. It's a text from Sam. It reads Hey.

I go to unlock my phone with my thumb, but before I can, it slides across the table out of my reach.

"Annie," Sophie says with a reprimanding intonation, "I told you."

"It's Sam," I say.

"I know," she says. "Here you are having a perfectly lovely Saturday morning, and here he is ruining it."

"He didn't ruin it," I say. "It was just a text."

"Reminding you of his existence and the pain he caused you. Continues to cause you," she says. "Look, pet, I understand it must be hard to sever ties with someone you loved for so long. But he's not in your life anymore. You're building a new life. Why let him poison the well? Take it from me, who has actually poisoned a well. From inside that well."

I don't like the way she's looking at me. I turn away, shoving some donut into my mouth.

"I was kidding about the well. Well, sort of. I don't want you to think I'm being insensitive."

She puts her hand on my hand. When she pulls it back, there's a ring on my index finger. Silver with a rough pink stone.

"Look," she says. "Something shiny."

"Sophie! It's so pretty!" I hold it up to the light.

"You like pink, yes?"

"I like pink."

"Thought so," she says. "It doesn't really suit me."

"Every color suits you," I say.

She basks in the compliment. I decide one of the things I like most about Sophie is how much she enjoys a compliment. I wouldn't think someone so beautiful would feed on compliments the way she does. It makes me feel less pathetic for my need, to know that someone could be so completely self-possessed and still savor validation.

"This muffin tastes bad," she says, pushing her plate away. "What in this world is more disappointing than a bad muffin?"

"A lot, Sophie. A lot of things."

She sulks, dramatically slouching in her seat.

"I'm sorry," I say. "It's very, very disappointing. You want some of my donut?"

"No, that's all right. I wanted all of this," she says, tapping the box, "but I think I wanted for the sake of wanting."

"So you *are* human."

"Bleh," she says, sticking out her tongue. "Don't insult me."

"Hey!" I say. "I'm human."

She retracts her tongue and sits up. "Are you?"

"Last I checked."

"Mm. Would you like to swim?"

"Yes! Yeah, that'll be fun."

"You can change upstairs in your room. I'll meet you down here."

"Are you going to swim?"

She shakes her head no.

"Why not?"

"I don't care for it," she says, sighing. "Not at all."

"Okay. You know, we could always get you a blow-up raft. They make fun ones now. Shaped like swans. And unicorns!"

She cringes. "I hate unicorns."

"What do you mean, you hate unicorns?"

"Another time," she says. "You go change. I'll make us lemonade and meet you on the steps."

"All right, all right," I say, heading off to "my room."

Being with Sophie in the house is a very different experience from being alone in the house. Without her presence, the house becomes cold and unnerving. I walk through the mirror hallway haunted by the memory of the face I saw in the bathroom upstairs. I clench my fists, my palms slick with nervous sweat. With each mirror I pass, I have to fight off momentary panic and reassure myself that the only reflection I see in my peripheral vision is my own.

This, of course, isn't true. There's a pale disembodied face hovering somewhere over my shoulder, behind my back. It appears for a second, but as soon as I turn to verify its presence, it slips out of view.

Sophie said this place isn't haunted, and she's been nothing but honest with me so far. So I shake it off. Must be my imagination.

Upstairs in my room, there are several bouquets of fresh flowers. There are clean sheets on the bed, which is made so neatly I'm hesitant to ever disturb it. There are even mints on the pillows.

It's so nice to be somewhere you're wanted.

I drop my bag on the floor and start to undress. I have my pants off when the bathroom door begins to move. It was wide open, but now it's closing. All by itself.

And here I am, standing defenseless in the middle of the room, stark naked below the waist like Donald fucking Duck.

"I'm naked!" I shout for some reason. If it's a murderer, that's more of an advertisement than a warning, and if it's a ghost, not really sure it would care?

I've gone from lifelong steady-handed skeptic to half-naked and shouting at unseen beings within a span of two weeks. The logic I've always relied on has become so slippery, impossible to grip.

The door closes. Shuts completely. I hear the click of the latch.

Maybe I'm being given some privacy?

Or maybe it's a draft. It's probably a draft.

I change quickly, put my pajama pants and sweater on over my swimsuit, then run down the stairs.

Sophie sits at the bottom with a tray of lemonade.

"What is it?" she asks. "What's wrong?"

"Nothing," I say. Suppression is a useful tool. Honestly, it's underrated.

"Follow me," she says. "To the swimming pool!"

She leads me down what she calls the gallery, the long hallway with all of her paintings.

"If you go right here, you'll find the conservatory. It's my little lair. Smells divine with all of the flowers. Now, through here . . . I don't really know what this space is meant to be used for."

We enter a hexagonal room. The ceiling is a skylight, glass angling up to an intense point in the center. There's no furniture in this room, no accents on the walls. We walk across it and the echoes of our footsteps seem to run circles around us before fading away.

Sophie opens a door that leads to a rickety spiral staircase. It's steep and narrow, and by the time we get to the bottom, I'm so dizzy I can almost feel my eyeballs knocking together inside my skull.

The pool room is not what I was expecting. An indoor pool is a luxury, but nothing about this room is luxurious. It's like a tiled cave.

The tiles were likely white at some point, but they've yellowed with age. They line the pool, the walls, the ceiling, though there's not really any distinction between the surfaces, since every one is curved. I imagine this is what it feels like inside a submarine. Acutely claustrophobic.

Sophie sets the lemonade tray down on a small glass table. She sits along the ledge, her dress fanning around her.

"Are you comfortable?" I ask. "You're really just going to watch me swim?"

"Is that strange?"

"A little."

She pulls a small leather-bound book out from behind her. No idea where it came from.

"I'll read," she says. "Or write. Or draw you."

"Very funny," I say.

I hope she was kidding. Most of the time, I can tell when Sophie's kidding. Most of the time.

I shimmy out of my pants and sweater, dip a toe in to check the temperature of the water. It's warm.

I step into the shallow end, which isn't actually that shallow. I dunk myself under and begin to do the backstroke. When I get to the other side of the pool, I let myself float there.

"How is it?" Sophie asks.

"It's great," I say. "What are you reading?"

"Some book of alchemy," she says. She fakes snoring.

"That bad?"

"No," she says. "I'm melodramatic."

"You? No."

"Sarcasm, darling."

I begin to swim around, do some laps. I was on the swim team throughout middle school but decided to quit freshmen year after Kim Schulman made a comment about my flat chest. I'd spent three years trying to convince myself that no one cared about my lack of boobs except me, only to have my paranoia validated.

I wonder what Kim is up to now. I bet she's married. I make a mental note to Internet-stalk her later.

And while I'm envisioning what her wedding dress might have looked like, if she wore a ball gown or something more fitted, I'm able to ignore the sensation working its way up my foot, around my ankle.

But as it becomes tighter, colder, more aggressive, I'm forced to open my eyes and look beneath me, directly under the spot where I'm treading water in the deep end.

At first, I think it's my shadow, until I see the distinct fingers.

With a single violent tug, I'm underwater.

The sting of water up my nose, inside my lungs, shocks me into complete stasis. I'm being dragged down to the bottom of the pool. The whirring in my ears is vicious.

I make the mistake of turning. There's a person there. Kind of. A person with grayish pocked skin and bulging eyes, the color in them like melted wax. I scream and water punches down my throat.

I thrash around, trying to get the thing away. I fight for the surface, but it becomes very clear to me very quickly that it will not let me go. I manage to move us over to the side, and with everything I have, I kick, smashing it into the wall.

But it's gone. It's my foot that absorbs the impact.

I float up to the surface. I throw myself onto the ledge, coughing up pool water and probably my lungs along with the rest of my internal organs. The gum I swallowed when I was six.

"Annie, what happened? Are you okay?"

Sophie reaches out and pulls me up over the ledge.

"Your foot!" she says.

I look down. It's mangled. Bleeding. I can't feel it.

"What the fuck, Sophie?!"

"What?" she asks, looking confused, hurt by my anger.

"There was a . . . a . . . a thing! A guy! A person in your pool! It just tried to drown me!"

She inches toward the edge, carefully craning her neck to see into the pool.

"It's gone now," I say. "It's . . . it's a ghost! It looked like a ghost!"

"Hmm," she says, tapping her lip.

"I thought you said your house wasn't haunted."

She doesn't answer. She won't look at me.

"I almost drowned," I say. "Is your house haunted?"

Without raising her eyes to meet mine, she mumbles, "Maybe a little."

"Sophie!"

"If I had told you, you would have never wanted to come over again!" she says. "You're not in any danger. They're just . . . inconvenient."

"Who are they? And I'd say almost drowning isn't an inconvenience. Death isn't an inconvenience."

"Well, I don't know if I'd agree, but . . ."

"Sophie!"

"I didn't realize they could swim," she says. "I apologize. Please, please don't be angry with me."

She grabs my hands and kisses them. "Please? I'll fix your foot."

I can't bring myself to look at it again. I know it's broken.

"I need to go to a doctor," I say.

"Pshh," she says. "I can fix it. And I promise I'll do something about the ghosts. They're just excited because you're new."

"Excited?"

She sighs. "I should have been honest with you. I thought it would be too much if I told you everything all at once. I didn't want to scare you away. I wanted you to still want to be my friend and to come over and for us to have a normal experience. As friends. Who can, you know, hang out."

Her eyes are wide and sweet and pleading. Most of the time, with Sophie, I feel like the clueless, uncool little sister, but every once in a while, I'm the big sister with the allowance money and the jeans she wants to borrow.

I don't know. I'm an only child.

"You can get rid of them?" I ask. "The ghosts?"

"Oh, yes. It's much easier since they're already dead."

I find this disturbing on multiple levels. First, I don't appreciate her nonchalant attitude toward literal ghosts. Second, it implies she's familiar with the difficulties related to disposing of living people.

She gathers up my pants and sweater. "Let's talk about this upstairs."

"How am I getting upstairs?" I ask.

She leans down and lifts my arm over her head so it's draped across her back. She shuts her eyes hard, and a moment later, I'm weightless. She opens the door to the spiral staircase, and I whimper at the sight of it. There's no way we're getting up it side by side, and there's no way I'm getting up alone.

Sophie reaches out and touches the wall. We climb the first step, her anchoring me as I float along beside her, and somehow we fit. It's like the stairs expand for us to accommodate us.

I hear a rattling sound and peer behind us to see the lemonade tray following us up the stairs. Carrying itself.

"I'm sorry," she says. "I'll take care of the ghosts, I promise. I didn't think they would bother you. I understand if you don't want to come here anymore."

There's such sadness in her voice, such defeat.

"Maybe not for a swim," I say.

Her smile is bright as a firework. "Really?"

"And I don't want to sleep in that room," I say. "There's a ghost in there."

"Is there really?"

"Yes."

"I'm so sorry, pet. Truly, I am."

"It's okay." I'm not capable of staying mad at anyone. I don't have the stamina.

She carries me to the conservatory. It's basically a fancy greenhouse, a giant glass room brimming with plants. It's balmy and smells incredible. There's a gorgeous array of colors from all of the flowers. There are rows and rows of herbs. Vines hang from the ceiling.

I'm reminded.

"Hey," I ask her, "did you put up a plant in my stairway?"

"Hmm?" She sets me down on a stool in a corner, next to a workbench. She wastes no time busying herself, grinding away with a stone and pestle.

"I noticed there was a plant hanging above the stairs up to my apartment," I say. I gesture to the room around us. "Wondering if maybe you had something to do with that."

"Hm . . . oh, yes," she says. "Mistletoe. It's often misunderstood and absurdly misused. It brings peace. When we met, I sensed you were in need of peace."

"Oh. Okay." I'm not sure how I feel about her sneaking into my stairway to hang a plant, but I know her well enough by now to know that her intentions were good.

"Is that weird?" she asks me after a minute of silence. "Was that a strange thing to do? Be honest with me, please."

"Kind of, yeah," I say.

"It's been so long since I . . ." She sighs. "I don't know how to be any other way. I suppose I'm out of touch. Terribly uncool."

"Are you about to heal my foot with magic?" I ask her. "Because that's pretty fucking cool."

She giggles. Her cheeks go pink and she hides them with her hands.

"I am!" she says. "I am about to do exactly that! Close your eyes."

I do. There's a moment of pain as she covers my foot in some kind of cold, wet paste. I hear her walking away from me, and when she returns, I hear the sound of running water and feel the spray of liquid passing gently across my foot.

"All done," she says. "You can open your eyes now."

My toes are straight; there's no blood, no swelling. And more than that, there's no more dead skin or calluses. It's like I just got a pedicure.

"Wow," I say. "Thank you."

"Don't thank me," she says. "I feel too guilty to be thanked. You're not still mad, are you?"

"No," I say. "But honestly, I don't think I've really accepted what just happened."

I don't think I'm digesting any of this information. About Sophie, about the town, about the fact that I was just almost drowned by a ghost that could somehow manifest in physical form. My brain doesn't know what to do with any of this. It's like being a doctor stumped on a diagnosis. *It's probably fine. Monitor the symptoms.*

"I can walk you home if you like," she says.

I shrug. "I don't have anything to do at home."

At least here, I have Sophie. I have company. I don't want to be alone, sad and thinking about Sam, about why he texted me this morning.

I wonder why he texted me this morning.

"What should we do?" she asks. "Are you hungry? Should I make the goulash? Do you want to read? Watch a movie?"

I notice a wet stain on her dress. I realize, in total horror, that it's my blood.

"Sophie," I say, "I think I bled on you."

I point.

"Oh," she says. A grin splits across her face. "Human blood. My favorite!"

That was definitely a joke.

"Come upstairs with me. We can go into my closet. Play dress-up," she says.

"Okay!"

I put my pajama pants back on, my sweater, my socks. My bathing suit is still damp, and now my clothes are damp, too. It's uncomfortable, and I look like a slouch compared to Sophie, who is the epitome of elegance despite her dress being stained with blood.

We go upstairs, to the east wing. Sophie opens a set of French doors and announces, "This is my room."

It's very black. Black-and-silver damask wallpaper, a monumental four-poster bed with black velvet curtains, a black crystal chandelier. There are bouquets of black roses in black vases all around the room. It's intense, severe, but somehow beautiful in its severity.

"Closet is through here," she says. She opens another set of French doors.

The closet is almost as big as the bedroom. We're surrounded by dresses, mostly black. They seem to sway on their own, to dance in a nonexistent breeze.

Sophie walks with purpose all the way to the back of the closet. She pulls some dresses aside to reveal an armoire. She opens the bottom drawer and begins sifting through it.

"You like to wear pants, yes?" she asks. "I'm going to find some pants for you."

"That's okay," I say. "I can wear these."

"They're wet," she says. "And besides, it's dress-up. You agreed."

"Okay, okay," I say. "Your pants will all be too short on me."

"Maybe," she says. "I can make you some."

"Make them?"

"I made all these," she says, gesturing to the rest of the closet, to what must be over a hundred dresses. "Don't be impressed. As I've said, I have a lot of free time. Here, catch!"

She throws me a pair of silky gray pants, then opens the top drawer and throws me a black cashmere sweater. "Try those."

She turns around.

I'm not getting naked right here in the closet.

"I'm going back to my room," I say. "My underwear is in there."

"All right, darling," she says. "But come right back. I want to see how they look."

As I walk back out through her bedroom, I again remember what's so easy to forget when I'm around Sophie.

This house is very, very scary.

I break into a light jog, hurrying to my room, where I can change quickly and get back to her.

I close the door, undress as fast as I possibly can, flinging my wet bathing suit across the room. It lands on top of the canopy. A problem for later. I put on my underwear, my bra, then the pants and sweater. They're both incredibly soft. The pants are too short.

I'm too afraid to check my reflection. I don't know whom else I'll see in the mirror.

As I go to power walk past the staircase, I remember that my phone is still downstairs on the dining room table.

Retrieving it would mean journeying solo through the ghost house. But it would also mean I can text Sam back. See what he wants.

Maybe he'll apologize for our last conversation.

Maybe he misses me.

I turn and travel quietly down the steps. I don't want Sophie to hear me. I don't think she would approve.

I run on tiptoes through the mirror hallway, looking only at the floor. When I get to the dining room, I see my phone on the table. I pick it up. The text from Sam hangs there on my home screen. Hey.

I lower my thumb down to unlock my phone.

"Annie."

I drop my phone.

Sophie is sitting at the table, looking thoroughly unamused.

"Sophie! You startled me!"

"Well," she says. She opens her hand and my phone flies into it.

"I was just getting my phone," I say.

She raises an eyebrow.

"I wasn't going to text him back."

She raises the other eyebrow.

"Sophie."

"Annie."

"I'm being honest," I say. "I just like to have my phone. I feel weird without it."

"I've heard that happens," she says. She hands me my phone. "As long as you're not tempted."

"I'm not," I say. I feel bad lying to her. I feel even worse for my own weakness. "It's just . . . I think the hardest part about a breakup is not talking to the one person you've always talked to. About everything."

"Pet," she says, softening. She stands up and puts her arms around me.

"It's like breaking a habit. It's hard."

"It's not something I've experienced," she says. "But I can see that you're struggling. Why don't we go back upstairs? I can show you some of my old dresses from back when. Then maybe we can make dinner. Relax in the library."

"Yeah, okay."

"And I can walk you home after," she says. "Or you can stay. Whatever you like."

I really can't imagine ever sleeping here again after what happened in the pool, but I don't want to come out and say that to her.

I nod politely and follow her back to her closet, where we spend hours going through all of her dresses, some that date back to the seventeenth century. And her hats! She has an extensive collection of hats.

"Notice none of them are tall and pointy," she says.

I did notice.

Later that night, after we eat leftover pastries for dinner and drink gin cocktails and read each other poems in the library, I tell Sophie that I'm going to go home, and she doesn't try to convince me to stay.

"I'll walk you through the wood," she says. She puts on a magnificent black feathered coat that she rediscovered in the back of her closet. She tells me that she's going to make me one to match, even though I express my doubts at being able to pull it off.

We walk in silence for a while, which is unusual for us. We rarely have a substantial lull in conversation.

It begins to get uncomfortable.

"What are you thinking about?" I ask her.

"Just remembering something," she says. "Something that happened in these woods a long time ago."

"Do you want to talk about it?"

She runs her hand along my arm. "Not really. Not a pleasant memory."

"I'm sorry, Sophie."

"I've come a long way," she says. "There's no reason to be sorry for the things that make us better."

"Yeah. But why do the things that make us better always have to suck so much? Can't there be a route to self-improvement with—I don't know—rainbows and cupcakes and, like, sitting on the couch?"

She laughs. "I think so! I believe it's possible."

"Good," I say. "Sign me up for that."

"Not everything can be easy. Not everything has to be so hard," she says.

"Yeah."

The silence rises again, putting space between us. I should let it be, allow it to exist, be content with it. Sam and I used to sit in silence, and it was fine. But something about this quiet I can't trust. I fear it'll continue to expand and expand until it swallows the promise of our friendship.

"Do you know those ghosts?" I ask. "In your house? Do you know who they are?"

Sophie sighs, and I know instantly it was the worst thing I could have said.

"No," she says. "No idea."

I find that hard to believe. She's lived in Rowan for hundreds of years. She's lived in that house for almost a hundred.

"No?" I ask.

"Annie," she says, "the more thought and energy you give them, the more they'll appear to you. They're attracted to that energy. It's quite similar to your ex-boyfriend. You give him power with your thoughts."

"You're right," I say. "I'm sorry."

"We can put it in the past now, yes?"

"Yeah."

"I'll take care of it," she says. "I promise, no more ghosts."

"Okay."

"Don't worry," she says. "They won't follow you home."

I hadn't considered that they might.

We come to the edge of the woods and she hugs me, rubs my back.

"Sweet dreams, darling," she says.

"Will you come over this week? For dinner?"

"If you'll have me," she says, releasing me.

"Any night," I tell her. "Whenever."

"I'll see you soon," she says. And with that, she turns and begins to walk back through the woods.

When I get home, I stand in front of the mirror, admiring the clothes Sophie gave me. I have to admit, I look exceptional.

It's late, but I'm not tired. I make myself a cup of tea and sit on the couch, examining my foot. There's no evidence that it was ever injured. The events of the afternoon seem so far away, like they happened in another lifetime or to someone else.

Sophie seemed so concerned that I was mad at her, but for some reason, with the way we left things, I wonder if she's mad at me. If I did something wrong.

I guess I shouldn't have asked about the ghosts, though how could I not?

I don't know how to navigate a new friendship, especially not with someone like Sophie.

I tap my finger against the mug, my new ring making a satisfying clink. It's such a pretty ring. Such a lovely gift.

My phone chimes. It's another text from Sam. This one reads You okay?

I adjust the ring on my finger. I don't respond.

THE PICTURE

A week goes by. And another. Another. I develop a routine. In the mornings, I get my coffee from the Good Mug. I make small talk with Oskar and whoever else is around from town. We talk about how it's getting cold outside, about how it's getting dark early. We talk about what TV shows we're bingeing, complain about the characters. We talk about what fruit is good at the market.

After, I go to school. The students are afraid of me. I find the rumors they spread about me ironic, considering my recent discovery about Sophie. They think that I'm the one with some kind of dark power, that I'm the one responsible for the now-infamous Chris Bersten spider incident.

But . . . they behave now. So . . .

I eat lunch in my classroom and avoid other staff, especially Jill, who has assumed that because I went to see her once about something work related, she has free rein to ask me personal questions. She asks, as I stand horrified in front of the vending machine in the teachers' lounge, if I'm single.

"Uh . . . yeah," I say, because for some reason I feel obligated to answer despite the question being inappropriate, verging on unprofessional. I never did learn how to set boundaries.

"This might be forward of me," she says, "but I figured it couldn't hurt to ask!"

She figured wrong.

"I know someone, a friend of my husband's. His name is Pascal. He's from Vermont, very handsome. Great catch. I really think you two would hit it off. If you're interested! Only if you're interested."

"Um," I say. "Thank you for thinking of me. But I just got out of a relationship."

"Oh, no!" she says with such an overt display of pity it's legitimately nauseating.

"I'm fine," I say, wishing Sophie were around with her understated empathy, with her lack of patience for despair. "Just not ready to date."

"You let me know if you change your mind!" she says. "He's really, really handsome!"

With that, she leaves me alone to squirm in the lingering discomfort of the interaction.

I tell Sophie about it that night while we're prepping potatoes in my apartment.

"I guess she was just trying to be nice," I say.

"A lot of people just try," Sophie says, lacerating a sprout. "Trying doesn't absolve you."

"Oof," I say.

She rubs salt on a clean spud and carefully inserts it into a tinfoil cage. "I didn't invent the truth, Annie."

"Didn't you, though?"

"Don't flatter me, pet," she says. "My poor ego can barely fit into this dress."

She's in a new dress. It's a deep purple velvet. From the remaining fabric, she made me a matching ensemble, pants and a top with cap sleeves. When she gave it to me, she told me, "We don't need to wear them at the same time." But we do. We are. We look like we're a late-seventies glam-rock duo.

I haven't been back to Sophie's since the ghost-in-the-pool incident. Now she comes over here. We cook and talk, and I've introduced her to Netflix. She says she'll never forgive me, but I know she already has.

"Would you consider it?" she asks me, now slicing some scallions.

"Consider what? Going on a date? With supposedly handsome Pascal from Vermont?"

"Yes."

"I don't know. Probably not."

She doesn't say anything. A spider gathers up the rogue scraps of blemished potato skin and onion, slowly rolling them toward the trash.

"Do you think I should?"

"I can't tell you what to do," she says.

"You can tell me what you think. I want your opinion."

"I think you'd be setting yourself up for disappointment," she says, "though I am who I am and live how I live."

"What do you mean?"

"I'm never going to advocate looking for a romantic partner, especially not a male partner," she says, and pauses to shudder. "I don't much care for men. Or romance. I think both are a waste of time. And I'm someone with a lot of time."

"Tell me how you really feel."

"That is how I really feel," she says, not picking up on my sarcasm.

"Yeah, I mean, I guess I get it," I say. "I understand where you're coming from."

A blatant lie.

I used to be convinced that no one was okay with being alone. I thought anyone who claimed happiness with their single status was sad and delusional. I still believe that, but now I know there's one exception. Sophie.

We put the potatoes in the oven and wait for them to cook. We shred a block of cheese, and when the potatoes are ready, we cut through their crispy, salty skin and stuff the cheese inside, along with the onions and some sautéed mushrooms. We eat them on the couch while watching a documentary about the British royal family, Sophie's new favorite subject.

"In my day, royals killed one another," she says. "Now they stand around and get divorced!"

"Is that a good thing or bad thing?"

"I don't know! It's all so horrifying. Yet fascinating."

She's obsessed.

At some point I start to doze off. Sophie puts a blanket over me and a glass of water on the coffee table.

"I'll see you tomorrow," she says, petting my hair.

Sophie never sleeps over. I couldn't really picture her sleeping on a couch; she's too glamorous for that. But I wonder if there's another reason. Some rule I don't know about. Does she sleep at all?

I wake up late the next morning and meet Sophie for coffee at the farmers market. It's starting to get chilly. Sophie wears a long, soft leather jacket that cinches at the waist. I wear a blue puffy coat that she finds hilarious. She pokes at it and giggles.

We walk around town and eat a late lunch at the diner. We each get grilled cheese and share a side of fries.

"Darling," she says, "I might go home after this."

"Okay," I say.

"Is that all right?" she asks. "I hate to abandon you, but I'm feeling so tired today. New moon. And with Mercury in retrograde . . ."

She rolls her eyes.

"Yeah," I say. "Of course."

I didn't know she could get tired. I'm always the one passing out early or calling it a night. Maybe she's sick of me. We have been spending a lot of time together.

When we're done eating, Tom hurries over to clear our plates. He doesn't leave a bill. He never charges us. Of everyone in town, I think he's the most terrified of Sophie.

She hugs me on the sidewalk.

"I'll drop by tomorrow afternoon," she says. "We can have tea."

"Only if you're up to it."

She winks at me, then turns on her heel and walks off.

On the way home, I stop in Simple Spirits and get a bottle of Pinot Grigio that Alex recommends. She's always got a sour look on her face. I can't tell if it's because of my association with Sophie or if she judges me because it's fairly obvious that I drink too much.

I tell myself that I'll have *a* glass. A single glass. I tell myself that I won't immediately change into sweatpants and pull my hair back in a low ponytail like I'm the backwoods murder suspect in a low-budget crime show reenactment.

Act like a real, functioning human being, I beg myself as I climb the stairs to my apartment. *Read a book. For the love of God, read a book!*

But sure enough, after five minutes of walking around my apartment, pretending I'm not about to do exactly what I'm about to do, I do it.

I change into sweatpants, pull my hair back in a low ponytail, open the bottle of wine, not bothering to get a glass, and sit on the couch. I reach for the remote to put something on TV, but "accidentally" grab my phone instead.

Sam texted me again last weekend. He wrote, Annie . . .

I was with Sophie, so I didn't respond. But I'm not with her now.

I know I shouldn't talk to him. It's better for me not to. A few days this past week, I woke up, and he wasn't the first thing I thought about. I didn't open my eyes and instantaneously feel the crushing ache that reminds me I'm without him. One day, I didn't even think about him until I was eating my lunch, picking the crusts off of my uninspired turkey-and-mayo sandwich, something he used to criticize me for.

"The crusts won't kill you!" he'd say.

"Where's your proof?" I'd ask.

He'd groan. "It's wasteful."

"I give them to you," I say. "No waste."

As I sat there decrusting my sandwich, I wondered if he'd known that one day he wouldn't be around to eat them. Maybe that was why he objected so strongly.

I lost my appetite, but I ate the sandwich anyway, not wanting it to go to waste.

Now, on my couch, trying to resist the urge to reach out to him, I come up with the idea to instead look at old pictures of us. For some reason, this seems like a good alternative.

A few pics in, I realize this is hands down the stupidest decision I've ever made.

The last picture we took together was a week before we broke up. We got ice cream sandwiches to celebrate the first warm day of the season, those magical hours in early spring when you no longer need a jacket, when the sun is high and bright, when the birds are extra chatty. It's one of the rare occasions when everyone in the city is in a good mood, probably because the trucks are out and everyone's eating ice cream.

Our fingers got so sticky from the ice cream sandwiches that, when we'd finally got some napkins from a generous street vendor and went to wipe our hands, the napkins stuck. Sam managed to take a selfie of us holding up our napkin fingers. We were making miserable faces, but you can see in our eyes that we were happy.

There's a video of us on Valentine's Day in which he's working his way through the massive box of chocolates that he got for me, eating all of the undesirables. The molasses chews and weird nougats.

"I'm doing this for you!" he says, grimacing as he bites into what looks like a chocolate-covered turd. "Ugh!"

"This is so romantic," I say, turning the camera around, capturing me laughing maniacally while he whines in the background.

I haven't spent a Valentine's Day single since I was thirteen. How will I cope with the endless stream of hearts and flowers and the onslaught of Hallmark gooeyness, knowing that I'm thirty and alone and that the person I have loved for so long doesn't want me anymore? Knowing that Jill is somewhere out there pitying me. Knowing that pretty much everyone pities anyone single on Valentine's Day.

Maybe not Sophie, but she doesn't count.

Panic floods my lungs, and suddenly I'm struggling to breathe. I can hear my heart pounding like an angry neighbor. I'm sweating. Or maybe I'm crying. Probably both.

In the midst of this anxiety fit, it seems I've dialed Sam.

Because it's ringing. Until it's not ringing. Until he's saying, "Annie? Hey!"

"Hi," I say. I clear my throat. "Hey."

"What's up? How are you?" he asks. "I thought you were ignoring me."

"No," I say. "Just busy."

"Molding impressionable young minds?"

"Sure," I say. I tuck my feet underneath me, making myself as small as possible. I feel safer this way.

"So you weren't ignoring me?"

"No," I say. "I'm actually busy. New job. New apartment. New friends."

"Other teachers?"

"No," I say. "They're all pretty cliquey."

"It *is* high school."

"Yeah," I say.

"Good you're making friends, though."

I don't know why I called him. Was it to hear his voice? Was it to figure out why he's been trying to reach me? Was it to ask him if it's really too late to fix this? To repair our relationship, go back to how it was at the beginning. Get the spark back. Have sex on the living room floor and afterward snicker at our carpet burns.

Can I? Should I? Ask if we can go back to the start? Be more assertive, push harder like I know I should have that day in April.

"I thought you might have seen . . . ," he says.

"Seen what?"

He doesn't respond, and enough time passes that I feel it necessary to pull the phone away from my ear to check that the call didn't get disconnected.

It didn't.

Finally, he says, "Tell me more about what you've been up to."

"Um . . . ," I say. "I've been hanging out a lot with my friend Sophie. She's . . . she's a really interesting person."

"Cool, cool," he says. He sounds distracted.

"Samantha."

"Andy."

These are the names we use when one of us is testing to see if the other person is actually listening.

"What's going on?" I ask him. "What's going on with you?"

"I've got a new archnemesis," he says. "I call him the Middleman. He goes around eating all the cream out of the middles of Oreos. Then he reseals the packages and puts them back on the shelves."

"What a monster."

"The worst this city has ever seen."

I could go on, indulge in the back-and-forth, but I really don't feel like it. I'm too sad.

"I meant, what's been going on with *you*? Alter ego. Otherwise known as Sam."

"Oh, oh," he says. "Right. Sam."

"Yep."

He takes another long pause. He exhales. It's the kind of exhale that precedes bad news. You know it when you hear it. The sound echoes in your bones.

"Annie," he says, "the reason I've been trying to get in touch with you, and why I thought you might be ignoring me, is I posted some pictures."

"Okay. On what. Myspace?"

Sam and I were never particularly active on what we jokingly called "the Internets." We both have dormant Facebook pages we use for occasional stalking of former classmates and tracking birthdays, but we were never the type to post updates about what was going on in our lives or to seek out new platforms.

"No," he says. "Actually, I didn't post. I got tagged."

"Okay."

"There's a picture of me with a girl."

"Okay."

"We're together in the picture. It's a picture of us together. I thought maybe you saw it."

"I didn't," I say. But . . . I've got my laptop now. So . . . in a matter of seconds, that will change.

"I thought maybe it upset you. I wouldn't have put it up myself."

"Yeah," I say.

It's on his Facebook. Tagged from Instagram? A picture of him looking at the petite redhead who is sitting on his lap, looking back at him. Her hand is on his face. His hand is on her ass. Their noses are almost touching. Their foreheads are touching.

There's nothing to interpret.

The photo is a bomb I've just swallowed. I'm listening to the faint tick, awaiting the inevitable explosion.

Pretty soon, any second, I'll be blown to smithereens. It'll hurt so bad I won't know what to do.

"I would rather have told you about it first," he says.

"You are telling me about it," I say. "I didn't see it. You're telling me. Now I know. I'm hearing it from you. There's a picture."

"Yeah," he says. "I wanted to tell you about Shannon."

Shannon.

"Okay, well, I mean, how long has this been up? Like, I'm sure there were still some people who didn't know we weren't together anymore. And this is how they found out probably," I say. "I mean, it's a little disrespectful. You're friends with my dad on Facebook."

"Does your dad not know we broke up?"

"That's not your business," I say. The explosion is budding. A heat rises within my chest.

"So no?"

"Yes, he knows. I told him I was moving and gave him my new address," I say. "Is that a satisfactory answer? Is that sufficient?"

I don't think I've ever raised my voice to him before. I don't like the way it feels. I'm out of control. I'm burning.

"Annie," he says. His voice is calm, and somehow that's worse. "There are going to be pictures."

"We broke up five minutes ago."

"We broke up five months ago! Six, actually."

"After almost ten years!"

"No," he says. "It was eight years, and the last two barely counted. We were together, but we weren't really. You know what I'm saying. It wasn't how it used to be between us. It wasn't the same."

I smell the smoke. I can taste it.

"This was your decision," I say. "And you made me leave."

"It was our decision," he says. "Don't pin this on me. It wasn't working and you know that."

"I thought we were going to get married! You blindsided me. You just gave up!" I'm yelling now. Crying and yelling.

"Annie. Come on. That's not true."

"It is true. You gave up, and I was the one who had to suffer for it. Pick up my whole life and start over. And you're just there. Doing the same thing. In our apartment. At bars with random girls."

"Shannon isn't some random girl," he says. "She's my girlfriend. We're together."

I look down, expecting to see my skin blistering. Fat translucent bubbles. Visual proof of the sensation I feel, of the pain. I touch my face, and there are no lesions, no gaping wounds, no sticky recessions of skin. I'm on fire. I'm on fire, but I have nothing to show for it.

"Annie?"

"Okay," I say.

"It happened," he says. "Sometimes things happen sooner than you expect."

"Sure."

"Sure?"

"What else do you want me to say?"

"Fair," he says. "I don't want this to change anything. She knows that we're close and that you're a part of my life. As friends. She's good with it."

"Good," I say. "I'm glad she approves."

"Annie, don't be like that."

"Like what?" I ask.

"All right," he says. "I reached out as a courtesy."

"A courtesy? A courtesy! Wow," I say. "Should I send a picture of you in to the *National Enquirer*? 'Good guys! They do exist!'"

"Why are you being so sarcastic?" he asks.

"I'm sarcastic. Did you forget this fun fact about me?"

"You're never sarcastic to me," he says. "We were always nice to each other. Always."

"I'm sorry," I say. "It's hard to be nice right now. I'm sorry."

There's a faint sensation on my hand. It's a spider. A big one. Big enough that I can see its individual eyes. So many of them, all looking up at me.

All of a sudden, it rears back. It lifts one of its front legs and waves it back and forth. It's also shaking its head.

It does not approve of my apology.

"That's okay," Sam says. "It's a weird situation. It's hard. I just thought you should hear it from me. Now you know."

"Now I know."

The spider plops back down on all of its legs. It's still shaking its head.

I wonder if it's Sophie. I wonder if she can see what the spiders see. She'll be so mad if she finds out that I called Sam. So disappointed. I can't tell her. I can't face her.

I move my hand over to the coffee table and gently wiggle the spider off. It crosses its front legs and turns its back to me to signal its discontent.

"Nothing's changed," Sam says. "We're still friends."

"Nothing's changed," I echo. How dense can he be?

Or is it me? Am I the one who's being unreasonable? We have been broken up for about six months. How did I not anticipate this? It actually never crossed my mind that he would move on. That he would really go on to date someone else. To fuck someone else. To get a new girlfriend.

I guess I was operating on the phantom hope that we might get back together.

I stare at the picture. I can't really see Shannon's face; she's in profile. She looks cute. Pretty. Beautiful even. Maybe.

I wish that I could prick my finger and fall into a long deep sleep, and that when I woke up, there'd be a hot guy there at my bedside totally enamored with me.

The spider begins to pace on the table. I don't know what it wants from me.

"All right, Annie, I'll let you go," Sam says. "We'll talk soon. I want to hear more about life in Rowan."

"Sure."

"All right. I am sorry, Annie. I am."

"Okay. Bye, Sam."

"Bye."

I hear him hang up. I can't move. I can't put the phone down. I can't do anything but cry.

There's a knock on my door.

I can't open it, but I don't need to.

I watch as the dead bolt unlocks itself. As the knob turns. As the door swings open.

Sophie's there. In her magnificent black feathered coat, and a new matching black feathered hat.

"Oh, pet," she says.

I don't ask her how she knows. I can't move my mouth. I remain motionless.

She pulls the phone from my hands and vanishes it somewhere. She sits next to me on the couch and pulls my head to her shoulder. She strokes my hair.

Sometime later, Sophie gets up and returns with a cup of tea.

"Drink this, and then go to sleep," she says.

"Are you leaving?" I ask. The tremble in my voice makes me sound like a child.

She puts a hand on my cheek and nods.

"You'll be all right," she says, "though the tea tastes terrible."

"What is it?"

"Mushroom. My own blend," she says. "It will make you feel better. I promise you that. You trust me, yes?"

"Yes," I say. "Thank you."

"I'll be back in the morning," she says. "If I stay tonight, tomorrow night will only be more difficult."

"Yeah. You're probably right."

"Probably?"

"You're right."

She smiles without teeth.

"I'm sorry," I say. "You were tired. You wanted to rest tonight. You must be so sick of me."

"Don't be silly. You were in distress. I'm here. I want to be here. That's what friends are for," she says. "Isn't it?"

"I'm a burden on anyone close to me," I say, thinking of Sam and every other person I've ever latched onto, squeezed and leaned on until they had enough. Old boyfriends, camp bunkmates, recess friends. I make someone the center of my universe until they buckle under the weight. It's habitual. Now that Sam is gone, I'm doing it to Sophie.

"You're not a burden to anyone but yourself," she says. "Drink your tea. Get some sleep. Good night."

As she leaves, I notice the spider from earlier is in her hair, its legs clutching the strands.

When the door closes, the silence rises up against me. It takes shape. I don't know what time it is. It feels like I'm neck-deep in a nightmare. I wish it were a nightmare.

I want to look at the picture again.

I want to analyze the look on his face. I want to compare it to the pictures of us.

The stink of the mushroom tea distracts me.

I slip off of the couch onto the floor, stretch my legs out underneath the coffee table. My arms are slack. I can't stiffen my wrists. I rock myself forward and sip from the mug.

Sophie was right. This tea is truly repulsive. It's thick. It drags its nails across my tongue, squirms down my throat. But once it's inside me, once it's settled, it begins to warm me. Soothe me.

I take another sip. And another.

A brightness erupts inside my head. It splits into twin stars, one in each eyeball, twirling in my vision. Spinning, spinning.

Another sip and I'm up. I'm testing out my new body. It's made of lightning.

I reach down and pick up the mug. There are little bits floating in it. Dark leaves. Tiny black seeds. Dried mushrooms. Flowers.

I finish drinking the tea. I swallow some of the flowers. The mushrooms. I don't know if I'm supposed to.

I trust that I'll be okay.

I dance around my apartment to music I can't hear. But it's there. I know it's there. The spiders are dancing, too. They wave their limbs. I wave mine. I have just as many. Just as many as them.

Too many.

I raise my arms up. I try to count them. They multiply quickly, split at the ends into several hands. My collection of fingers, I notice, is not all fingers. Some of them are different. Ribs. Rib bones. I've got rib bones functioning as extra fingers.

Because I am a creature, an amalgam of bones. I'm a femur, a kneecap, a fragment of jaw. One of my arms isn't an arm, or not just an arm. It's extended by vertebrae.

I'm rearranging.

My torso is a sack of transparent skin. I can see my organs pulsating inside, wet lungs, a pulpy red heart, liver dark and smooth, stomach like a naked bird. I reach up for my head to see if it's still there, and it is, only the texture is wrong. My distorted skull feels something like cardboard. Like an empty box. There are voids where my eyes should be.

But then how am I seeing?

My tongue. My tongue is like a huge sponge, wagging out of my mouth, spit bubbling, popping, murmuring.

I try to speak, but my tongue has expanded. It extends to the far reaches of my mouth. It presses up against my cheeks. It's like a marshmallow in the microwave. It's going to explode. My tongue is going to explode.

I stuff my fingers in my mouth to try to make space. So many fingers. So many rib bones.

That's when I realize I don't have any teeth.

I begin wailing, but the sound is trapped behind the wall of my tongue.

My teeth. Where are they? Where did they go?

I pull my hands out of my mouth. They're covered in something. A slimy membrane. Glossy saliva. I try to shake it off, but that only forges my fingers together, so my hands are now like oven mitts.

Fleshy, webbed mitts.

There's a dense noise ahead of me. A hearty plop.

I feel around in the bog of colors and find it.

My tongue.

Wearing a crown of my teeth.

"There you are," I say, only I can't make words without my tongue or my teeth. And even if I could, it wouldn't matter, because the laughter is too loud.

Who's laughing at me? Why?

Or am I laughing? Is it me?

It is.

I pull at the dog-eared pages of the universe and fold myself up inside of it.

BAD REACTION

I am violently ill. I'm hunched over the toilet in my bathroom, throwing up some kind of gluey water-bile mixture. It's the kind of vomiting that involves the entire body. It's brutal.

I've been puking for some time when I realize I've been puking for some time. When the fog disperses and the events of last night return to me, when my thoughts become clear.

I called Sam. He told me he has a girlfriend. Sophie came over. Comforted me. Gave me weird mushroom tea. I felt okay for a while, I think, but now I'm hard-core praying to the porcelain God.

When the last bits have trickled out and all that's left is spit, I deposit a dollop of toothpaste on my tongue, lift a handful of faucet water to my mouth and swish. I don't have any mouthwash.

When I come out of the bathroom, my eyes shrivel inside my head. It's bright out. It's daytime. Not morning. Day.

I scan my apartment. It's a mess.

What the hell happened last night?

I stumble into my bedroom, where I find my phone on the floor. The screen is shattered. I attempt to turn it on. Nothing happens.

"Damn it!" I croak. If the sound of my voice is any indication, I've aged five thousand years overnight.

I fall back on my bed. What was in that tea?

I take a series of deep breaths and must pass out again, because when I open my eyes, it's cloudy and raining outside, and my phone is gone.

I hear movement in the other room. Sophie humming to herself.

"Sophie," I call. "Sophie?"

Footsteps.

She pokes her head through the doorway. "Yes, pet?"

"What's happening? What time is it?"

"It's three thirty," she says. "How are you feeling?"

I prop myself up on my elbows. "Pretty bad. What was in that tea?"

She cocks her head to the side. "Was it too strong?"

Images sweat from my subconscious. They're heinous. Abstract. A collage of Bosch paintings.

"I think I had some kind of trip," I say, scratching my neck. "Or an allergic reaction. I . . . I might have hallucinated or maybe had nightmares. I don't know."

Sophie comes in and sits on the edge of the bed. Her hair is in a long braid draped over her shoulder. She's wearing a velvet dress with a corset top and long sleeves. She looks great, as always.

I probably look like a hag.

"I may have been a little heavy-handed," she says, nibbling on her thumbnail. "It's been a long time since I last made that blend. I'm sorry."

"I got sick," I say.

"Oh, no!" she says. "It was supposed to make you feel better. Soothe you. Maybe boost your mood."

"Well," I say, rubbing my temples, "I think it was a successful distraction."

The picture flashes before my eyes. Sam. And Shannon. *Shannon.* Worse than any echoing nightmare, than any Bosch painting.

"I see you've destroyed your torture device," Sophie says, holding up my smashed phone. She sets it on the nightstand.

"Yeah. I don't know what I'm gonna do. I can't really afford a new one."

"You'll be better off without it," she says. She stands up. "Let me make you something to eat."

"Thanks, but I'm not hungry," I say, sinking back into bed.

"Why don't we watch television?"

I think about it.

"Annie," she says.

"Okay," I say. "We can watch TV."

She helps me out of bed and over to the couch, where she settles me under a thick knit blanket.

"I made this for you," she says.

It's soft and warm, a pretty baby pink. It smells like lavender. "Thank you."

"You're welcome," she says. "May I choose the program?"

I hand her the remote.

"Are you sure you don't want something to eat?"

"No," I say. I'm too afraid I'll throw up again, though there is a sour taste lingering on my tongue I'd like to evict.

"More tea?" she asks. "Different tea? Have I ruined it for you?"

"Maybe," I say.

"Oh, dear," she says. She doesn't seem too bothered. She turns on the TV and selects a series about international luxury real estate properties.

I find it depressing.

But that's probably because I'm depressed. All I can see is that image. Sam and *her.* Someone else. All I can feel is the twist of the knife, the slow death of possibility. This isn't temporary.

I still love him, but he doesn't love me.

It's gone. Whatever he felt for me, he doesn't feel it anymore. Not at all.

I lost it. I fucked up. I wasn't enough.

"You were right," I tell Sophie, who's totally engrossed by this show, now featuring a gorgeous villa in the Italian countryside with its own spa.

"About what, pet?"

"I shouldn't have called him," I say. "I wish I didn't know."

"Someday you won't care," she says. She puts her arm around me. I rest my head on her shoulder and she rubs my back. "Shall I make you a revenge dress? Like Princess Diana?"

"You have to stop with the Windsors," I say. "And I have nowhere to wear a revenge dress."

"That's the thing about a revenge dress, darling. You can wear it anywhere, everywhere, whenever your heart desires."

I sigh.

"You don't seem like a vengeful person," she says. "I am."

"No," I say. It seems like the polite response.

"It's true," she says. "You should know that about me, Annie. I don't mean it, like, you know . . . It sounds a bit cryptic. It's not a threat. I'm just saying it's my personality."

"You'd wear a revenge dress?"

She laughs a little. "Among other things."

"Yeah," I say. "A bit cryptic."

She laughs again, then turns up the volume on the TV.

We spend the afternoon like this—side by side on the couch. At some point she goes into the kitchen and comes back holding two caramel apples.

"Where did you get these?" I ask her as she hands me one. It's on a long wooden stick.

She winks at me. That's her answer.

I don't have an appetite, but I eat it anyway. It's delicious. Worth the risk of getting sick again.

It actually makes me feel better, somehow settling my stomach.

"How do you always know what I need?" I ask Sophie.

"I've told you," she says. "I consider myself very intuitive."

A memory crawls out of a cobwebby corner in my mind.

"On my birthday, I went out with this girl from my old job, and she insisted on taking me to see a psychic."

Sophie nods slightly to signal that she's listening. Juice from her apple streams down her chin. She wipes it with a small black cloth, then tucks the cloth into her cleavage.

I wonder what else she has hiding in there. How deep it goes.

"Yes," Sophie says. "What happened?"

"Yeah, so we went to this random psychic in the Village. She told me that I had a dark fate or something along those lines. Actually, she said she sensed a darkness. She couldn't see my fate."

"Why are you telling me this?" Sophie asks. I thought she'd be more interested in the story.

I shrug. "I don't know."

She smiles. Boops me on the nose. "You want me to tell you that she was full of shit?"

I laugh. "I guess. Maybe, yeah. That's what I'm after."

"She probably was, yes. It's very likely. Or it could be that your future *is* uncertain. That you're in a place where your path diverges, and not even fate itself knows which way you'll go."

"Oof."

"Don't despair," she says, running a thumb under my pouty bottom lip. "I'm also full of shit. To be honest, pet, I don't even believe in fate."

"No?"

She scoffs, waves a hand in the air. "If it does exist, I've eluded it so many times."

"You're special, though."

"So are you."

Now it's my turn to scoff.

"Fate is just another invention to trick us into complacency. Inaction. If one assumes that they cannot change their circumstances, they won't try. When you think about it, really, there's a myriad of ways we're conditioned to passivity. Women, especially. Of course, I realized all of this a long, long time ago. It saved me. It could have just as easily drowned me."

"Yeah," I say.

"Literally," she says. "They tried to drown me."

"Who?"

"The townspeople," she says. Her tone is casual. She's not looking at me. She's browsing shows on the TV. The remote is making that *bloop-bloop* sound as she scrolls.

"When?"

"As I said, a long time ago."

"In the well?"

"No, that was a different occasion. There were many attempts over many years," she says. She shakes her head.

"That's awful," I say. "I'm sorry."

"Oh," she says, "don't be. I'm here, aren't I?"

"You are."

"I'm on your couch with you watching Netflix!" she says. "And they're all dead."

She pats my knee twice. "I should get home. I've got so many chores to do around the house that I've been neglecting."

"Busy taking care of me," I say. "Your sad, pathetic friend."

"Next time you insult yourself in front of me, I'll tie your tongue in a knot," she says, putting her coat on. "Will you come over next weekend, please, pet? I really miss having you around. The ghosts won't bother you. I promise."

"I'm skeptical."

"You don't trust me?"

"It's not that," I say. "I'm scared."

"Don't be," she says. Like it's that simple. "It'll be fun. Come over, yes? Come Saturday around noon. I'll make us treats."

"Okay."

"Yes! Lovely," she says. She kisses me on the forehead. "You'll be all right, darling. Better than all right."

"Thanks, Sophie."

"I left food in your icebox," she says. "Fridge. Whatever you call it. Good night."

As soon as she's gone, as soon as I hear the door close, I open my laptop and go straight to Facebook to look at the picture again.

I *stare* at it.

I know I shouldn't be doing this, but there's a nagging evil inside me, a little devil brandishing its pitchfork, compelling me. Punishing me. Its sole mission is to deprive me of any momentary relief I might have if I were to escape the hard evidence of my heartbreak.

Eventually, the screen blurs and my eyeballs recline.

I shut my laptop.

I put myself in the shower. I turn the water as hot as it will go so I can disappear into the steam, let it transport me somewhere else. If I can't see anything, I can pretend I'm anywhere.

I pretend I'm in the spa of that Italian villa from the luxury real estate show.

I pretend I'm in a Diane Lane movie. I masturbate.

Afterward, I put on soft cotton pajamas and carry a sleeve of crackers and a glass of water into my bedroom. I settle in bed and eat the crackers slowly while staring out the window. I'm too lazy to get up and close the curtain.

It's a mystery hour. The sun has been setting earlier and earlier. The daylight selfish, sparing. Soon my entire day will be spent in darkness. The drive to work. Teaching in my basement classroom. My drive home after.

Why bother to get up at all?

I put the remaining crackers on my nightstand and roll over. I didn't brush my teeth today and I can smell my own breath. Acrid. Stale. My hair is still wet from the shower. I couldn't be bothered to dry it, and I know when I wake up, it'll be a tangled nightmare. I'm also 99 percent sure I forgot to put on deodorant.

I should just live like this. Abandon my ablutions. Let my teeth go yellow with rot, gums red and receding. Allow my skin to break out, forget exfoliation. Let the dead flakes congregate, create societies of zits on my face. Evil empires.

I should let my hair gnarl together. Form a giant nestlike mass on top of my head. I could keep things in there. Credit cards. Snacks.

I should develop a smell so terrible that no one will ever come near me. Create a force field of stink.

Wouldn't that be easier? To be left alone in my misery. To lean into what I feel, match my exterior to my interior.

I won't do it, though. I'll wake up in the morning and floss and brush my teeth and my hair. I'll put on deodorant and perfume. A little mascara. Apply some tinted lip gloss.

I'm not brave enough to be who I am.

HOPE IS STUPID

"Can I have lunch in here, Miss Crane?"

Madison stands in the doorway of my classroom, holding a thermos in one hand and a copy of *The New Yorker* in the other. I would much prefer to be alone for the opportunity to put my head down on my desk and whimper softly to myself for the next forty-five minutes, but . . . I'd feel guilty saying no to a student who's just looking for somewhere to be. I've been that kid.

I still am that kid.

"Sure," I say.

She sits in the desk directly across from mine. "Beth is absent today and I cannot deal with the rest of them. I cannot."

She unscrews her thermos. I get a whiff of an earthy smell.

"It's kombucha," she says. "I brew it myself. It's really good for you."

"Is that all you have?"

"I eat. Don't worry," she says. "I just don't really believe in lunch."

She opens *The New Yorker* and I gather a stack of papers that I've been putting off grading.

When the bell rings, she screws the top back on her thermos and smiles sweetly.

"Thank you for letting me hang in here, Miss Crane," she says on her way out, her eyes wide, her expression earnest. She looks so young right now. She *is* young. It's easy to forget that kids these days don't act like kids.

Kids these days. Oof. Let me just disintegrate into dust and be carried off by a gentle breeze.

"You're the only cool teacher here," she says.

I wish it were possible to catch a compliment, to hold it in the cage of your hands like a firefly and never let it go.

But . . . it isn't. The high is transient.

After school, I stop at the Verizon store in Aster to get a new phone. The guy who sells it to me seems annoyed by my very existence, and to be honest, I find it deeply relatable.

I go to Tops Friendly Markets and get a rotisserie chicken and a liter of ginger ale. Then I stop at Simple Spirits for a bottle of bourbon.

"What's the occasion?" Alex asks me, her eyes narrowing with their usual judgment.

"Had a hankering," I say, surprising myself with my lack of shame.

If I want to drink straight from a bottle of bourbon on a Monday night, that's nobody's business but my own.

I let this attitude keep me company as I plow through a hefty fraction of the bottle while eating the rotisserie chicken with my hands, sitting on the kitchen floor.

When I'm done, I leave the carcass on the counter and go straight to bed.

On Friday, I run into Jill while getting coffee in the teachers' lounge.

"Hey!" she says. "I was just thinking about you."

I don't say anything. I search the fridge for half-and-half.

"Are you sure you don't want to meet Pascal? We saw him last weekend and I just really think you guys would hit it off."

"There's no half-and-half," I say. I give a long, defeated sigh as I pour 2 percent milk into my tumbler.

"We could all do dinner. Or drinks?" She's persistent. "Double date."

Of course, I'm thinking about the picture. Of course, I'm thinking about Sam and *Shannon*.

I wonder how he'd feel if he saw me with someone else.

Probably indifferent.

"Sure," I say. "Let's do it."

"Really?" she squeals.

"Yeah," I say.

"It's going to be so fun," she says. "When are you free? Next weekend?"

"Whenever."

"Yay! I'll talk to my husband and see what we can see! I love setting people up," she says. "I'm good at it, too."

"High success rate?"

She nods, her ponytail bobbing.

"All right," I say. "I have class."

"I'll let you know about plans!"

I give her the thumbs-up on my way out. I hate myself for it.

On my walk back to class, I begin to regret my decision to accept Jill's offer. What have I just gotten myself into?

Why am I willingly subjecting myself to a blind date? A blind *double* date. And they already know one another, so they'll either be rehashing shared memories the whole time with me just sitting there pretending to be engaged, or they'll be asking me questions about myself. Questions like: Where did you grow up? Do you have any brothers or sisters? Did you play sports in school? Do you like *Star Wars*?

And what if Pascal sucks? What if he chews with his mouth open or watches golf for fun? What if he owns a red hat?

How is it that when trying to climb out of a hole, I always seem to dig myself deeper?

The next morning, I stop at the Good Mug for coffee on my way to Sophie's. No one is there, except for Oskar, who is pouring coffee beans into the grinder.

"Morning," he says. "What can I get for you?"

"Thinking," I say. "I'm heading to Sophie's. Wondering what I should bring her."

He frowns.

"What is it?" I ask.

He shakes his head. "Nothing."

"Let's go with vanilla cinnamon," I say. "Two larges, please."

"Yep," he says.

I turn toward the windows to observe the street. It's getting cold out, but the flowers haven't died yet. They're not as vibrant as they once were, but they're hanging on. I wonder if Sophie has anything to do with that.

"You shouldn't go out there," Oskar says, so low I can barely hear him.

I turn around. He's frothing milk.

"Sorry?" I ask.

"You shouldn't go out there. To the woods."

"To Sophie's?"

"Some people go out there," he says, "and they don't come back."

The hiss of steam interrupts him. He begins to pour the milk into cups in the slow, meticulous way he always does. His jaw is clenched, but that's its permanent state. He gives nothing away.

"What do you mean?" I ask.

"Eleven," he says, setting the cups down on the counter in front of me.

I stare at him, waiting for him to elaborate. Why the hell would he say that?

"Cash or card?" he asks.

I search my bag for my wallet. My pockets. I find it in my jacket and promptly fumble it onto the floor. When I reach down to get it, I narrowly avoid smacking my head against the counter.

Oskar doesn't ask if I'm okay. He just stands there, stoic.

I hand him my credit card. He swipes it and gives it back to me. When he does, he grabs my hand. It's so quick and unexpected I almost scream.

He's looking at me, his blue eyes bright and intense, like the sky on an all-too-perfect day. I wait for him to say something, to tell me something else. Explain. But he just releases my hand and says, "Have a good one."

"Yeah," I say. "You, too."

I take the coffee and step out onto Main Street. I start toward the woods, toward Sophie's, but my body is reluctant, my legs suddenly rubber.

What did Oskar mean?

Does he not know that I know the truth about Sophie? Is that what that was about?

I guess if I knew only what Sophie was and not who she was, I'd fear her, too.

I continue in a daze toward the woods.

It requires a lot of focus to walk through the woods holding two large lattes. It's a feat of balance, especially on rubbery legs.

I also have never gone to Sophie's without having Sophie herself to guide me, so I have to pay close attention to every familiar tree, every distinct dip in the ground, every unique rock. I get myself to the well. Part of me is tempted to peer in to see how far down it goes, but I'm afraid to get too close.

And the hut, too. I'm curious to look inside, see what it's like, but I don't have the nerve.

The circle of headstones I'm totally good with avoiding. All set there.

When I walk down the hill to her house, I see the front door is already open, and she's standing there in a black gown with a plunging neckline. She's waving to me. Waving me in.

"I'm coming," I say.

"I'm impatient," she says.

"I brought coffee," I say, handing her one of the cups.

"My sweet! Come, let's drink it in the parlor. I've cleaned it up."

She leads me to a room I've never been in before, one with silky wallpaper and dainty furniture. There's a baby white marble fireplace, an excess of reedy plants, a few watercolors depicting bucolic landscapes. We sit on two pretty but uncomfortable chairs, drinking our lattes.

Sophie tells me about her week, about a new balm she made for her cuticles and about how Monday is Halloween and no one in town likes to celebrate because of her.

"I don't know what they think," she says. "I threw a party one year, and nobody came! I like those tiny little chocolate bars just as much as the next person. It's beyond aggravating."

"Yeah," I say, debating whether to disclose Oskar's weird comment.

"There's such a stigma," she says, sighing. "You know I don't believe in self-pity, but if I give myself one night a year to feel sorry for myself, that's the one. I'll probably mix myself a cocktail in a cauldron and get bloody drunk."

"A cauldron?" I ask, because I can't help myself.

"Mm," she says.

I don't have a response, which results in an awkward pause. The quiet recalls Oskar's voice. *Some people go out there and they don't come back.*

I look up at Sophie, and she's looking back at me. Her amber eyes have gone dark.

"What is it, pet?" she asks, her chin ascending.

"Um, no-nothing," I stammer. The coffee cup begins to crumple in my hands. I'm clutching it too tightly.

"Oh, I don't believe that," she says. "You can tell me."

"Really, it's nothing." Why would Oskar say that to me? Why would he say it if he didn't have good reason?

Have I been too accepting? Have I glued on my blinders for the sake of this friendship?

I always thought I was an exceptional judge of character. That I could see people for who they really are deep down. But isn't that the kind of arrogant thinking that gets people called to the witness stand? Ted Bundy had a wife, didn't he?

Oh, God. Would I have married Ted Bundy?

"Annie," Sophie says, coolly examining her nails, "we're friends, yes? Friends don't keep secrets from one another, now, do they?"

"No," I say. I don't have a choice now. "It's just . . . It's Oskar."

She raises an eyebrow.

"He said something to me. I just . . . It was weird. I thought it might . . . I don't know. I thought it might hurt your feelings. You know, the stigma."

She laughs. "Oh, pet. You don't need to worry about Oskar hurting my feelings, though I am curious. What did he have to say about me?"

"It wasn't anything bad," I say.

She laughs again. Louder this time.

I swallow. "He said that I shouldn't come out here. He said . . . he said . . ."

She leans forward. Closer to me.

Closer. Closer.

"He said . . . he said some people come out here and don't come back."

She latches onto me, her hand on my knee. She sinks her fingertips into my skin. Her eyes are wild. A sneer possesses her lips. "Did he really?"

I nod.

She lets go, settling back into her chair. "He still blames me. I suppose it's easier than accepting any responsibility himself. He can't bring himself to confront the reality of what happened. It's too painful for him."

"What happened?" I ask, nerves churning.

"His wife. Helen. Erik's mother. She was unhappy. She was very young when she married Oskar, when she had Erik. She felt trapped, completely overwhelmed. So she came to me. We spent some time together. She was so lost. I thought she was seeking friendship, direction." Sophie's eyes catch on something. Some memory. She's quiet for a moment. "Then she left."

"Left?"

"One morning Oskar woke up and she was gone. He came storming over here, of course, accusing me. I hadn't a clue where she went. He didn't believe me. He asked to come inside. I didn't much like the idea of letting an angry man into my home, for him to turn the place over, searching for someone I knew wasn't here. He threatened to call the police. Imagine! I said if he did that, I'd harvest his teeth, pluck them from his jaw one by one and use them for jewelry."

She sighs, stroking her bare collarbone. "A shame he relented. He does have nice teeth, don't you think? They would have made a beautiful necklace."

If I had any sensation left in my body, I'm sure I would feel my chin dropping into my lap.

"Anyway," Sophie says, noting my expression, "I had nothing to do with her leaving. All I did was listen and give her advice. He was the one who drove her off. He was very dismissive of her needs. But no, as far as he's concerned, and perhaps the entire town, it's my fault."

"Where did she go?"

"She talked about California," Sophie says, and sips her latte. "Maybe there."

"Maybe?"

She stares at me. Seconds pass. In these seconds, babies are born, people die, stars burn millions of miles away and I may or may not let out a silent, nervous fart.

"Helen isn't dead," Sophie says finally, "or missing, if that's what you're wondering. She resurfaced several years ago and has been in touch with Erik. I've not been informed of her whereabouts. From what you've just told me, it seems her reappearance has not absolved me. A stubborn grudge from a stubborn man."

"I'm sorry," I say.

"No, that's all right. I suppose it's best that you know," she says, "and that I was the one to tell you. Now, do you have any more questions? Any other concerns?"

I shake my head. "I'm sorry."

"Don't be. Already in the past," she says. She sits up straight and smiles, her eyes bright again. "Now! Darling. Will you come? I have a surprise for you in the ballroom."

Any lingering nerves are immediately mollified when she reveals her surprise. She's set up a shuffleboard court.

"Have you ever played?" she asks.

"I haven't," I say.

"I'll teach you."

And she does. She teaches me. We spend the day playing shuffleboard in the ballroom, taking breaks to drink raspberry lemonade and eat shortbread cookies.

I feel guilty for entertaining any suspicions about Sophie. I mean, she went out of her way to make a shuffleboard court for us to have a fun afternoon together. She baked cookies and made lemonade. She dropped everything to come over when I was upset; she cleaned my apartment and made sure that I was okay. She's the most generous person I've ever met.

I look at her now, dancing around to *Blackout*-era Britney Spears, and all I feel is an overwhelming love for her.

How could anyone not love her? How could anyone fear her?

"All these songs are about sex," Sophie says. "Why is society so obsessed with sex?"

I shrug.

"If this singer is truly seeking a partner, someone should tell her good conversation is much harder to have than good sex. That should be her primary concern."

"Yeah, somehow I really don't think it is."

"I can't help everyone," she says. "Are you hungry? Do you want to make pizza?"

Half an hour later, I'm covered in flour and Sophie, in her black dress, is somehow not. Yet we've both participated in making the dough. Kneading side by side. Now it sits in a bowl covered by a damp cloth near the oven, and we're chopping vegetables.

"Onions make me cry," I tell Sophie.

"Not me," she says. "But I don't think I can have a proper cry anymore. I don't think it's physically possible."

"You don't cry?"

"I have," she says. "I get sad. But emotions become . . . less and less over time. I feel things. And at times, I feel them intensely. But there's a perspective that comes with age. It's all fleeting. I savor the joy. The sadness, I let it pass. Crying takes a lot of effort. Not a lot of things inspire me to exert myself."

"You want to chop the onion? I'll trade for the broccoli."

"Yes, darling," she says. "Do you want artichokes? I think I have some down in the cellar."

"Sure," I say.

"I'll get them." She wipes her hands on a rag and pauses for a moment. "You shouldn't go into the cellar."

"Right, right," I say, thinking it's one of her cryptic jokes.

"No, pet," she says, "I'm serious."

"Oh," I say. "Okay."

"The ghosts are there now. Don't worry. They can't leave. And there weren't that many. It's not as if the place was crawling with them."

"Okay." How many ghosts does she consider not that many? I'm of the strong opinion that any number of ghosts is too many.

"They're trapped down there, so, you know . . . best for you not to go."

"Not a problem."

"Great," she says. She opens the door to the pantry, then leans down to open the cellar. There's an outburst of moans. Eerie, ghastly bellows.

"Oh, shush," I hear Sophie say. Then she lowers her voice and begins to speak a language I don't understand. Maybe Latin? Whatever it is, it shuts them up. There's no more moaning.

She emerges moments later, holding a jar of artichoke hearts.

"My second favorite type of heart to have on pizza," she says.

This is a joke. I can tell because of the look she gives me after she says it.

"What am I going to do with you?" I ask.

"What kind of cheese do we want? Goat?"

We cook the pizza on a stone over crackling red flames in the fireplace. We eat it at the dining table. Sophie lights some candles, but the room is so huge that a few small candles don't make much of a difference. It's dark, and where it isn't dark, shadows dart in and out of the space afforded to them by the candlelight.

"Is it cold in here?" she asks me.

"It's a little cold."

She stands up. As she walks over to the fireplaces, I hear her snap her fingers. There's a loud pop, and suddenly a fire roars in the first fireplace. In the new light, I watch Sophie throw a yellowish powder into the second fireplace, and a fire appears there instantaneously. She snaps her fingers again as she comes toward me. She sits down next to me and takes another slice of pizza.

"Fancy," I tell her, staring at the two big healthy fires.

Shapes emerge in the flames. On the left, a lion. On the right, a regal bird. They change. A wolf, a mouse.

"Ooh!"

The shapes swirl and disappear.

"Do you think you'll stay over tonight, pet?" she asks, pouring me some wine.

"Sure," I say.

"Really?"

I hesitate. On one hand, I know for a fact that this house is haunted and that one of the ghosts attempted to kill me. On the other, I don't want to go home. I'm having a great time. It'd be a bummer to trek back through the woods to spend the night alone in my apartment, thinking about Sam and potentially being too sad to masturbate.

If Sophie says she trapped the ghosts in the basement, she trapped the ghosts in the basement. I heard them down there.

"We can stay up late," she says. "We could play more shuffleboard, or watch a film, or read. I can make hot chocolate. I've got some cream I can whip."

"All that sounds great," I say. But we're too full after dinner for hot chocolate. Instead, we split another bottle of wine and Sophie puts on *Jaws*, which surprises me.

"I heard everyone talking about it when it first came out, so I had to watch. Have you ever seen it?"

"Yeah, a few times. It's one of my dad's favorite movies."

"I quite enjoy it," she says. "But of course, I always root for the shark."

I think she's kidding, but at the end of the movie, when Brody blows up the shark, she sighs, shaking her head like she hoped for a different outcome despite knowing there wouldn't be one.

We walk upstairs arm in arm, and she kisses me good night. A quick kiss on each cheek. One of the few things I remember about my mother is that she used to kiss my cheeks like that. Kiss, kiss. Then she'd say, *Good night, mini muffin.* I don't know why she called me that, but she always did.

"What is it?" Sophie asks. "Are you afraid?"

"No," I say. "Just had a random memory come up."

"Mm," Sophie says. "A good one, I hope."

She winks and heads toward her room.

"Good night," she says.

"Night."

In my room, there are two new lamps and a giant box of chocolates on the nightstand. The extra light contributes to increased coziness. The fear I previously experienced in this space is gone.

I change into the pink silk pajamas that Sophie laid out for me. I eat the chocolates in bed while reading a book of collected poems. When I fall asleep, it's deep and dreamless.

The next morning, over pancakes at the diner, I decide to come clean with Sophie about my most recent stupid decision. My upcoming blind date.

I've been nervous about her response, but she doesn't have much of a reaction.

"Any step away from the past is a step in the right direction," she says.

"I guess," I say. "I'm just worried it's going to be a shitty experience, and then I'll feel worse about everything."

"Why? Are you not happy as you are? With how things are?"

"I mean, kind of. Not really."

She sighs. "You don't need a boyfriend, darling. You need perspective."

"Probably."

"Does the coffee taste funny to you today? It tastes funny to me." And with that, the subject is changed.

I don't think about the date again until the next day, when Jill comes prancing into my classroom wearing a bat costume. Apparently, the staff was meant to dress up for Halloween—information I might have learned if I cared enough to pay attention to memos, which I don't.

"What are you?" she asks me.

"Forgetful."

She laughs. "You're so funny. I told Pascal how funny you are."

"No pressure."

"You want a Mounds?" She offers me a fun-sized candy bar. I take it. It's very warm. Molten inside its wrapper. "I have good news. You have plans Friday."

"Cool."

"With me! And my husband, Dan. And who knows? Maybe your future husband. Pascal!"

"Again, no pressure."

"Seven work for you? Have you been to Rhineland?"

"No."

"You're going to love it. They have this cheese dip appetizer that might be my favorite thing ever. So seven?"

"Yep. See you there," I say, instead of what I want to say, which is *Kill me now.*

"Great!" She hands me another Mounds before flapping out of my classroom.

As soon as she leaves, Madison enters. She's always early.

"No costume?" she asks. She's wearing Ouija board knee socks and a blouse patterned with skulls.

"No," I say. I toss her the Mounds.

"Here," I say flatly. "Happy Halloween."

The rest of the week I spend every spare minute brainstorming viable excuses I could use to get out of dinner. A variety of illnesses. A head cold. A chest cold. The flu. Allergies. Strep throat. A stomach virus. Food poisoning. Pink eye. Ringworm. Or maybe the death of a relative? I have a lot of dead relatives. It wouldn't be a lie to say that my grandpa died. It was six years ago, but he did die.

I wasn't raised religious, but a common warning from my grandmother (still alive) is that you get out what you put into the universe. The ole "What goes around comes around." Karma.

Since things already aren't going so hot for me, I can't risk any cosmic consequences.

By Thursday afternoon, I've resigned myself to going.

When I get home, I open my closet, readying myself for a long, frustrating solo fashion show in which I get to confront how terrible I look in everything I own, but instead I find a new dress hanging front and center. It's a deep yellowy gold. Crushed velvet. V-neck, A-line.

I try it on. It's a perfect fit. There's never been a more flattering dress.

There's a note tucked into the sleeve.

To what's ahead. Have fun on your date. XO, Sophie

I'm so moved by the gesture I could cry.

The dress reframes the way I look at the date. It *could* be fun. That's a possibility. Pascal could be really hot. He could be nice and smart and charming. We could hit it off. He could want the same things that I want. Maybe we'll get married at the courthouse and have an intimate brunch after. Maybe we'll honeymoon in Barcelona, hold hands and kiss in the streets, have strangers come up to us to tell us how in love we look. Maybe we'll buy an old house with character, with good bones, and we'll fix it up ourselves, then post pictures so people can marvel at the before and after.

Maybe we'll have a tradition of sleeping in late on Sundays, and we'll wake up in each other's arms just shy of noon, spooning so we don't have to endure morning breath.

What if I get to have one of those great stories? Like how some couples talk about how they met, like how he found her glove and then chased after her and then they kissed in the snow and the rest was history? I could say I was with someone for almost ten years who I thought was my soul mate, but then we broke up and I moved here and got set up on a blind date and found my actual soul mate.

I look at myself in the mirror, in this dress, and it's hard not to feel a spark of hope. It's impossible not to consider the chance.

BONE TO PICK

On Friday, I rush home after school to shower, blow-dry my hair, put on makeup, put on the dress, accessorize. I wear my black boots, black stockings and a black faux-leather jacket. I wear my mother's earrings, black diamond studs. I even wear red lipstick.

But then I change my mind and wipe it off.

On the drive over, I'm too nervous to listen to music. I listen to my phone calmly providing directions and to my own heart anxiously throbbing.

I open my mouth to speak words of affirmation like *You can do this!* or something along those lines, but what comes out is "Fuck fuck fuck fuck fuck fuck fuck!"

My hands are so sweaty I can barely grip the steering wheel.

"Get it together," I snarl at my reflection in the rearview mirror. I take a few deep breaths as I pull into the parking lot. I find a space far away from the restaurant, hoping it'll give me time to walk off my nerves. I don't let myself linger in the car. I force myself out into the frigid November night.

Having to slog across the parking lot doesn't do much for my nerves. My sweat freezes my hair to my temples. I almost twist my ankle in a pothole. By the time I open the door to the restaurant, I'm even more agitated than I was before.

It's a kitschy place. A lot of wood. Ceiling beams wrapped in colorful lights. There are ambiguous flags on the walls, many of them featuring lions or crests, many of them both. The tables are close together and people are drinking out of beer steins. It might be German themed.

I might be on a blind double date at a German-themed restaurant.

Am I going to have to eat sausage in front of strangers?

"Annie!" Jill is waving at me from the bar, her ponytail going wild.

There are two men next to her. One I recognize from the photos on her desk. He's pretty standard-looking. Guessing that he watches football on Sundays in his lucky sweatpants and that he enjoys trips to Home Depot. He probably has strong opinions about women in politics. I don't know what they are. But I bet he has them.

The other guy, the guy behind Jill's husband, is . . . not bad-looking. He's got a stubbly half beard and dark hair that he's obviously put some effort into styling. His nose is substantial, and I like it. I want to touch it. Run my fingers over it. He's got full lips and big eyes. Almost a unibrow but it works.

I walk over, nearly smashing into a waitress passing by with a tray of food. I choose to play it off like it didn't happen, as the waitress huffs away in her truly unfortunate lederhosen-inspired uniform.

"Hey," I say to Jill.

"Hi!" she says. "Can I hug you?"

"Sure."

She throws her arms around my neck. I guess I never realized how short she is. I feel like a giant. I should have worn flats.

"This is my husband, Dan," she says.

Dan stands up and shakes my hand. I knew he would. He looks

like a handshaker. I bet he'll give his children handshakes instead of hugs.

Maybe I'm projecting because my dad never hugged me. I'm familiar with parental affection in the form of an awkward pat on the back, a firm handshake. The occasional coveted high five.

"And this is Pascal," Jill says, her voice lilting.

Pascal doesn't stand up. He waves. "Hi," he says.

I can't tell if he's shy or disappointed.

"Hi. I'm Annie."

"I know," he says, and sips his drink. So, not shy.

"Let me check if they'll seat us," Jill says, and skips over to the host.

"So," Dan says, "heard you used to live in the Big Apple."

"Yeah," I say, "for twelve years. I just moved here."

"I never understood why anyone would want to live there. Smells like garbage!"

"Not all the time," I say. Once you've lived in New York, it becomes like a sibling. I can bash it, call it names, but no one else can.

"Table is ready," Jill sings.

Dan chugs his beer. Pascal doesn't say or do much of anything. I can feel my anxiety metastasize. My legs go weak underneath me, and I'm afraid I won't make it to the table. I'm afraid they'll give, and I'll fall flat on my face in front of the entire restaurant.

Maybe the other diners are too busy eating giant pretzels to notice.

I get to the table and am seated next to Pascal and Jill, across from Dan, who appears to be scrutinizing me.

"You're pretty tall," he says.

"Your server will be right with you," the host says before quite literally running away from us.

"How tall are you?" Dan asks.

"Five nine," I say, putting the menu up in front of my face. If he can't see me, maybe he'll forget I'm here.

"That's tall for a girl," he says.

I shrug. "It's not that tall."

"Did you play basketball?"

"Nope."

"Volleyball?"

"No," I say, "I played soccer."

"Soccer?" he asks.

"Yeah."

"Huh," he says. He sounds skeptical.

"Pascal, did you play any sports in high school?" Jill asks.

"Erm," he says. "I ran track. And I was the captain of ski club."

"Ooh, that's cool," Jill says. "Annie, do you ski?"

"No," I say. "Sorry."

The waiter comes by. Dan orders another beer and Jill gets a vodka cranberry. Pascal gets a whiskey neat, which is telling. I also order a whiskey.

Jill asks for the pretzel appetizer and the beer cheese dip. Beer cheese doesn't sound too appealing to me, but I'm operating under the belief that this dinner is a bad dream, and soon I'll wake up in my apartment with a lump on my head. It seems to be an effective coping mechanism.

If I were to accept this situation as reality, I'm fairly certain I'd immediately be crushed like a bug under the sheer force of unpleasantness.

"I love this cheese," Jill says, understanding her role as the load-bearing wall. "I love all cheese, but this cheese is my all-time favorite. Dan says I'm cheesy."

"You are cheesy," he says.

"See?" she asks.

Where is my whiskey? I wish Sophie were here. I'd love to see the look on her face as she witnessed this conversation.

I understand now why she would choose to live mainly in isolation. I understand now why I spent years content to stay home with Sam and not interact with other people. It's too much of a gamble. Some people are terrible.

Like Dan, who is blatantly staring at me.

"What do you teach? Math?" he asks me.

"English and ASL," I say.

"What's ASL?"

"American Sign Language."

"Can you say something in sign language?"

"Yes," I say.

The waiter sets my whiskey down. Pascal reaches for it, thinking it's his, and our hands touch.

I look up at him, and he's looking back at me. His face is void of expression. A brick is more emotive.

He retracts his hand. I gulp my whiskey.

"What's everyone getting for their main?" Jill asks. "I was thinking the brat with the potato salad. Or maybe the schnitzel."

Nothing on the menu calls to me. I think my appetite has been permanently destroyed by this interaction.

A pretzel that's so large and twisty that it resembles a crusty brown octopus is plopped down in the center of the table, along with a cast-iron bowl of bubbling orange cheese.

Jill and Dan dig in, ripping at the pretzel and dunking it in the cheese. Double-dipping. Pascal stares into the depths of his whiskey. Mine's already gone.

When the waiter comes back to take our order, I ask for another whiskey.

"What will you have to eat?" the waiter asks.

"Oh," I say, "I guess the mixed green salad. With chicken."

"A salad?" Dan asks.

"Is that not acceptable to you?" I ask, because the whiskey's in me now, lowering my tolerance for bullshit.

Dan raises an eyebrow. Jill laughs a nervous, high-pitched giggle. Pascal pulls a classic Pascal move and does absolutely nothing.

The waiter flees. Dan gnaws on a chunk of pretzel and says, "One of the things I liked about Jill was, on our first date, she ordered a cheeseburger. I like a girl who eats."

"I definitely eat!" Jill says. "I can eat."

She takes another piece of pretzel and drenches it in cheese, then pops it into her mouth as if she's trying to prove a point.

"So," I say, desperate for a change of subject, "how long have you two been married?"

"Three years," Jill says. "But we still act like newlyweds."

Something happens under the table and they both giggle and squirm. I throw up a little in my mouth. I swallow it back down, chase it with whiskey.

I shouldn't have allowed myself to hope that this night would go any better than the way it's going. That was my mistake.

I see the picture. Sam. Shannon. Her on his lap. Their faces so close. Their cheeks red and slick with that happy glow.

"How did you meet?" I ask them.

"We met in college," Jill says. "He played football and I was a cheerleader."

"I was dating her friend at the time," he says. "Then I traded that one in for a better model."

I gasp midsip, spitting a little whiskey back into my glass. I guess I'm the only one offended by this comment. Jill seems tickled by it.

"Excuse me," I say. "I'll be right back."

"Are you going to the bathroom? I'll go with you," Jill says.

"No," I say. "I . . . I forgot something. I have to make a call."

I book it to the bathroom and lock myself inside a stall. I press my forehead against the door, let it hold my weight.

"Don't cry," I whisper to myself. "Don't cry."

I pull my head back and notice the graffiti on the stall door. I put the toilet seat down and sit on top of it with my head in my hands. I read the graffiti to distract myself.

RL ♡ NJ

Jess & Rocky 4everrrr

I love Dick!!!

It's okay, Annie.

I stop. Read it again.

It's okay, Annie.

"Sophie?" I say, tracing my fingers over the words written in what looks like red Sharpie. When I bring my hand away, the red has transferred to my fingertips. I rub my fingers together. It spreads. It's fresh ink.

"Sophie? Is that you?"

Don't worry.

The words have changed.

And they change again.

It's one night.

"It's miserable," I say. "How did I ever think this was a good idea?"

It's okay. You're okay.

"It's okay. I'm okay."

The night is yours.

"What do you mean?"

Take it back.
Give them hell.

I run my fingers over the words again, and this time they disappear from the door altogether. There's nothing there. It's all on my hands now. They're covered in sticky red ink.

I come out of the stall, and there's a woman there with a flat mouth who's looking at me like I'm a foul creature.

I wonder if she heard me talking. She must think I was talking to myself.

Or she sees my hands covered in red and thinks I'm indecent.

I avoid her on my way to the sink.

It takes a long time to wash the ink off of my hands. It requires a lot of soap, an aggressive lather. As I wash them, I look at myself in the mirror.

I hear Sophie's voice in my head.

Take it back. Give them hell.

Why should I let these people ruin my night? Why should I let stupid Dan make me feel bad?

When I get back to the table, I sit up straight and pull my chair in. They're all looking at me like I owe them an explanation. I don't give them one.

"We were just talking about jobs," Jill says. "Pascal works for his family's logging business. In accounting."

"Cool," I say in a tone that makes it very clear I do not think it's cool. I finish my whiskey and wave over the waiter. "May I have another, please?"

"What's that?" Dan asks. "Your third?"

"You can count!" I say.

Jill does her awkward laugh. It sounds like a dying motor.

"Logging," she says, "is really lucrative. Right, Pascal?"

He nods.

"Pascal is from Vermont. Vermont is beautiful," Jill says. "Have you ever been, Annie?"

"I don't think so," I say. "Too busy burrowing in my NYC trash mountain."

I look at Dan, who is busy examining the cheese he's spilled on his shirt.

It occurs to me as he dips his napkin in his water glass and begins to pat away at the congealed orange glob that maybe this isn't the best approach. Maybe I should accept that this night isn't going my way and take the loss with grace, instead of getting drunk and sarcastic, doubling down on the unpleasantness and actively contributing to a collective misery.

When the waiter brings my next whiskey, I ask for a ginger ale and push the whiskey away. But it's too late. I know I'm already buzzed by the motion of the room, by the way my eyes are reluctant to focus. I've been too nervous to eat anything all day, and while I've built up my tolerance over the past few months of excessive drinking, it hasn't made me insusceptible.

I take a deep breath and spread my napkin across my lap.

"Did you grow up in the city?" Jill asks me.

"No," I say. "I grew up in Connecticut. But I went to the city for college and never left. Well, until now, I guess. Obviously."

"Why leave?" Pascal asks. It's the first question out of his mouth all evening, and it's rude.

"Personal reasons," I say.

"What's that code for?" Dan asks.

Code for "none of your damn business." "Long story."

"We've got all night," he says.

But then the food comes, and everyone's distracted.

I stab at my sad salad. Droopy romaine. Pieces of tough gray chicken. A pool of watery dressing at the bottom of the bowl. My stomach withers.

The good news is that the rest of the table is preoccupied with eating, so the quiet that ensues isn't painful; it just is. I let it exist, find some sanctuary inside it. I'm getting through it. I'm doing it. I'm surviving.

"How's your salad?" Dan asks.

"Good," I lie.

"Here," he says, leaning across the table and plopping a greasy chunk of sausage on my plate. "You need some meat on your bones."

I gawk at the sausage, at its charred skin peeling away to reveal a too-pink center, the most unappealing, cratered texture. It oozes liquid onto my already damp, overdressed salad.

I push the plate away, unable to stomach its appearance.

"Uh-oh, better call the guidance counselor," Dan says. "We've got a problem."

He points to me and then mimes making himself throw up, indicating he believes I'm bulimic.

Jill slaps his hand, a playful rebuke.

"Fine," Dan says. "Don't take my advice. But if you're wondering why Pascal is so quiet . . ."

"Dan!" Jill says, but it's through laughter. She's genuinely charmed by everything he says. It's mind-boggling.

"All right," I say. "Thanks for the tip."

"There it is! Some gratitude. You're welcome," he says, smiling. A big dumb, self-satisfied grin. He has no idea how much of an asshole he's being. I imagine it started in his youth, a few bad off-color jokes that people laughed at to be polite, or because they had terrible senses of humor, or because they were family and loved him so much they'd marvel at anything he said or did, or because his primary audience was a bunch of prepubescent peers. And as time went on, he continued to get this positive reinforcement. If the occasional person didn't laugh at his bad jokes or bullying or general shtick, he'd assume it was their fault, that they were no fun, sticks-in-the-mud. In adulthood, he's surrounded himself with like-minded idiots to insulate himself from any negative feedback.

And through this lifelong cycle of validation and fortification, his ego has transformed into something large and dangerous. I picture a Godzilla-like creature with an enormous, destructive body and a teeny-tiny brain. Terrorizing those smart enough to recognize it, entertaining those too stupid to realize they've created a monster—and monsters can't be unmade.

Watching him chew, opening his mouth to shovel more food in before he swallows what's already inside, I'm certain he doesn't have an ounce of self-awareness. I'm also certain it's no excuse, though nothing I can say or do in the next hour will magically change him. Make him realize that he's been horrifically rude the entire night and apologize profusely.

Pascal, too. If he's not attracted to me, fine. Ouch, but fine. The least he could do is make minimal conversation. Not sit there making small, erratic movements like a malfunctioning animatronic puppet whose memory has been wiped of words.

I think about Sam, about what it would be like if he were here. We'd be making fun of the decor, drinking soda because we'd be too embarrassed to drink out of beer steins and too happy to have any need for hard liquor. We'd order cheeseburgers and he'd get fries and I'd get onion rings and we'd share. We'd speak to each other in bad German accents. Maybe we'd call each other Hansel and Gretel.

"How's everything?" the waiter asks.

"Great!" Jill says.

"Can you bring more of the cheese?" Dan asks. "And another pretzel."

"Okay," the waiter says. "I'll be right back with that."

"Are you still going to be hungry for dessert?" Jill asks Dan. She turns to me. "They have the best dessert here. Have you ever had Black Forest cake?"

"Yes," I say.

"Yeah, right," Dan says. "Look at her. She's never had a piece of cake in her life."

I open my mouth to defend myself, to say that I eat cake all the time and that I'm just naturally thin. That this is the way my body looks and has looked since I was about fourteen. But I zip my lips back together. What difference will it make?

My insecurity comes knocking. Maybe I am so thin it's repulsive. Maybe Pascal is disgusted by me. There was this guy in high school who told me he thought having sex with me would be like having sex with a pile of bones. I cried about it for weeks. Years, even. I'll probably cry about it tonight.

"Ow," Dan says. His face, which has been locked in the same dumb-happy expression all night, has suddenly changed. His eyes are dark, small and concerned, his eyebrows sinking. His lips bulge along with his cheeks, his mouth full of too much food.

"What is it?" Jill asks.

He reaches up, puts his fingers to his lips. Something thin and sharp and pale begins to protrude, to stab itself through. He grabs it, holds it up to the light.

It's a bone. A tiny white bone.

"What *is* that?" Jill asks. "Is that a bone?"

It's so small; it's like a fish bone or a bird bone. But I thought he was eating sausage?

He sets the bone down on the table, then returns his hands to his mouth as it births another bone. This one is considerably larger.

"Oh, my God!" Jill says.

Dan sets the second bone down next to the first, then goes back to his mouth to pull out yet another bone. This one is so big I don't know how it fit in his mouth in the first place.

Jill gasps so loudly that it gets the attention of the diners at all of the surrounding tables.

Dan sets the third bone down. I think he's going back for more, but instead he grabs his napkin and spits the rest of the contents of his mouth into it. When he pulls the napkin away, his mouth is dark, and I realize the darkness is blood. He's bleeding from his mouth. He plops the napkin down on his plate, and it unfolds to reveal the beigy pulp of chewed pretzel, chunks of pink sausage, tiny spiky white bones and a lot—a lot—of blood.

Jill is horrified. Her hands are on her face; her mouth is contorted into a scream position, though no sound escapes. Pascal's eyes are wide, nostrils flared. Dan looks utterly exhausted. He's ashen, eyes barely open. Blood drips from the sides of his mouth.

I look at the bones, back at Dan, back at the bones. And for some reason, the reaction that rises from inside me, from the core of me, is laughter. I start laughing.

It's quiet at first. But . . . it builds quickly.

I can't control it. The look on his face—I can't describe it.

I'm laughing so hard my obliques begin to ache. Tears drip from my eyes, travel with a delightful sensation down my face.

I'm aware they're looking at me. Jill's horror is now directed toward me, along with Pascal's big eyes. And Dan, of course, is staring at me in complete shock, his expression wounded and stupid.

The nearby diners, too. All too curious to go back to their own bad meals and boring conversations.

It's too much. I can't catch my breath.

I turn in my seat so I have room to hunch over, so my spine can curl the way it wants to, so the tension in my neck releases. I stay like this, laughing, until the waiter comes over and asks if everything is all right.

"It is not all right!" Jill screeches. "There were bones in my husband's food!"

"What?" the waiter asks.

"Look!"

My laughter begins to subside as I peer up to see what the waiter's reaction is. I'd say it is mainly confusion.

Dan's skin looks the color and consistency of cement. There are rust-hued stains on the sides of his mouth from the blood. He's not bleeding anymore. His jaw is slack, and in the dark void of his mouth, I can see teeth. His teeth. Still attached. His tongue is extended slightly. Also still attached.

He's fine. No major damage has been done. I use my napkin to dab away my remaining laughter tears.

The waiter stares at the bones.

"Well?" Jill says.

"I'm sorry about this," the waiter says, reaching to clear the plate with the bloody napkin on it.

"This is ridiculous!" Jill says. "He could have choked and died! Are you okay, honey?"

Dan nods his head but doesn't say anything. I bet it's the first time in his life he's ever been speechless.

"We're not paying for this!" Jill says. "I want to speak to a manager. This is unacceptable. Disgusting."

She's shouting, and her voice carries throughout the restaurant. Silverware begins to clink, clink, clink all around us. The sound of people setting down their forks and knives and spoons, too afraid to take another bite.

The manager comes over and apologizes. She offers to escort Jill and Dan to her office, I assume to prevent the rest of the diners from hearing any further details about the fiasco. Jill helps Dan up, and as he stumbles to his feet, another chuckle escapes me. I cover my mouth, but it's too late.

Dan looks at me, his eyes focusing after being blank and dead for a few solid minutes. His expression is a mix of confusion and fear. Or maybe it's suspicion. Whatever he's thinking or feeling, it's definitely about me. Jill, too, only her feelings are clear. Anger. Disgust. She glowers at me as I sit with my hand clapped over my mouth.

The manager ushers them away. Dan now possesses a wobbly wide-legged gait, like he's just had a colonoscopy. Jill follows at his heels, her hands placed on his back as if she's pushing him or worried he'll fall. They turn a corner and disappear.

I exhale and take a sip of ginger ale, and when I set it down, I realize Pascal is still here, sitting right next to me.

"Why'd you laugh?" he asks.

"Nervous reaction," I say, proud of myself for coming up with a quick plausible lie.

"Huh," he says.

A minute goes by, and in it I come to the conclusion that there's nothing else to do but leave.

"All right," I say, standing, "I'm going to go."

"You're leaving?"

"Yeah."

"Okay," he says.

"Nice meeting you," I say. "Good luck with the logs."

He seems offended by my words, which admittedly came out more venomous than intended. I do genuinely wish him luck with the logs. Without a personality, they're probably all he has.

I hurry out of the restaurant to my car. I take off my shoes the second I sit down and toss them in the backseat.

I don't know why exactly, but I feel good. I drive home singing a song I make up as I go.

By the time I pull into the driveway, I'm so full of energy it's coming out of my ears. I leave my shoes in the car and run into the backyard, saying a quick hello to Mr. Frog.

The grass is dead and scratchy underneath my feet, but I don't care. I like the feel of it. I dance on top of it, singing my song from the car.

And when you hate someone you meet,
they will get a tasty treat,
bones on their tongue and in their cheeks,
bones to make them hush and make them bleed.
Bones are the escape you need;
you can sing and dance alone,
all thanks to the bones.

Above me, the moon is full and shines silvery white.

So bright, so bright, so bright.

But the brightness isn't just above me. It's in front of me. Glowing toward me.

There's a light on.

Downstairs.

The light is coming from a downstairs window.

I notice it now. The other car. It's parked in the street in front of the house.

Lynn.

She's home.

And she's standing in the window, staring at me. She's been watching me. I don't know for how long. Long enough.

I should be mortified. Right now I should be experiencing the excruciating sting of embarrassment. I've felt it for less.

And yet.

I face the window. I step forward so I can be fully illuminated, so my smile is not masked in shadow. I wave to the face behind the glass. To Lynn.

With a quick swish of the curtains, she's gone, and the light goes off.

"Oops!" I say to myself. And to the moon, "Oh, well."

I lay myself down in the grass, waiting to feel some belated humiliation.

It never arrives.

I revel in its absence. It's liberating.

I laugh and laugh.

RALPH

The next morning, I head to Sophie's first thing. I decide to stop in the Good Mug for coffee. I wait for Oskar to comment on the two coffees, on the fact that one of them is for Sophie, but he doesn't. He does ask me if I'm feeling all right.

"I feel great," I say. "Why?"

He shakes his head.

It's nippy, and there's a shimmering layer of frost on the ground, but it's not bothering me at all. I like the way it makes me feel, how it reminds me of my body. *You're here,* the cold says. *It's now.*

I trot up to Sophie's door and set the coffees down so I can knock twice. The door opens itself and I step inside. Sophie is at the top of the stairs wearing a long purple velvet robe with black fur trim.

"Pet," she says, yawning, "good morning."

"Am I too early?" I ask. "I have coffee."

"I'm tired is all," she says, descending the steps. "Thank you for the coffee. How was your date?"

I hand her the cup and she removes the lid to sip. She looks at me, her eyes bright and eager.

"You don't know?" I ask her.

"Know what, darling?"

"About the date?"

"What do you mean?"

"We talked," I say. "Last night. On the stall?"

I was so sure. I didn't doubt for a second.

"The stall?" she asks.

"Are you messing with me?"

She leans back, puts a hand over her heart. "No, darling. I'm sorry. I don't know what you mean."

"Oh," I say. "I guess I had too much to drink or something. I could have sworn . . ."

"Tell me," she says. "Come. Let's sit."

We sit on the stairs and drink our coffee as I give her a play-by-play of the night. I tell her about handsome, terrible, bland Pascal. I tell her about Dan and his repulsiveness. She scoffs.

"Some men are so foul you wouldn't even bother to save their blood," she says.

"Sorry?"

"Never mind," she says. "Continue."

I tell her about how the restaurant was tacky and the food was gross, about how I drank straight whiskey and escaped to the bathroom. I tell her about how I saw the graffiti, the message that I assumed was from her. The red ink.

She keeps shrugging and shaking her head like she had nothing to do with it, like she has no idea what I'm talking about. I'm not sure I believe her. Part of me hopes she's lying, because the alternative is scary. Did I hallucinate? See what I wanted to see? Was I drunker than I realized?

I tell her about how I started to get sassy, but then realized it was futile.

And then I tell her about the bones.

She's silent as I recount the story. She doesn't sip. She doesn't move. I don't think she breathes.

"I laughed. I started laughing. It took me over. I thought it was the funniest thing I'd ever seen, the funniest thing to ever happen. He was bleeding from his mouth, spitting out bones, and I was laughing. I laughed. The whole restaurant was staring."

Last night, the laughter made me feel immortal, but in the yellow light of day, I feel ashamed of it. It was crazy to laugh. Why did I laugh? What was so funny?

"I thought maybe it was you," I say. "Like the spider. I thought it was a curse."

"It wasn't me, pet," she says, stroking my hand. "It was you."

I have a flash of memory. Me spinning around and around, a swirl of trees, the house. The moon hovering above me. My feet numb. A mist like a silver aura delicate as lace. My voice. A strange song.

I remember how it felt. How *I* felt.

I conjure it. The feeling. The feeling of watching Dan spit bones from his wretched mouth. The feeling of dancing on the grass, in the moonlight. Of being seen by Lynn and not caring. Not caring at all.

I wasn't myself. I'm not myself.

Or maybe . . . maybe I'm more myself than I've ever been.

"But how?" I ask. "How?"

Sophie puts a finger to her lips, a thought haunting her face.

"What?" I ask.

She smiles widely. "Nothing at all, my dear," she says. "Let's go out for breakfast. We can talk over pancakes."

"You're obsessed with pancakes."

She shrugs. "What can I say? They are cake disguised as breakfast. I'll go get dressed. How'd the dress work out, by the way?"

"It was perfect. Thank you."

"You're welcome, my pet," she says, walking upstairs.

I'm left sitting on the steps drinking cold coffee and questioning everything.

I let my eyes wander around the foyer. They distinguish each detail. The shape of the crystals dripping from the chandelier, not quite teardrops. They're too sharp, and in this exact light, at this particular time of day, they look dangerous, like the kind of icicles that kill people.

The colorful silhouettes the crystals project onto the walls, they're in constant movement. They make me dizzy.

I put my face in my hands and rub my temples with my thumbs. It smells like incense in here, a scent so rich it's almost rotten. I'm finding it hard to breathe.

There's a pain in my chest. A gnawing.

Once Sam and I were watching some show on the History Channel about medieval torture, and there was one type where the torturers would adhere a bucket of rats to your chest and then heat the bucket so the rats would panic and chew through you.

"That's actually happened to someone," I said to him, "to multiple people."

"I don't want these anymore," he said, setting the bowl of Cheetos we'd been snacking on down on the coffee table. Then he used his foot to push them farther away.

"I feel bad for the rats," I said.

He laughed.

"They didn't do anything! Must be scary for them."

"Yeah," Sam said, still laughing, "too bad for the rats. Not the guys getting eaten by them."

"I feel sorry for the people, too," I said, because I did feel sorry for them, and because I didn't like it when Sam laughed at me like that, like I was crazy in a not-adorable way. But then I decided to be honest. "I feel worse for the rats, though."

I thought about how terrifying it must have been for them, to be minding their own business, happily nibbling on garbage and scurrying through the streets, only to be scooped up and find themselves in a situation in which they thought they'd burn to death if they didn't eat through some smelly dungeon human.

"Pet," I hear. Sophie emerges from her room in a dress that looks pretty much identical to the robe. I don't know why she bothered to change. "You look upset."

"Just thinking about rats," I tell her. "Do you think I have too much empathy for rats?"

I ask because I know she won't laugh at me. She won't think I'm crazy in a not-adorable way. She would never.

"Rats are selfish creatures," she says. "They want to survive, and they do whatever they can to survive. I admire them."

"Yeah."

She reaches for my hand and helps me up.

"Shall we?" she asks.

I follow her out the door. I hear it lock behind us.

We walk in silence for a while, the ground chomping beneath our feet like it's something alive, like it's something we bring to life with our contact, with our presence.

"Are you still thinking of rats?" Sophie asks me.

"No," I say, "I'm back to thinking about last night. What do you mean, it was me?"

"Here," she says. "Open your palm."

I do. In it, she deposits a large spider. So large I can see its face perfectly without having to squint. Countless eyes and a smile. A big lively grin.

"This is Ralph," she says. "He and I are good friends. He's very cheery."

"Is this real?" I ask her.

"Annie," she says, "there's only so much I can tell you, only so much I can teach you. I can show you things about the world, about yourself. Beautiful, wonderful things. But I can't make you believe them. There are some things you need to discover on your own. Do you understand?"

"I . . ."

I look down at Ralph, whose smile is so big it takes up most of his dark, fuzzy face.

He's the most adorable creature I've ever seen. And she's right. He is very cheery.

And suddenly, I'm cheery, too.

"He's amazing."

"I thought you two might hit it off," she says. "He's good company. Almost as good as me."

When we arrive at the diner, we sit in our usual back booth and order pancakes. Sophie pours maple syrup into her spoon and lets Ralph stick his face in it.

"Should he eat that?" I ask.

"I don't know," she says. "But he loves it."

"This is so weird."

I almost say that I can't believe it, but I stop myself. Instead, I say, "There's a lot I used to believe wasn't possible."

She smiles, picking an apple out of thin air and tossing it to me. She says, "I know."

INTERLUDE

In the weeks after the date, Jill, along with the rest of the staff, avoids me like I'm a leper on fire. I assume Jill told them what happened and I have to admit that between the Chris Bersten spider incident and the bone-date incident, they're fully justified in being wary of me, though, since the date, there have been no other suspicious occurrences on my end.

It's unclear if it's a phenomenon I can control. My curiosity has been outwrestled by my extreme apprehension. I try not to give it too much thought. I'm well aware I can't avoid it forever, but that's a problem for future me.

Present me has melded herself to her routine. It's a source of stability, instilling a much-needed sense of normalcy in my life. There's comfort in the simplicity of doing the same thing every day, every week. There's beauty in the ritual.

I get up, stop for coffee at the Good Mug, go to work, pretend the whole school doesn't suspect I've got evil powers—which is TBD, I guess—come home, take a shower, eat an easy dinner like a frozen burrito or scrambled eggs or peanut butter on bread, drink a glass or bottle of wine or occasionally something stronger, watch a TV show and, depending on any romantic story lines in the show, maybe fit in a quick ugly cry or go straight to bed. Most weeknights I'm asleep by nine p.m. at the latest.

The weekends, though . . . The weekends I spend with Sophie. On the weekends, I'm not lonely at all. I'm eating homemade strudel, dressed head to toe in silk and soft velvet. I'm lounging around the library reading old books, or in the conservatory tending to flowers. I'm playing shuffleboard or dancing or watching an old movie where the actors are all hams. There have been no ghost sightings since Sophie captured all the ghosts and put them in the basement.

It's been blissful.

But fleeting.

I'm too ashamed to admit to Sophie that I can't maintain my happiness on my own. That when she's not around, I'm a pathetic mess who eats meals off of paper towels and uses her sleeves as tissues. She gets impatient at any mention of Sam or if I make any implication that I'm unsatisfied in my singledom. So I try to keep this aspect of my life, of my routine, to myself.

But. Sophie's not stupid. When she suspects I'm having a particularly rough time, she'll send me home with Ralph. She's done it on multiple occasions.

"Why don't you take Ralph this week, pet?" she'll say, and Ralph will crawl out of her pocket and into her hand, then make his way into my hand. He'll look up at me, smiling his big silly smile, and we'll walk home together.

I made him a tiny bed out of a cereal box. It's got a tall headboard and a sponge for a mattress. I covered the headboard in orange construction paper because orange is his favorite color. I covered the sponge with an old pillowcase.

He loves it.

He also loves to watch TV with me. I'll let him use the remote, pick whatever he wants. He particularly enjoys HGTV and home-makeover shows. Also cooking competitions.

"You're so silly, Ralph," I'll say, and he'll smile, march his little legs.

It's astonishing how normal it is to love a creature you're not supposed to love.

It's astonishing what you'll accept when you want love. When you need it. You'll welcome it in any form, from anyone, anything, regardless of circumstance, however peculiar. However fantastical.

I wonder all the time if I'm desperate, and I definitely am, but the truth is, anyone would be happy to love Ralph. And be loved by him. He really is great company. The most adorable spider.

And he does help. If I cry, he cries. His cries are terrible. He makes this horrible, high-pitched squeaking noise. It's enough to discourage me. Also, he's too cute. After one look at him, it's hard to be sad about anything. Even Sam. And dying alone.

Ralph does not like Sam. If I pull up pictures of Sam or open my phone to text Sam, Ralph goes crazy. He'll run up the walls. Stomp his legs. Turn the volume all the way up on the TV. He'll demand my attention. Usually, he distracts me for long enough that I give up on Sam.

At night, I put his bed on my nightstand and he climbs on. I pull a fuzzy washcloth over him as a blanket. He vibrates with glee. He likes to be cozy.

I don't blame him. December has been ruthless. It's already snowed three times. Two delayed school openings and one magical Sunday at Sophie's watching flurries fall through the big windows in the ballroom while drinking hot chocolate with chunky marshmallows.

My dad doesn't call to ask if I'll be coming back to Connecticut to celebrate Christmas with him. He doesn't text. He does send an e-mail with the entire content of that e-mail in the subject line.

I respond quickly, telling him no, I won't be able to make it, though I don't have any alternate plans and the idea of spending the holidays alone is daunting. Sam was big on Christmas. We'd spend it with his family in Maryland, dress up in matching pajamas and eat strictly carbohydrates, watch all the stop-motion specials. He'd often declare that it was his favorite holiday, which I've since come to suspect was a tactic to deflate the significance of all other holidays, specifically my two favorites: Valentine's Day, for obvious reasons, and New Year's, which Sam found particularly baffling.

"It's a clean slate," I'd tell him.

"It's another day," he'd say. "It's just another day in a series of days."

"I like resolutions. It's hopeful!"

"You can make resolutions literally any day."

I would pout and eventually give up on whatever grand ideas I had for an intimate, lavish, champagne-soaked NYE dinner, a spin class and a couples massage on New Year's Day. Mason jars filled with resolutions.

It's bad enough I have to suffer through the carols and commercials reminding me of my ex-boyfriend's favorite time of year. The thought of having no one to kiss at midnight is a devastation I hadn't accounted for in my log of sad, unfortunate single-person stuff.

When I lament to Sophie about the holidays, she makes a sour face.

"I don't approve of the sentiment," she says, shuddering, "but I do enjoy the decorations. Some of them, anyway. The trees are my favorite. Beautiful."

"Yeah." I sigh.

"You should celebrate the winter solstice with me," she says. "I'll throw us a marvelous party."

"That sounds nice."

"What is it, pet? You still look down."

"I've always liked New Year's. Staying up until midnight. Making resolutions. But it's pretty pathetic if you're single."

She balks. "Please, Annie Crane, never say anything like that again. We're celebrating."

We decide Sophie will host me for the winter solstice, and I'll host her for New Year's Eve.

In preparation, I buy garland and string lights and sparkly silver pinecones. I buy two bottles of champagne. I have to go back out to buy a stepladder and thumbtacks to adhere the lights to the walls. I go out a third time to get replacement champagne, since I drink one of the bottles to ease the stress and agitation of hanging the lights.

But of course, Sophie puts me to shame. When I arrive at her house for the winter solstice, she opens the door for me in an extravagant purple gown. It has intricate beading and embroidery, a corset back and a long train. Her hair is in a braided updo laced with flowers. A whole flower arrangement, actually. The way she has it, it's like the flowers are growing out of her head.

There are more flowers. Everywhere, on every surface. Massive arrangements. There are candles. There's a roasted chicken, and sweet potatoes and carrots and an apple slaw. For dessert, she made a fruitcake with a maple glaze. There's blackberry wine.

"Only for special occasions," she tells me as she pours me a generous glass.

After dinner, around nine o'clock, Sophie brings me upstairs to give me a present. It's a dress, nearly identical to hers, except mine is a warm pink.

"Thank you! Thank you!" I say, as I go into her closet to put it on. When I reemerge in the dress, I do a spin, and Sophie throws a hand over her brow from the drama of it all.

"Gorgeous," she says. "My Annie."

She made Ralph an outfit as well. He wears a small navy bow tie and top hat.

"You look very handsome," I tell him.

He beams.

We go down to the ballroom and drink another bottle of blackberry wine and dance by candlelight. I don't know if it's the wine or the intimacy of wearing matching dresses, but something possesses me with the courage to ask.

"Can I ask you something?" I shout over the music. We're listening to Britney again, Sophie's favorite.

"Yes, darling," she says.

"How does it work?"

"How does what work, pet?"

"The . . . the . . . I don't know! Like, how did I project graffiti onto the bathroom stall? How did I do that thing with the bones? It wasn't intentional. It just happened."

"Strange, isn't it?" she says. "How things just happen."

She grabs my hands and spins me around and around.

"Sophie."

We stop spinning. She cradles my face in her palms. "You have to surrender, Annie."

"To what?"

"No, no," she says, laughing. "You must surrender everything for everything."

She twirls away from me.

I realize she isn't going to elaborate.

So I surrender to the night. I surrender to dancing wildly and to blackberry wine. I pour a drop out for Ralph. He drinks it, hiccups, stumbles a few steps, then passes out on his back.

Just shy of midnight, Sophie leads me out to the backyard. There's a bonfire. I'm drunk, and through my eyes, the world is opaque, the sky velvety, lush, constellations like strings of pearls. I watch Sophie lay wreaths of winter jasmine. She circles around the fire like the obedient hands of a clock. She's barefoot.

There's this moment when, through the fine ribbons of smoke and curtains of yellow flames, I think I see her, though I also feel her next to me, braiding flowers into my hair.

"There's someone else," I tell her. "Who is it?"

She isn't there to answer. Only her shadow. Beside me. Somehow independent of her. Untethered, tucking a pansy behind my ear.

I wake up the next morning with a dry mouth and a hangover.

"Dear, dear," Sophie says, looking particularly radiant over a breakfast of eggs and fresh biscuits. She can't have slept much, so I don't know how she looks so well rested. She made me a face cream with rose hip and orange peel. She said it was the one she used, and it made my skin soft, but sadly, it did not make me ethereally beautiful.

She brews me an herbal tea that I'm hesitant to drink, considering the last time she gave me a home blend I hallucinated. She insists it will alleviate my hangover. I relent, and she's right. I do feel better.

"What are your plans for the week?" she asks me.

I sigh. "To be either drunk or asleep, ideally."

"Why don't you stay here? Stay the week. I can give you clothes. You have a toothbrush. What more could you need?"

"Nothing," I say. "Nothing at all."

So I stay with Sophie. I stay with her through New Year's, the decorations and champagne back at my place pointless.

I don't mind. I'm happy to be with Sophie. Happy to be occupied.

And most of all, happy not to be alone.

Like Sam, Sophie doesn't understand my enthusiasm for New Year's.

"I've been alive for so many years," she says. "I think it's made me a bit indifferent. Besides, I honor the passing of time on the solstice."

"Oh," I say.

"But you enjoy New Year's, so we shall celebrate!"

"We don't have to."

"We don't *have* to do anything, darling. We're free," she says. "And freedom means doing what you want. I think I'll make duck."

She makes us duck and brussels sprouts. She makes us flower crowns. She has us write resolutions on pieces of parchment with quill pens, fold them and burn them over a special candle she made and placed inside a pewter bowl. The candle smells like sage. When we burn the parchment, the flame turns purple.

"Is that good?" I ask her.

She doesn't answer.

I have a lot of lofty resolutions, like being more patient, like not forgetting to put on deodorant, like learning to make things the way that Sophie makes things—food and soaps and tonics and balms.

Like overcoming my uncertainty and figuring out how to wield whatever power I had that night at Rhineland.

Like finally getting over Sam.

As midnight approaches and we sit watching the grandfather clock in the library, I confess to her my sadness about not having anyone to kiss at midnight.

"Is that your measure of joy?" she asks, deadpan. "Kissing a man?"

"I guess not," I say. "When you put it like that . . ."

"You have to let it go, Annie," she says. "Promise me. At the stroke of midnight. No more of this self-pitying talk about being single or alone or missing Sam. He gave you a gift. Look at where you are now. This is only the beginning."

"You're right," I say. "I'll try. I can promise you I'll try."

"Good," she says. "I'm very serious about promises."

"I know."

"Very, very serious."

"I know, Sophie. I promise you, I will try."

She smiles and moves herself closer to me on the couch, resting her head on my shoulder. Ralph has fallen asleep on my knee, his legs spread out flat, his top hat askew.

When the clock strikes midnight, the lights flicker, and I have a strange, evanescent vision. I see a version of myself I don't quite recognize parting the dark, standing before me and wearing an alien grin.

I rub my eyes and blame the wine.

"Happy New Year, pet," Sophie says, raising a glass to me. "May it be your best one yet."

"Happy New Year, Sophie."

When I leave a few days later to go back to my apartment and my routine, Sophie sends Ralph with me.

"Why doesn't he live with you for a little while?" she says. "Keep him."

I don't do much of anything the first week of January, but I do teach Ralph how to play fetch.

RESOLUTIONS

"I never make New Year's resolutions," Madison says, licking the remaining yogurt from her spoon. Beth is still in the Poconos skiing with her family, meaning Madison will be eating lunch in my classroom for the next two days so she doesn't have to brave the cafeteria alone. "If I want to do something, I do it."

"That's good," I say. I haven't made any progress on my resolutions, and I've already come dangerously close to breaking my promise to Sophie. Last night I pulled up Sam's Facebook page for a split second, then x-ed out of it before I could see anything.

"I think a lot of people make resolutions so they can tell themselves they're trying to be better, instead of actually just being better," Madison says. "You know what I mean?"

I don't much appreciate being dragged by a fifteen-year-old.

On my way home from school, I stop at the grocery store and buy ingredients. I buy fresh herbs and a clove of garlic and a garlic press. I buy tinfoil. I buy lemons and green beans and red potatoes and a small whole chicken. I buy butter and a nice bottle of olive oil. The oil is twenty-five dollars, which makes me feel very adult but also breaks my heart a little. A single tear may or may not fall as I insert my debit card at the cash register.

When I get home, I follow a recipe I found online. I almost quit as soon as I'm tasked with "removing the giblets from inside the cavity." But I press on.

"I'm doing it!" I yell, reaching inside the dead bird. "I'm doing it."

Ralph waves his front legs in a show of support.

I do it. I roast a chicken. I also make green beans and buttery mashed potatoes.

I cook a beautiful meal by myself, for myself.

Well, I share some with Ralph. He gets a shallow ramekin of chicken juice. He nods off immediately afterward, wearing a satisfied grin, chin resting on the rim of the dish.

It feels good to deliver on my resolutions. To do something just for me.

After I finish, I sit at the dining room table with my hands clasped in my lap and my plate still in front of me. The only things left on it are a few skinny chicken bones.

I stare at them. They're delicate and pale. A grayish pink. They have a vague shine.

I wonder now, in the elastic minutes I spend studying these bones, who gets to decide what's beautiful.

Before tonight, I probably would have said that chicken bones were grisly, unsightly things. I would have thrown them right in the garbage without a second thought. But why? What's ugly about these parts?

This bird fed me. I should cherish its bones.

I fed me. I should cherish myself.

I clamp my eyes shut. My fingers curl in tight, my hands embracing like long-lost friends. I focus. I breathe in. That golden scent of butter, of citrus and rosemary. The warmth of it all nuzzles against me.

There's a contentment I've never known brewing within me. I can feel it, its gentle swell.

Surrender, a voice says.

Sophie says. I say.

It glides through me with slick fins. Down to my toes. Up, in the narrow canals of my ears. But when it gets to my chest, something happens. My nerves rupture, and they drown it. It drowns.

I open my eyes.

I open them to a tall tower of chicken bones floating above my plate.

I gasp, and they fall. There're more of them now, so many, and they rain down on me. I push myself away from the table. Ralph takes cover under the ramekin, a makeshift fort.

Maybe it lasts only a few seconds, but it feels like longer. It stops eventually.

There are chicken bones scattered all over the dining room. On the table, on the floor.

"I think it's safe now," I tell Ralph.

He emerges cautiously.

"I don't know what happened," I say.

He shakes his head. He doesn't know, either.

"Well," I say, looking down at all the bones, "I guess I'm magic!"

I start to laugh.

"I'm fucking magic! I can't . . . I mean, I can't believe it. I can't believe I just did that. I made that happen. Don't know how, but I did. Me! Can you believe it?" I ask Ralph.

Of course he can.

I decide to save the chicken bones.

I gather them all and put them in a pot with water, along with my final lemon sliced thin, some rosemary and salt. The Internet says to boil, so I boil. Then I reduce to a simmer and let the pot sit while I work on lesson plans, while I brush my teeth and wash my face. While I tuck Ralph into bed. While I tuck myself into bed.

I lie on my back, facing the ceiling, trying to breathe out my lingering adrenaline so I can sleep.

I choose not to fixate on my failings, because maybe I'm not any closer to having control over whatever it is, whatever I'm capable of. But I know that I'm capable.

I didn't always know that.

I flip over onto my stomach. I smile into my pillow.

In the morning, I wake up to bone broth.

"I made this!" I tell Ralph, letting him taste a small spoonful. He gives an enthusiastic squeal.

I get dressed and sail out to my car. I run into Lynn on the driveway. She's walking up with a coffee cup I recognize from the Good Mug.

"Good morning!" I call out to her.

She gives a quick wave, then puts her head down and cuts across the yard, beelining toward the front door.

It occurs to me that the last time we saw each other, I was dancing barefoot in the backyard. For some reason, this compels me to say, "I made bone broth, if you'd like some! It's broth from bones."

If my goal was to let her know that I'm not weird, shouting the word "bone" at her twice before sunrise probably wasn't the best move.

She gives another wave and then disappears into the house.

I save the broth and take it to Sophie's on Saturday. She doesn't think I'm weird. She thanks me and teaches me how to make soap from wood ash and pig fat.

"Don't worry about Lynn," she says when I tell her about our encounters. "She travels, sees a lot. She has an open mind."

Lynn doesn't seem that open-minded to me, but I guess it's a lot to ask of someone to shrug off their upstairs neighbor frolicking around the yard on a cold November night, singing to herself.

"I'm glad for you, pet," Sophie says. "It's a nice thing, to cook for yourself. To be good to yourself. To commit to and feed your own happiness."

"Yes," I say. "I used to think, 'Why put in all that effort just for me?' But I get it now."

"Mm," she says, straining some strawberry juice for the soap.

The next weekend, Sophie teaches me how to make rose petal salve, how to make ginger oil. We roast and grind cinnamon. We dehydrate mint and make tea. We slice open vanilla beans with sharp knives and scrape out their insides. We bake cakes we adorn with fruit.

I teach myself how to make lamb stew. I teach myself how to bake salmon so it's well-done, the way I like it. There's no one else to consider, and for the first time, that feels like a gift. I dance around the kitchen to music of my choosing.

One morning, I wake up and there are flowers at the foot of my bed. I don't know how I know, but I know. I picked them in my dreams.

I take them to school and display them in a vase on my desk.

"Who are those from?" Madison asks, picking fuzz from her glossy bottom lip.

"They're from me," I say.

She doesn't bat an eye. "Nice."

"You're a special person," I say. "Don't let anyone tell you otherwise."

She sits up a little straighter.

"Thank you," she says, the compliment coaxing a rare smile.

When I get home, my apartment is crowded with flowers. A hundred floating bouquets. Pink and yellow roses, cobalt delphinium, pastel snapdragons, white calla lilies, red carnations.

I pick one of the carnations for Ralph.

"This is for you," I tell him. At first he's sheepish, but then he accepts it. He cherishes it the rest of the evening. He carries it with him to bed, cuddles it as he sleeps.

"I grew my own flowers," I tell Sophie.

We're in the conservatory watering plants. It's balmy in here, and the humidity clouds the glass walls, the glass ceiling. Without any view of the world outside, the room is claustrophobic, overcrowded with plants and kneading fists of hot air. I draw a flower in the condensation on a window. It's gone in seconds, engulfed in fog.

"You did?" she asks, spritzing a leafy fern. "That's lovely."

"With my mind," I say. "I made them appear."

"Mm," she says, unfazed. Because, of course, right? No big deal. "Annie, these plants are thirsty."

"Oh, yep. Sorry." I lift my mister and begin to spray.

I've been useless lately. I can't stop thinking about the chicken bones. I can't stop thinking about the flowers. About what else I might be able to do. The possibilities have become the bright stars of my obsessive thoughts.

My questions breed. I can no longer keep up with them. I look at Sophie, too perfect with her hair in a romantic updo, a few strategic curls framing her face, and there's so much I want to ask her, so many things I want to know that I just can't seem to articulate.

"It's all new to me," I say. "I feel annoying bringing it up, because I know it's not new to you."

"Nonsense," she says, playfully spraying me with her mister. I'm comfortable around Sophie, but not comfortable enough to spray her back. "I'm here for you, pet. Anything you need. Anything at all."

"How about a haircut?" I ask. I'm joking, though I could actually use a haircut. My hair has been dried out by the weather. It's coarse and brittle. My ends are atrocious.

"Happy to," she says.

"Really?"

She sets down her mister and takes me by the hand, leading me up to her bathroom. It's dark and Gothic, all black marble. In the center of the room there's a round tub that's roughly the size of an aboveground pool.

"I never use it," Sophie once told me about the tub. She refuses to submerge herself in water. I wonder if it's because the townspeople tried to drown her. She didn't seem too bothered by the incident when she offhandedly brought it up a few months back. Maybe she was kidding. I don't want to pry. I figure she must take showers, because she appears very clean and never smells anything but dreamy.

Above the vanity hangs a large mirror with a frame that's a giant silver Ouroboros. Its fanged mouth is open, and its tail is just inside, closing the circle around the mirror. It's got big rubies for eyes, like two red golf balls.

Sophie sits me on a black velvet stool and positions me in front of the mirror. She produces a pair of antique scissors. They're ornate, perhaps Victorian era. But they're not rusty. They're freakishly shiny.

"Fancy scissors," I say.

"Thank you," she says. "My murdering scissors."

"Sophie!"

"They're great for cutting hair as well," she says, grinning. "Your face, darling. Oh, I'm sorry. Bad joke."

"No," I tell her, "it was a good joke. As long as it was a joke."

"Of course," she says. "I wouldn't use scissors to murder someone. Terribly inefficient."

"I do appreciate your morbid sense of humor, but . . ."

"But what?" she says, beginning to snip away at my ends. "I'm going to cut it dry. I was thinking shorter. Is that all right?"

"I've never had short hair."

"Let's try it. If you don't like it, I have a serum. It'll make your hair grow like that."

She doesn't snap her fingers, but I hear the sound.

"Okay," I say. "Let's do it."

Maybe if I look different, I'll feel different. Why didn't I think of this sooner?

I've been in a good place for the past few weeks, but it's nothing I can savor. It's tentative. Regression looms. I worry I'm in constant danger of slipping back into sadness and self-loathing.

Maybe this haircut will anchor me in the embrace of who I'm becoming. It'll be a visual, tangible change.

"Tilt your head down, darling," she says.

Listening to the crisp snips of the scissors, I do and watch as my hair gathers on the floor. It's cathartic.

Sophie begins humming. I'm sure she's got a gorgeous voice, but I've never heard her sing before.

"Do you sing?" I ask her.

"Not with witnesses," she says. "Do you?"

"No, but I play the guitar. Or I used to. I haven't in a while."

"Why not?"

I shrug.

"Hold still," she says.

"Sorry."

"That's all right."

"I learned to impress boys," I say.

"Darling," she says, "you're in desperate need of new motivation."

"This was back in high school. Sixteen years ago. But yeah, you're right."

My motivation hasn't changed much since. When Sam and I first met, he mentioned that David Foster Wallace was his favorite author, and an hour later I was in my dorm room reading *Infinite Jest*. I would have never read a book that long in college on top of all of my coursework had it not been for a boy. I thought it was whatever, but naturally I didn't tell Sam that. I told him I thought it was brilliant.

And a few years ago, when Sam decided he wanted to take up running and train for a marathon, I was awake at four a.m. right there with him, even in the winter, ready to go in head-to-toe Nike. At the time, it seemed like I was merely adopting a good habit, a healthier lifestyle, but in retrospect it was clearly all for him. To spend more time with him. To support him.

"I want you to play for me," Sophie says.

"Guitar? Oh, I haven't played in forever. It'd be terrible."

"I don't care."

"You'll care. Besides, my guitar is shitty. And I don't have strings or anything. I'd have to get all new strings, tune it. All that."

"Too much trouble to go to for your dear friend Sophie?" she asks.

"I mean, if you really want me to, I will. You're the one with the scissors. Whatever you want."

"My favorite phrase. Look, pet. Look how beautiful you are."

She reaches around and lifts my chin. My hair grazes the tops of my shoulders. I swivel my head, shake it back and forth, back and forth. I feel so much lighter. How heavy were my dead ends?

I never realized how much bullshit is bound to the bottom of your hair. How it carries with it the years and experiences, all it has witnessed, has endured. The reason you can't let go of your past is that it's still attached. That weight on your shoulders, the strain on your back and neck. It's your dead ends.

Cut your hair! I'm going to scream it from the rooftops and while running down the street, all across America. *Cut your hair!*

"I love it. Sophie! I love it."

"Here," she says. She takes one of the many crystal bottles from the vanity and pours a drop of yellowish liquid into her palm, then rubs her hands together. She moves her hands through my hair, giving it some texture, some shine.

"You're the best," I tell her. "You're everything."

"Please," she says, blushing.

When I get home the next day and show Ralph, he holds his face like Macaulay Culkin did in *Home Alone.*

"You like it?" I ask him.

He nods. He's wearing a new hat Sophie made for him. It's green and pointy and has a teeny pom-pom at the tip. He looks very, very cute.

"You're such a good boy," I tell him, tickling his chin. I sit on the couch and he climbs onto my lap. I pet his back with my index finger. I like the way his fuzz feels.

"I'm happy," I say to him or maybe to myself. Then I say it again because it's true and because I like the way it sounds.

VALENTINE'S

"There's something different," Oskar says, his eyes catching on mine. It's early the next morning, and he's rolling up the sleeves of his flannel while the espresso machine whirs behind him.

"My hair," I say. "I cut it."

He doesn't say anything to this, just grunts and begins to steam milk.

"A compliment is common courtesy," I say, delighted by my own audacity.

"Do you care what I think?" he asks, wiping a hand on his shoulder rag.

"No, not really."

He grunts again. "Latte?"

"With honey."

He taps the cup on the counter and pours the milk. Concentration wrinkles appear on his forehead.

"The cut looks good," he says, still focused on the latte. "But it's not the hair. It's something else."

"Oh," I say.

He puts a lid on the cup and slides it toward me.

I hand him cash and wait for him to meet my eye again, but he doesn't. A customer comes in behind me.

"Morning, Ed," Oskar says. "Usual?"

I walk out to my car, considering the possibility that Oskar was flirting with me. Stranger things have happened.

I sink into the front seat and remove the lid from my latte to sip at the foam.

There's a perfect heart. He made a heart with the milk.

He *was* flirting with me!

I'm smug in this belief until I get to school, where there are hearts all over the fucking place. Pink and red streamers. Paper roses. Everywhere.

Valentine's Day is Friday.

I'd forgotten.

I'm not thrilled to be reminded in this manner.

The halls are unceremoniously undecorated in my wake. Tape unsticks. Streamers rip. A cardboard cupid gets decapitated.

Several students and a custodian bear witness to this mysterious instantaneous destruction.

"Looks like they, uh, need to use better adhesive," I mumble as I do my best to pretend my subconscious is not wreaking havoc on the hard work of the student council.

I take shelter in my classroom, locking the door while I interrogate my emotional state.

I've always fancied myself a gold medalist in mental gymnastics. If there's something that's difficult to process, I've typically got no problem split leaping right over it. But that's not going to work anymore, at least not if my avoidance manifests itself in very public supernatural tantrums.

I sit at my desk, running the sleek, blunt ends of my hair through my fingers. I close my eyes.

I grant myself permission to think about Sam.

I think about our first Valentine's Day together. We decided to stay in and order Chinese food. He said it'd be romantic to spend it at home, where we were most comfortable, but I wondered if he'd waited too long to get a reservation. I wasn't disappointed. Not really. I liked to be home with him.

After we finished eating, I went to dive into the box of chocolates he got me, but he insisted we have fortune cookies.

When I cracked open the first cookie, I realized why.

He'd written the fortunes. They said things like *I love your smile* and *You're the funniest person I know.*

"How'd you do that?" I asked him, amazed.

"There's this thing called the Internets," he said, grinning. "You can get anything on there."

I saved the fortunes. I still have them. They're in an envelope in a folder. Also in that folder are my passport, birth certificate, and Social Security card. It makes me sad that I ever chose to store those fortunes alongside the most crucial pieces of evidence of my identity, to think that I once considered them of equal importance.

I don't anymore. I really don't.

"I bet I'm still the funniest person he knows," I say.

I breathe into the thought. It's the sweetest peach. When I open my eyes, I find a small crystal bowl of gummy peach rings there on my desk right in front of me.

I pop one into my mouth.

Now that I'm thinking about it, Valentine's Day doesn't scare me.

I spend the week planning my solo Valentine's Day. I decide to make myself beet salad, mushroom risotto and a chocolate layer cake. I decide to wear my comfiest pajamas and watch the Anne Boleyn documentary that's been in my queue for months.

I stop in the Good Mug every morning, interested to see if Oskar is consistent with his latte art. He is.

On Thursday, he asks, "Do you have plans for tomorrow?"

I inspect him for the slightest hint of emotion, for the anticipative twitch of an eyebrow, a nervous slip of the fingers, something, anything. Any microscopic clue to his motivations.

I get nothing.

I decide to be honest.

"Yes," I say.

Still nothing.

"I'm making dinner."

Nada.

"How about you?"

"Alone?" he asks, sweeping some coffee grounds off of the counter with the heel of his hand.

"Sorry?"

"You'll be alone?"

There's no pity in his tone. Only mild curiosity.

"There something wrong with a person choosing to spend Valentine's Day in their own company?"

He looks up at me, his eyes so blue I'm defenseless against them. They demoralize me. Hold my exhale hostage.

My insides pickle as I wait for him to speak.

Is he going to ask me out?

"Sophie," he says. "I didn't know if she ever let you be alone."

Seconds pass, flat and colorless. I listen to the slow clap of my heart.

Oskar does not relent. I seem to have unwittingly entered a good old-fashioned staring contest. His eyes are merciless.

The understanding expands, and with it my embarrassment, occupying every last crevice of my existence.

Oskar was never flirting with me. He doesn't give a shit if I spend Valentine's Day sobbing into a self-bought Whitman's Sampler repeatedly viewing *The Notebook* or having an orgy with street magicians I met on Craigslist. His interest in me is purely related to my association with Sophie.

He's engulfed in his vendetta. I see it now. It hangs around him, a red agony.

"Sophie is my friend. My best friend," I say. I've never said it out loud before.

I travel back to the moment I met her, across the street in Simple Spirits. I remember how gorgeous she looked, how I was in awe of her. If someone had told me then that she'd become my closest friend, I'm not sure I would have believed them. I definitely wouldn't have believed the rest.

But . . . who knows?

Maybe the hardest thing for me to believe would have been that Sophie would want to be my friend. That she would take a special interest in me, take me under her wing. Maybe that was the most severe bend in my reality. After that, it was easy to believe in magic, to accept that ghosts are real and to play with cute spider accomplices.

"She's no one's friend," he says.

I look down at the ring she made for me, the pale pink stone with its starry glint. I think of the things she's given me, the things she's shown me. I can't listen to anyone speak badly about her.

Also.

I have to believe in her. I have to believe she's good and right. Because I'm like her.

Because the coffee cup that was just on the counter is now floating into my outstretched hand.

Oskar goes rigid. His jaw unhinges just a little, just enough that I don't need to squint, I don't need a microscope to confirm his dismay.

The cup arrives in my hand. I summon a lid.

"You know, all Sophie does is try to help people, and you and everyone else in this town just want to blame her for anything that goes wrong. It wasn't her fault that Helen left."

He winces when I say Helen's name.

"Thanks for the coffee," I say. I decide I don't feel like paying. I turn to leave.

"She's a plague on this town!" he shouts, thick, ugly veins swarming his neck.

Really? A plague?

I sip my coffee and give him a sweet church smile.

"Then move," I say.

I step out onto Main Street and walk to my car with my shoulders back, my head up, a regal posture. But on the drive over to school, my confidence begins to pill like a cheap sweater.

The embarrassment spiral beckons.

Doubt waits there, too.

I know Oskar has a major chip on his shoulder when it comes to Sophie. I know this. Still, for him to be so adamant in his animosity . . . is there something I'm missing? Some part of the story that Sophie may have left out? I have known her to be not particularly forthcoming with the whole truth, and she does tend to be deliberate in her edits. Case in point: the ghosts.

I guess if I thought someone had kidnapped my spouse, and then, when I confronted them about it, they threatened to wear my teeth as a necklace, I'd also be pretty miffed.

Maybe that is the whole story.

My intuition yawns, awakening briefly from its endless slumber to deliver a message before rolling over and going back to bed.

That's not what's bothering you, Sherlock.

Right.

My insecurity returns like a villain in a sequel. The same but worse.

I'm not upset about Oskar's grudge against Sophie. I'm concerned with his perception of me.

I shouldn't have told him that I'm spending Valentine's Day by myself. And I definitely shouldn't have done the floaty-cup thing.

I've opened myself up to judgment and maybe worse. I've made myself vulnerable.

I try to take a deep breath, calm myself down, but it's like there's cellophane over my lips.

Am I ashamed to be associated with her? With Sophie? Am I embarrassed by this newfound power?

I mean, I was sad before, but at least I was normal.

Spite-floating hot beverages in a local café is not normal.

Have I made a mistake?

I pull into the school parking lot and sit in my car, take a few minutes to compose myself.

When I open the door and step out into the brutal February wind, there's Jill. We make eye contact. She turns to Rebecca Deacon, an uppity AP history teacher. She whispers something in her ear. Rebecca looks at me. Now we're making eye contact.

Is it too much to ask never to have to make eye contact with any other living being ever again?

I offer a weak smile that goes unreciprocated. They huddle together and scramble away from me.

This is how it is to be like Sophie. To be different. To be feared.

I put my head down and hurry to my classroom. The day crawls by, the clock mocking me from above the door. After school, I force myself to go to the grocery store to get the ingredients for my Valentine's Day dinner tomorrow night.

As I stand beyond the automatic doors sanitizing my hands before selecting a basket, I realize something. It seems to fall out of the sky and strike me with the force and precision of a ballistic missile.

None of this has been by choice.

Sam and I didn't break up. He dumped me. And if he hadn't done that, there's no way I'd be out here proclaiming how wonderful it is to make risotto for one. I've spent the past few weeks convincing myself that I'm becoming empowered, but I know that if someone, if anyone, wanted me, I wouldn't be here.

Maybe independence is just the flag we wave to distract from the pain of being alone.

And if everyone's afraid of me, alone is all I'll ever be.

I'm tempted to abandon my list and instead purchase multiple frozen pizzas, a bag of cherry Twizzlers and an enormous jug of Arizona iced tea, but I suspect that will only make me feel worse.

I stick to the list. Then I stop at the pet store to get Ralph some live crickets as a special treat.

I leave them out on the stairs, so he doesn't see. I planned on surprising him tomorrow morning, but then end up crying as I put the groceries away and, for a while after, sitting on the couch, catching what seems like a disproportionate amount of snot with my bare hands.

This of course upsets Ralph, who lies on his back and flails his legs around for the duration of my sob session.

Afterward, I feel too guilty to let his gift wait until tomorrow.

"I got you something," I say, wiping my hands on my pants.

He perks up.

"Wait here," I say.

I take a few steps toward the front door. I spin around quickly, catching him right behind me.

"I said, wait."

He looks up at me with so many eager eyes.

"Okay, okay," I tell him. I open the door and get the crickets.

When he sees them, he squeaks with excitement.

"Not all at once," I say.

At least I'm not totally alone. At least I've got Ralph.

But as I watch him hunt one of the crickets, as I watch him devour it, slurp up its juices, a chill slithers up my back and wraps itself around my neck.

—

I embrace the next morning with all the enthusiasm of a goat entering Jurassic Park.

I do my best to rally, to put on a decent outfit and use concealer on the zit that has appeared on my forehead, the approximate size of a demoted planet.

I go to the Starbucks drive-through in Aster for coffee. Whatever I get, it's 50 percent caramel and I'm not complaining.

The day is benevolent and moves quickly. When I get home, I take out all of my ingredients and spread them across the counter. I watch several YouTube videos on how to cook beets for the salad. It's more involved than I had anticipated. Salads are always too involved.

"No, this is good," I say, scrubbing the beets. "Cooking is relaxing."

Roughly ninety minutes later, my kitchen is a catastrophe. I'm dripping sweat. My purple beet-stained fingers are covered in Band-Aids, but I have a lovely three-course meal prepared and a sense of accomplishment.

I've never understood why people take pictures of their food, but . . . here I am. I grab my phone and snap a few photos to commemorate the occasion.

For your pathetic moments scrapbook? a malevolent voice asks me.

I tell it to fuck off.

I set the table and pour myself a glass of Pellegrino.

"Still or sparkling?" I ask Ralph.

He doesn't get the joke.

"Crickets later," I tell him.

He rubs his front legs together.

I sit down to dinner. I put on some Icelandic folk music, then change my mind and play Fiona Apple.

I admire the salad for a moment before attacking it with my fork.

"It's good!" I tell Ralph a few bites in.

He's pleased to hear it.

He's not eating with me. He's saving his appetite for the crickets.

I'm enjoying my risotto when the malevolent voice returns.

I wonder what Sam and Shannon are up to right now, it wheezes.

Probably not listening to "Criminal" while grating an obscene amount of Parmesan cheese onto their food and contemplating the texture of mushrooms.

The thought of them together gets me. It renders my food tasteless. It zaps the color from the room, the world.

I carry my plate into the kitchen and scoop whatever's left into Tupperware.

I stand over the kitchen sink, staring at the Everest of dirty dishes that awaits me, and begin to chant.

"You're okay, you're okay, you're okay.

"You're good, you're good, you're good."

I refocus my energy on decorating the chocolate cake with raspberries and cream. When I'm done, I put it down on the coffee table. The whole cake. I don't bother to slice it. I'm honest with myself about what's about to go down. I get a glass of milk and a fork.

I get the remaining crickets for Ralph. They died overnight, but Ralph seems happy to munch on their corpses.

I settle in to watch the Boleyn documentary.

I'm about to take my first bite of cake when I hear my phone chime.

I look over at Ralph. He's busy with the crickets. He doesn't even notice as I hurry into the kitchen, where I left my phone charging on the counter.

I want so badly for it to be him.

I hate that I want it to be Sam. That I want him to rescue me from this sad Valentine's Day. From myself.

It's not him. It's Nadia.

Hey, girl, happy V day!!! There's an excess of heart emojis.

I resent them.

Same to you, I reply. She and I text every once in a while. Most of the time, I'm happy to hear from her. Not right now, though. Not today.

Whatcha up to?

I step out of the kitchen. I look over at the chocolate cake on the coffee table, then at Ralph sucking on a cricket. I sigh.

She's texting me only because she knew I'd be around. I'm probably the only single person she knows.

Hanging at home, I type. You?

Same! she replies.

It's a comfort to know I'm not the only one.

Another text. I bought myself so much chocolate LOL.

My resentment begins to fade.

I made myself cake, I say. I send her a picture.

OMG!! Amazing!

Ralph does a little burp. It appears he's vomited up some cricket guts. Now he's eating the vomit.

I take my phone into the bedroom, sit on the window bench and stare out at the empty street.

What's new with u? Nadia asks. Miss u!

I guess it is kind of nice not to be totally alone tonight. To be catching up with a friend.

Not much, I tell her. How about you?

Just started dating someone! Really excited about him!!

Nope. Never mind. No, thanks. I can't handle hearing about someone else's happiness. I know it's shameful, but I just can't.

Remember I told u about the hot history teacher Mr. Collins? He's out of town right now, but we've been hanging out a lot & I was thinking of u because remember that psychic we went to on your bday?

I watch the little ellipses as she types another message. Is there anything more dread inducing in this world than those fucking ellipses?

That psychic said I was going to meet the love of my life and his name wasn't going to be his name, and Ben's real name is Winston but his dad is also Winston, so they call him by his middle name, Benjamin. Weird right?

I can't.

There's more, she types.

Of course there's more.

He's from Miami and says he'll probably move back there when he's finished with his master's. But he said he's also got family in San Diego and it's nice there, too.

She's still typing.

It's exactly what that psychic said to me. That I'm going to move somewhere warm like California or Florida. There are other warm places but she wasn't like u might move to New Mexico or whatever.

I press my head against the window, smoosh my forehead into the cool glass.

> Crazy right??? Imagine if I end up with him & that psychic was right about everything.

I let the phone fall from my hand. I close my eyes.

Nadia either doesn't remember what the psychic said to me or doesn't care.

Imagine if the psychic was right. Right about everything. About my bleak, ambiguous fate.

I sense a darkness. That's what the psychic said to me all those months ago.

I didn't need her to tell me. I sensed it then. I sense it now.

How could I not?

I sit in its palm.

I open my eyes, and there's nothing but black.

At first, I think I'm being dramatic, projecting the absolute dark, manifesting my fears.

But then it moves.

It's moving.

I back away from the window. My view outside is completely obstructed.

Obstructed by a swarm of spiders.

Layers upon layers of them crawling over one another.

To witness it, the sheer number of them, atrophies my muscles. I stand petrified in the middle of my bedroom.

"Sss . . . sss . . . sssss," I stutter. "Sssstop! Stop it!"

The spiders disperse with unnatural speed.

My view is returned.

I slump down to the floor. I rock there, holding my knees close to my chest.

DEVELOPMENTS

Simple Spirits doesn't close until ten. I put on my coat, my gloves, my hat and my ugliest, warmest boots and trudge out to Main Street.

Under the honey glow of the streetlamps, I see that it's desolate. It's always quiet at night, but not this quiet. I walk up to Simple Spirits and find it dark.

I try the door. It's locked.

I knock.

"Alex?" I say, my voice quavering with desperation. "Alex, it's nine twenty-six. Are you there? Are you open?"

I knock again.

I listen.

I hear voices.

But the voices aren't coming from inside Simple Spirits. They're coming from somewhere else. Somewhere close.

I step back from the door, back onto the sidewalk.

To the right of Simple Spirits, there's a Tudor-style antique shop. I've never been inside, but there's a carousel horse in the front window that I always admire. On the other side, on the left, there's the little white cottage.

The lights are on.

I've lived here for six months and I still don't know what's inside. I figured it was vacant.

I follow the stone walkway up to the door, which is slightly shorter than me. I'm about to lean over to peer into one of the small round windows when I hear someone speak my name.

"Annie is a sweet girl. I don't think we have anything to worry about."

I recognize that voice. It's Rose's.

I hunch under the window, out of view. I listen.

"She's corrupting her." Oskar.

"Lynn saw her out dancing in the yard." Alex. "Late at night. Singing to herself. Ya can't deny that's a little strange."

"Harmless," Rose says. "It's harmless."

"Until it isn't," Oskar says.

The horror of it blooms in me. It's an endless unfurling of embarrassment.

They're all talking about me. Why are they all hanging out late at night talking about me? Gossiping about me? About . . .

A bead of sweat descends from my hairline down to my temple.

"Oskar, I appreciate you keeping us in the loop and raising your concerns. I understand why you have them, given your history, but Annie isn't dangerous. She's a sweetheart."

"She is a very sweet girl." Deirdre, I think.

Are the two really mutually exclusive? Sweet or dangerous?

"Doesn't matter," Oskar says. "She won't be sweet when Sophie's done with her. Don't you see what's happening here? She's being manipulated."

"Annie moved here without knowing anyone. She doesn't have people. I don't think her friendship with Sophie is as destructive as you're implying," Rose says. "It might even be a good thing. Don't forget, a lot of what we have, we have because of Sophie. There are benefits."

Oskar starts to laugh. It's an icy, annihilating laugh.

"What?" Rose asks. "Our crops, our property, our health. Our entire way of life here in Rowan is possible because of Sophie. Deirdre?"

"Mm, yes," Deirdre says. "We do have something special here. It's not like this everywhere."

There's a branch poking me somewhere very inconvenient, but I'm too afraid to move, to make any sound.

"I'm tired of living like this. Under her thumb," Oskar says. "It's on us. We let it happen, and we're letting it happen again. We have a moral obligation to do something. If not for our sakes, for Annie's."

"I don't think it's a good idea," Rose says. "To interfere."

"I hear what you're saying, Oskar. I do," Alex says. "But ya know, I have to agree with Rose. I don't think there's anything we can really do here. We've all heard the stories."

"They're not just stories," Oskar says. "It's history. Our ancestors. Many of whom died under mysterious circumstances after making enemies with Sophie. Anyone who moves against her suffers or ends up dead. That's not a coincidence. Come on, Rose. How can you defend her? She curses people. Makes tonics out of their bones!"

My heart plummets. I'm nauseous.

"We don't know that for certain. And even if those things did happen, they happened a long, long time ago," she says. "You know as well as I do, Oskar, there is no Rowan without Sophie."

"I can't believe what I'm hearing," he says. "You're all terrified of her. Just admit it. Alex?"

"She is an . . . imposing figure. She can be a bit intimidating. But I don't *dislike* her," Alex says.

"Yes. I don't dislike her," Deirdre echoes.

"Tom?" Oskar asks. "Back me up here."

"I've learned to live with the old bitch," Tom says. "But there can't be two."

This unleashes something ugly from the depths of me. I experience a sudden and lawless swell of anger. It ignites like a match meeting a pool of gasoline.

The window shatters above me, sending shards of glass hurtling in every direction. There's a symphony of clinking, followed by profound silence.

For a moment, I'm too shaken to do anything. A tear sizzles on my hot cheek.

"Hello?" Rose says.

I take off running.

The air is freezing. I swallow big gulps of it as I book it down Main Street. Violent shivers rattle my whole body. Panic combs my veins.

I don't stop to look behind me, to check if anyone came out and is now watching me flail into the night. I keep going until I'm home. I lock my doors.

There's so much anxiety rioting inside me I'm afraid my body can't contain it. I pace around the apartment. I peek into the bedroom. Ralph is there asleep, snoring lightly under his washcloth blanket.

I go into the kitchen and get a glass with trembling hands. I fill it from the tap.

I take a sip, wishing it were whiskey.

And it is. Suddenly, it is.

I wish it wasn't just a glass. I wish I had a bottle.

And suddenly, I do. It's there, just chilling on the counter. A full bottle.

I take it into the living room. I sit down on the couch, where I promptly begin stress-eating the chocolate cake and drinking the magic whiskey and wondering what the hell I should do.

What did Tom mean, there can't be two? Are he and Oskar going to try to run me out of town? Would Sophie allow it?

And on the subject of Sophie, what did Oskar mean when he said that thing about her enemies ending up dead? About making tonics out of bones?

I wish I had some evidence to exonerate her from these accusations, but I don't. Because who are those ghosts in her cellar?

Because what if . . . ?

What if the people aren't wrong to fear her? What if I'm wrong to trust her?

I mean, she's magic. She has power. So far, she's used it only *for* me, I think, but she could just as easily use it *against* me, couldn't she? How have I overlooked that?

Could Oskar be right? Could Sophie be manipulating me? Corrupting me?

Am I just an oblivious idiot? Someone who will buy into anything that provides her with an ephemeral hope, a respite from her pain. Someone who will throw herself at anyone who pays her any attention. Someone so desperate for acceptance that it doesn't matter who's doing the accepting. Am I someone who would enjoy their time in the socialist utopia before ending up dead with a Kool-Aid mustache?

Yeah, probably.

But I'm also the kind of person who lets fear conquer her thoughts, her actions, rule her life like a callous boy king. My whole life, fear has made me cautious and small. It was only when I met Sophie that I started to feel like I could be brave. Like I didn't have to sit on my hands all the time being polite, swallowing my own needs and desires so as not to bother or inconvenience anyone else. That I felt like I didn't have to tolerate a flat, unobtrusive paper doll existence. That I could want more and not feel wrong to want it.

I remember what she told me in the ballroom on the solstice: *Surrender everything for everything.*

I'm too scared to get bangs. How am I supposed to surrender everything for everything?

It's all too much.

I crack.

I text Sam.

> Do you think I'm the kind of person who would participate in the Peoples Temple Agricultural Project?

As soon as I hit SEND, I remember it's still Valentine's Day. I realize he's probably with her. *Shannon.*

"This is the longest day of my life!" I shout into a pillow.

I need to put myself to bed. I shovel a few more forkfuls of chocolate cake into my mouth and take another swig of whiskey.

When I'm setting the bottle down, my phone brightens.

> Jonestown?

Yeah, I type. Would I drink the Kool-Aid?

> It was grape Flavor Aid.

> Grape?!?!

> You wouldn't have drunk it because it was grape & we're leery of people who choose grape.

> Why have grape when you could have cherry?

> I'm looking it up now. Flavor Aid had cherry, raspberry, tropical punch, pink lemonade, orange-pineapple, strawberry, mango, kiwi-watermelon . . .

MANGO?

Mango and they chose to go out with grape.

No, thank you!

See? You're fine.

Thanks, I type.

It's the longest interaction we've had in months. It feels so good to talk to someone who knows me. It feels so good to talk to *him*. Sam.

Also, it's Valentine's Day, and he texted me back right away. Maybe he's not with Shannon. Maybe they're not together anymore. Maybe.

My stomach flips.

What if?

I miss you, I tell him.

A minute passes. It's a bleak minute.

Then,

I miss you, too.

SOME DECEPTION

I pass out on the couch, cake crumbs crusting my mouth, my phone clutched to my chest. I wake up there to the sound of a door shutting. I blink into the morning.

"Annie, darling?" I hear, followed by the distinct click of the dead bolt turning. The knob twists, and the door swings open.

Sophie stands there dressed in all black. Feathers and velvet and lace and fur. Her hood covers her eyes and casts a shadow over the rest of her face.

I look up at her, at this hooded figure, and feel an extraordinary, suffocating fear I've experienced only since I came to Rowan.

This fear is interrupted by the pitter-patter of many tiny legs clambering in from the bedroom.

Ralph.

Sophie removes her hood.

She's beautiful, smiling. Amber eyes electric.

"Hello, little friend," she says to Ralph. She lowers herself to the floor and pats his head with a long elegant finger. He shimmies with satisfaction.

"Annie," Sophie says, turning to me, "I was worried."

Panic sits on my chest.

Worried about what?

I prop myself up on the couch, my hangover announcing itself with some feral yelling.

"What do you mean?" I ask, releasing a cloud of my breath. I suspect someone could get drunk from merely smelling it.

She stares at me. "It's Saturday. You always come over on Saturdays, pet. I thought something might have happened to you."

"Oh," I say. "No, no, I'm fine. Just . . . overslept."

I follow her eyes to the half-empty bottle of whiskey, to the small remaining mound of chocolate cake.

She opens her palm and Ralph climbs into her hand. He cuddles her thumb.

"Annie," she says, still smiling, "I know that's not true."

My throat constricts.

"I . . . It is. I didn't . . . I mean, I did. I overslept."

She settles herself next to me on the couch. She smells like violets. "I'm not angry with you. I'm concerned."

She begins to stroke my hair with her free hand, Ralph still in the other. My hair snags on one of her rings. I whimper. "So sorry, darling."

She doesn't sound sorry.

"I have to pee!" I blurt out.

I bolt into the bathroom and shut the door behind me. I need a minute to think, to collect myself. Also, I really do have to pee.

I sit on the toilet, self-conscious because of the trickling sound despite knowing I have bigger, more pressing concerns.

I can't forget about last night, what I overheard. When it comes to Sophie, I've always been keen to let certain things slide for the sake of our friendship, but it's at the point now where I can no longer ignore my mounting distrust.

There's also the issue of Sam.

I broke my promise. I told her that I was done with him, but then I went and told him that I missed him.

And he said it back.

He misses me.

If there's a chance that Sam and I can make things work, that I can go back to him and my magnificently normal, uncomplicated life, that I can escape this Grimm-worthy mess I currently find myself in, isn't that a chance I have to take?

I need to get rid of Sophie. I've got too much to figure out. I can't have her here.

But I can't risk pissing her off. She has magic.

A voice speaks quietly from somewhere inside me. *Yes,* it whispers. *But you have some, too.*

I flush, wash my hands with an emphatic lather and take a series of deep breaths.

When I open the door, Sophie's gone. So are the cake, the bottle of whiskey . . .

"Sophie?"

I find her in the kitchen washing the dishes.

"Hey, Sophie," I say. I want to get it out while I still have the nerve.

"Darling," she says, drying her hands on the air. She points to the table. There are two cups of coffee and a glass of water beside a small vial of something. "Let's sit."

The chairs pull out for us. I lower myself down. I keep forgetting about my hangover. It keeps reminding me. My head throbs.

"Ginger concentrate," she says, tapping the vial with a long nail. "Will make you feel better."

"Right. Thank you. So, Sophie . . ."

"I know you're not fine, pet. I'm sure yesterday was difficult," she says, playing with the steam rising from her coffee. She forms it into the shape of a doe, and it runs around in a circle before disappearing. "I don't understand the point of it. Valentine's, whatever. But I imagine for you, it was something like picking at a scab. You were upset. Are upset. I can smell your distress, darling."

What does distress smell like? Like whiskey and BO?

"I've made it so you feel you can't talk to me about *Sam*"—she pauses to shake off her revulsion at having to speak his name—"and while I don't approve of falling into complete despair over someone who hurt you, I suppose I can understand occasionally lamenting the loss of what once was. Memories have their purpose, and nostalgia is not a danger in small doses. It can be good to remember what has made us who we are, to reflect on what has made us stronger."

She reaches across the table for my hand.

"You never have to hide your feelings from me, pet. I apologize if I've ever led you to believe otherwise."

If last night didn't happen, if Nadia didn't reach out to confirm the eerie accuracy of the psychic, if I didn't go in search of liquor and stumble upon that conversation, if Sam didn't tell me that he missed me, maybe Sophie's words would be a salve. But now I can't get past my suspicion. I can't silence the constant hiss of doubt.

"Sophie," I say, making my voice soft as baby skin, "I appreciate you coming by, but you have nothing to apologize for. I'm not upset, really. I just overindulged last night. I made myself dinner and cake and I went too hard on the whiskey. I'm sorry I didn't come by. I didn't mean to worry you. But I've got a pretty bad headache that I think I need to sleep off. I think I want to take it easy for the rest of the weekend. Hang here. Alone."

"Oh," she says. A coldness sweeps across her face. All of the color and kindness about her drains in an instant. Then an inkling of a smirk appears at the corner of her mouth. "All right, pet."

In spite of my doubts, I don't want her to be mad at me. It's a horrible feeling. It's unbearable.

"I'm sorry," I say. "Maybe next weekend."

"Maybe," she says, gathering her cloak. "Maybe."

She leans toward me and clamps her hand around my chin. She looks at me, through me. I feel her gaze deep in the back of my skull.

Then she kisses me gently on the forehead.

She runs the back of her hand along my cheek. She turns to leave. She's at the door when she stops and says, "I almost forgot."

She reaches into the dark depths of her cloak.

"I brought a gift."

She produces a black satin pouch.

"For a very good boy."

She sets the pouch down on the coffee table and leaves without another word.

When I hear the second door shut, I get up and go to the front window to watch her walk down the street. I wait until she disappears before I collapse back onto the couch with a big sigh of relief.

Ralph is on the coffee table peeking into the black satin pouch.

"What you got there?" I ask him.

I look. It's dead flies.

"You're spoiled," I tell him, pouring out a few.

I watch him eat. When he's done, he gives a little burp and promptly falls asleep on the arm of the couch.

I get up and drink some water. I eat peanut butter on bread while standing in the kitchen, willing my hangover to subside.

I return to the couch, licking peanut butter from my fingers.

I check my phone.

I have a message from Sam. It reads Annie.

Yes, I reply.

I really do miss you.

Ralph stirs at the sound of the text, but then yawns and rolls over onto his back, snoozing through it. Which is lucky, because he's usually very diligent about policing any communication I have with Sam.

I take my phone into the bedroom and close the door as quietly as possible. I get in bed under the covers. I read and reread the texts.

What would it be like if Sam and I had never broken up? If we decided to work on things. If we sought couples counseling. Why didn't we do that? Why didn't I ask? Why was I so afraid to fight for what I wanted?

In some other timeline, in some alternate reality, I'm back in our apartment and we're waiting for takeout, watching old cartoons. We're playing with each other's hands like we used to when we first started dating.

Why did we ever stop doing that, and why did it become so impossible to start again?

Maybe these months apart have been good for us. Maybe he's learned to appreciate me, and I've learned how to be more self-sufficient, and maybe now things will work.

Maybe my time in Rowan was just a weird, short chapter in my life that I can close and never open again. Never have to think about the people in town arguing about whether or not I'm a threat. Never have to worry about Sophie, about random ghost attacks, or curses, or tripping on mushroom tea. I could just forget it. Leave and not look back.

I'm here, I text Sam. You can call me anytime.

Like now?

Yes.

I get up and lock the door to the bedroom. I stuff a sweater in the gap between the bottom of the door and the floorboards so Ralph doesn't come crawling in.

For an increased sense of privacy, I sit inside my closet in the narrow space between my suitcase and my dirty clothes. I close the closet door and sit in darkness, waiting for Sam to call.

What if he doesn't call? What if I just locked myself in my own closet for nothing?

The fear doesn't have time to marinate. My phone rings.

"Hello?"

"Hey, Annie," he says. His voice reaches through the phone and takes my heart in its fist. It hurts. It really hurts.

"Hey, Sam."

"How are you?"

"I'm good." I search for something cute and clever to say but come up short. "I . . . I cut my hair."

"You did?"

"Yep."

"How short?"

"Pretty short. It's at my shoulders now."

"I bet it looks good," he says.

"Yeah? How much you want to bet?"

"Seventy thousand dollars."

"Yes, but how much in gold?"

"Bars or doubloons?"

"*Pfft*. Doubloons, Sam. Don't you know me at all? Always doubloons."

He laughs. "I know you, Annie. I know you."

"Yeah," I say. "So, what's up?"

"I don't know," he says. "I miss you. I've been thinking about you a lot lately, and I miss you."

"Do you?"

"Yeah. I've missed you since you moved out."

"When I first moved here, I told you that I missed you and you didn't say it back."

"I didn't know it then. It took me a while to realize."

"Okay. What about Shannon?"

"This isn't about her," he says. "It's about us."

The smell of my dirty socks is fairly potent, and it contributes significantly to how surreal this moment is. Is this really happening? Does he really miss me? Do my feet really smell that bad?

"I want to see you," he says. "I want to talk in person. Can I come see you?"

"Come here?" I ask, trying to angle toward my suitcase.

"I think it would help give us both clarity if we saw each other again."

"Clarity on what?"

"Annie."

"Clarity on what?"

"If we made the right choice."

I've been waiting for this since the moment he broke up with me. I've wanted it so badly. But now that it's here, now that it's happening, I'm surprisingly salty. Why did it take him so long?

"If you don't want me to, I won't come," he says.

"No," I hear myself say, "I want you to. I want you to come."

"Yeah?"

"Yes." It's his voice. It's unraveling me. I picture chaos inside my skin. Muscles dissolving. Bones crumbling into dust. I'm spineless. "I miss you so much."

I hear a faint tapping. Ralph is awake. He's at my bedroom door.

"Next weekend?" Sam asks. "Saturday?"

"Yeah," I say. "Yeah, Saturday. You have my address?"

Ralph's whining now.

"Somewhere. Actually, can you send it to me?"

"Yeah," I say. "I have to go. I'll text you my address. Let me know what time Saturday, okay?"

"Probably later," he says. "I have to rent a car. It's a long drive."

"Okay," I say. "We'll talk soon."

"Annie," he says.

"Yeah?"

"If I come, I'll probably have to stay over. I don't think I can make it there and back in one day."

"Okay," I say. Ralph is going nuts, wailing away.

"Is that okay?"

"Yeah, yeah, it's fine. I really have to go. Bye."

I hang up and stumble out of the closet. It's hard to walk with no spine.

I move the sweater and open the bedroom door.

Ralph is standing there wearing a giant frown. I can see it in his eyes. He's suspicious.

"Sorry," I say, faking a yawn. "I was asleep. Must have dropped my sweater."

He marches past me into the room. Fortunately, he's too sleep-drunk to do any investigating. He climbs up the nightstand to his bed. He turns his back to me and resumes his snoozing.

I take my phone into the bathroom and sit on the edge of the tub. I send Sam my address and then delete my text and call history.

I set my phone down and curl up in the tub. It feels safe. Quiet and safe.

I used to think that if Sam ever came back, I would be ecstatic, I would be instantly freed of any and all sadness, but right now I can't shake this sudden, indomitable dread.

What if we're too far gone? What if we can't be put back together? Not with all the king's horses and all the king's men or superglue.

What will I do then?

TOIL & TROUBLE

With every day, the dread morphs into something more and more like excitement. Sam and I are talking again. Texting constantly. I get to school early and stay late since it's impossible to text at home with Ralph around.

By Friday, I'm full-on giddy.

Tomorrow, Sam says, adding a bunch of emojis. A series of smiley faces and a single slice of pizza.

Are you bringing pizza? I ask.

Pizza sold separately.

What about batteries? Are they included?

I'm a windup, he says.

You sure are.

After school, I stop at the grocery store to stock up on food and assorted beverages. I get wine from the liquor store in Aster, as I'm still avoiding everything and everyone in Rowan.

When I get home, I clean my apartment from top to bottom. I use Q-tips to dust the baseboards, an old toothbrush to scrub the grout in the bathroom. When I'm done, the place stinks like bleach and Lemon Pledge. I light a candle to mask the smell.

This is all highly suspect to Ralph, who watches me from the bedroom doorway, narrowing his many eyes. He's used to me sliding dust bunnies under the couch with a socked foot and pretending they aren't there. This level of cleanliness must be alarming.

I realize I won't be able to have him here tomorrow when Sam arrives. I also realize if I don't show up at Sophie's for our weekend hangout the second Saturday in a row, she'll likely come here looking for me.

I can't have that.

I decide that tomorrow morning I'll swing by Sophie's, drop off Ralph and make up an excuse to leave early, before Sam gets here. I'll tell her that I'm behind on grading assignments or that I'm coming down with a cold.

I could also be up-front with her, tell her the truth. That's probably the best course of action, but it also happens to be the most terrifying. She won't approve, but I'm not sure what the extent of her disapproval will be, how wrathful her response.

I've been trying not to think about it.

I've been trying to focus on Sam.

I stay busy cleaning. I do laundry. I bake chocolate chip cookies. I pick out an outfit. My favorite jeans that make it look like I have an actual butt and a pink silk blouse that Sophie made for me. It's pretty and feminine and a little sexy. I set the clothes out on my dresser.

I attempt to go to bed at a reasonable hour but am too excited to sleep.

I sit on the bench in my room and stare out the window at the moon.

In the morning, I spend an exorbitant amount of time in the shower. I shave everything. I scrub everything. I scour my body, buffing off layers of dead skin and drenching what remains in thick, creamy lotion.

I blow out my hair. I'm meticulous with my application of makeup. I can't look like I'm trying too hard, but I can't look like myself, either. I need to look much, much better.

All of this is very stressful for Ralph, who sits on the coffee table with a set of legs in his mouth, his eyes wide.

"I'm getting pretty," I tell him.

This doesn't seem to ease his worrying.

I haven't put that much thought or effort into my appearance lately. My blow-dryer has accumulated dust. My foundation has solidified. Ralph's never seen me go through this beautification process. He yelps when I take out my tweezers. I think he must view this all as a form of self-harm.

If I were to consider the merit of this concern, it would truly fuck up my day. And perhaps my life.

Instead, I ignore Ralph and carry on primping. At around ten a.m., I check my phone. Sam texted an hour ago saying he's on his way. I would be nervous to see him, but currently all of my anxiety is tied up in having to face Sophie, who once openly admitted to me that she's vengeful, who is adept with curses and, allegedly, using human remains to make tonics.

I take a few deep breaths. I put my wallet, phone and keys in my pockets and go to pick up Ralph.

He skitters backward, just out of my grasp. Poor thing. His adorable round face is twisted. He's afraid.

To be fair, so am I. But I need to do this if I want my reunion with Sam to happen without any supernatural interference. I can't have Ralph or Sophie jeopardizing my chance at a happy ending.

"Come on, buddy," I coo. "We're going to see Sophie."

His expression relaxes, eyes light up at Sophie's name. He hurries into my hand, nodding his little head from side to side.

"Sophie will be so glad to see you," I tell him. "You're such a good boy."

He squeaks with excitement. I feel guilty for lying to him. He's so innocent.

He taps my palm, points to the door.

"Right," I say, swallowing the lump in my throat. "We're off."

It's bitter cold out. I put Ralph in my coat pocket so he doesn't freeze.

"You okay, buddy?" I ask, peeking in.

He nods, but I can see he's shivering.

I hurry down Main Street, into the woods, past the well, the graves, the hut. Icicles drip from the collapsing roof of the hut, and they add a certain menace to it. A chill drags across the exposed skin of my neck. I should have worn a scarf.

The ground is slick in some spots, and I almost fall twice, Ralph yipping nervously.

"I got you," I tell him. "You're okay."

When Sophie opens the door for us, I'm so winded all I want to do is to collapse at her feet.

"Come in, darling," she says. "You're frozen. Come. I've got a fire going. And I have something to show you. A surprise."

"A surprise?"

"Yes," she says. She looks down. "You brought Ralph?"

He's climbing out of my pocket.

"Yeah," I say. "He wanted a visit."

She huffs. "Annie, it's too cold for him to be outside. He's not even wearing his hat."

"I'm sorry," I say. "He wanted to come. How could I say no to that face?"

Ralph cocks his head to the side, either confounded by the lie or charmed by the compliment.

Sophie sighs, taking Ralph and setting him on her shoulder. "All right."

"Sorry," I say. "I didn't realize how cold it was."

"Oh, of course you didn't, pet. I know you take good care of Ralph," she says. "And he keeps eyes on you."

What does that mean?

"Uh, yep," I say. My nervous voice sounds exactly like a pubescent boy's. It's indistinguishable.

"Hurry," she says. "I'm very excited about the surprise. I have absolutely no restraint. None. Come, darling."

She starts skipping away from me.

"Coming, coming. I still can't feel my toes."

"I'll thaw you out," she says, turning toward me to reveal a devilish grin.

Impatient, she grabs my hand and drags me the rest of the way to a room I've never been in before. The walls are pale blue, and there's a gold fireplace, a gold chandelier. Everything orbits around a beautiful grand piano. There's also a massive gold harp in the corner, and I can see cobwebs on it from here. There are a few petite antique chairs scattered around. Sophie sits me down on one of the chairs and tells me to close my eyes.

"They're closed," I say.

"Don't open them yet," she says. "Not until I say."

"I won't."

It's quiet for a minute, except for the hostile crackling of the fire burning in the fireplace. I get whiffs of smoke, hints of heat.

"Sophie?" I say.

She doesn't respond.

My immediate reaction is fear.

I was stupid to come here.

She's more powerful than I am. I couldn't hold my own against her if it came to that. I need to leave.

I open my eyes.

She stands in front of me smiling. She's holding a guitar.

"Surprise!" she says, presenting it to me.

I'm an asshole. Here she is being thoughtful and generous, and here I am scheming about how I can get away from her. Did I let Oskar get in to my head, let his hostility tarnish my perception of her? He doesn't know Sophie like I do. I have no reason to fear her.

Well, I mean, except I kind of do . . .

"You like it?" she asks.

"Yes," I say, taking the guitar. It's beautiful. "This is . . . too much. I don't deserve this."

"Nonsense," she says. "And it's just as much for me as it is for you. I told you, you have to play for me."

"This is so nice, Sophie. Too nice. Really. You're too good to me."

"I want you to focus on your own gifts. Your talents. I want you to continue to feed yourself," she says, pushing a stray hair out of my face. "When I met you, you were starving."

"Is that why you made me pie?"

She laughs. "No. The pie was because I wanted pie. It was selfish pie. Feeding myself."

"You shared with me."

"Only because I really like you, Annie. I don't go around sharing my pie with everyone."

"This sounds super sexual," I say.

She gasps. "Oh, dear!"

I forgot Sophie can be scandalized. I forgot how old she is. I stifle a giggle.

"Don't laugh at me," she says, fake pouting.

"Sharing pie with everyone."

"Stop!"

"Okay, okay," I say. "Sorry."

"This is the thanks I get," she says, "relentless teasing."

"No, I'm sorry. I'm very grateful for the gift. This really is a beautiful guitar."

She sits in the chair across from me, tucking one ankle under the other. Ralph settles in her lap.

"Play something for me, pet."

"I'm rusty," I tell her. "Out of practice."

"I don't mind."

"Let me practice first. I'll be too embarrassed otherwise."

"Don't be. It's just me."

"I know. I want it to be good. Put on a proper concert."

"Oh, I'm not looking for that. Come, darling. Play."

I hear my phone vibrate in my jacket pocket. Ralph stirs.

"Actually," I say, "I can't stay long today. I've got a lot of work to do. Grading and lesson plans. Fun stuff."

I wait for her to react. She doesn't.

Outside, the sky clouds over. The only other source of light in the room is the fire. It flickers belligerently. Casts intense shadows. Sophie sits in front of it, and when the flames lick up high enough, they appear over her shoulders like wings.

She uncrosses her ankles. Ralph gets up. His face has changed. The happiness is gone. His eyes are black and lifeless, like caviar. His mouth, ever wide and smiling, shrinks. Even his movements are different. Less fluid. He climbs down Sophie's leg onto the floor.

I clear my throat. "I wish I could stay, but I should head out soon. Get to it."

She's looking at me. I wait for her to speak. A minute passes.

"You know I'd rather be with you," I say, wanting out of the silence. "I'm sorry."

"For what, pet?" she asks. "For abandoning me or for lying about why?"

My dread bursts like a blister. I might throw up.

"Sophie," I say. What does she know, and how does she know it? "I'm sorry. I was afraid to tell you."

"Tell me what?" she says, rolling her shoulders back. "Go on."

"Sam reached out. He said he wanted to see me. He misses me. He wants to make sure we made the right choice."

"Is that so?"

"Yeah. I thought . . . I don't know, Sophie. I thought it'd be worth seeing him. Figuring it out."

There's a faint growling. I look around the room, searching for the source. It's Ralph.

Did he get bigger?

"Shh, shhh," Sophie tells him. He quiets, retreating underneath her chair.

My heart beats haphazardly. I put a hand across my chest and feel its unsteady insurrection.

Sophie stands. She begins pacing back and forth in front of the fire. Every time she passes, the flames burn black.

"The first time I saw you, I recognized you," she says. "I knew you were just like me."

The fire dances frantically behind her. It spits and howls.

"But you didn't know. What you were. What you could be. I thought if I showed you . . ." She trails off. "Perhaps I pushed you too hard. I wanted it for you more than you wanted it for yourself. That was my mistake. To put so much faith in someone who has none."

"Don't be mean, Sophie."

The fire snuffs itself out.

Or maybe it was me. Maybe I extinguished it with my mind.

She snaps her fingers and the fire reignites.

"And you want to go back to being ordinary?" she asks me with a smug grin.

The piano begins to play. Badly. The keys scream.

"Stop," I say.

"I'm not doing anything," she says. "That's all you, darling."

"I meant, don't tell me that I want to be ordinary," I say. "That's an . . . an oversimplification."

"Is it now?" she asks.

"I just want to be happy," I say, shouting over the piano.

"I know, pet. And I'm trying to help you. All I've ever done is try to help you. Have I not been a devoted friend?"

The harp is going now, too. The chandelier swings over our heads.

"I suppose it doesn't matter," she says, her grin widening. She gestures around the room. "You can't go back now. It's too late."

"No, it isn't," I say. Everything stops. "I'm done with this, Sophie. I don't want it. I'm done."

The room goes still and quiet, except for the fire, which seems to be whispering secrets to itself.

I move to stand, to leave. To run if I have to.

"Sit," Sophie says. "We're having a discussion."

"This isn't a discussion!"

"You're right," she says, sighing. "A disagreement."

We're both distracted by the sound. A chair tipped over, and it tipped because Ralph has outgrown the space underneath it. He's now roughly the size of a golden retriever.

I run.

I sprint out of the room and down the hall. I can hear my bones cracking awake.

"Annie," Sophie calls. She's following me. "Annie, stop this."

Ralph's following me, too. I hear his many footsteps.

My legs carry me to the right, toward the kitchen. I'll leave through the kitchen door, the side entrance.

"You're afraid of me," she says.

"You're chasing me!"

"Only because you're running." She speaks calmly from inside my head.

"Stop!" I tell her. My lungs seize up, my legs ache, but I go faster. I push harder. I blow into the kitchen. I'm almost there.

But it doesn't matter, because here's Ralph. Giant and fuzzy and fanged, blocking the kitchen door.

He opens his mouth, and a drop of his viscous slobber emerges, landing on the floor with a sickening smack.

"Annie," I hear, this time from outside of myself. She's coming.

What will happen when she gets to me?

I stand vulnerable in the sweaty armpit of crisis. I decide my best option is to hide. I scuffle into the pantry, through the hatch doors, down the steps into the cellar. I reach up and pull the doors down. I turn the handle, locking them in place.

It's pitch-dark with the exception of the thin sliver of light where the doors meet. I crouch on the steps, attempting to silently catch my breath, my hand clapped over my mouth.

I hear the clean click of her heels against the kitchen tiles. They're unhurried.

"Why do you fear me?" she asks. "I'm asking in all sincerity, pet. I've never understood people's fear. What about me is so terrifying? I'm kind. I'm giving. It keeps me up at night, darling. Truly."

I hear the faucet running, the tick of the stove igniting. Is she making tea?

"I don't smile when I don't feel like smiling. I don't pretend. I'm entirely honest about who I am. Is that my great offense? Or maybe it's that I live alone in the woods. And what's more damning: that I live in the seclusion of the trees or that I live alone? Or that I'm happy about it all? That I've made these choices, that I have these gifts, and I embrace them? I'm not ashamed of who I am. Of what I am. What is it about a woman in full control of herself that is so utterly frightening? Can you tell me, Annie?"

I begin to sidle down the steps, hoping to further conceal myself inside the dark of the cellar. But the deeper I submerge, the louder it gets.

The strange moaning.

Sophie is still talking, but it's hard to pay attention with the moaning. It sounds vaguely like a draft, like wind funneling through a small space. That's what it must be, because it's cold down here. It's freezing. Almost as bad as outside. I have to release my jaw to keep my teeth from chattering.

I don't know how long I'll be able to last down here. I'm a sitting duck.

I realize I'm oddly calm, considering. Either this is such a surreal situation that I haven't yet processed it or I've switched into some extraordinary survival mode I didn't know I had.

I remember my phone in my jacket pocket. My lifeline. I reach carefully, quietly into my pocket and slowly lift it up close to my face.

It illuminates with a text from Sam.

Halfway there ☺!

My brief moment of joy at the thought of him, at being able to feel his arms around me again, smell his familiar smell, talk with him, joke with him, touch him, is dragged away when I see the face floating before me lit by the glow of my phone.

It's a pale creature with bloated eyeballs protruding from receding sockets. I've never been this close to it before. Not when I saw it in the mirror. Not when it tried to drown me. It's wearing a dusty, tattered pin-striped suit. It's a man.

And when he opens his mouth, revealing rotten teeth and the prolific stench of decay, he says one word.

"Help."

The scream comes from some unknown part of me, some deep cavity of my being. It gives me away. The cellar doors fly open. The ghost wails and hobbles backward where the light can't reach him. I look down and see symbols on the ground. Red paint. White powder.

I see the others. There are more of them, all in various states of deterioration. Some look like people; they possess solid physical bodies. Others are less formed. One is just a floating orb.

"Annie," Sophie says, her tone like that of an annoyed parent, "I told you not to go in the cellar."

At the moment, she's the lesser evil. I stumble up the stairs, where she waits for me with her hands on her hips.

"Are you ready to have a civilized discussion?"

My mind is a white blizzard of fear.

"I made tea," she says, gesturing to the table set with two steaming cups.

Whatever emergency composure I thought I had dissolved the second I came face-to-face with the ghost that tried to drown me. This is too much. It's too fucking much!

"Come," she says, gently guiding me to my chair.

"I see you've met Theodore," she says, rolling her eyes. "He built this house, you know."

"He asked me for help. Why?"

"He wants to be released. He wants to leave, to move on, to rest," she says, "or, at the very least, to be able to roam about the house like he used to before you came around."

"Wait. What?"

"The ghosts are bound to me, Annie. It's a very long story involving several failed attempts against my life and several successful curses. They're a part of my history, part of me. I can never forget, and they can never rest. I wouldn't want them to after what they did to me."

I'm exhausted. I don't have any fight left.

"Whatever you're going to do to me, just do it," I say. "Just get it over with, please."

For the first time since I've known her, she seems genuinely shocked.

"Annie?"

"You can grind my bones for tonics or whatever."

"Ah," she says, and sips her tea. "Seems I'm still the subject of town gossip. I always think that maybe things are different now, that maybe this will be the generation to grant me some compassion and understanding. But it's never different. Their fear, it gets passed down. I should have known."

She drops a sugar cube into her tea and stirs.

"Is it true? Have you hurt people?"

"I have only ever defended myself. I'm otherwise perfectly pleasant. You know this," she says. "Those headstones, those graves in the woods, those were my sisters, my friends. They were burned at the stake. Hanged by their necks. Drowned. I couldn't save them, and I have to live with that. All I can do, all any of us can do, really, is embrace our power. Not restrain it for the benefit of those trying to do us harm. I've protected myself when necessary. I've saved myself. And, yes, on occasion I've taken some revenge. I think it not unreasonable, considering the circumstances."

She gives a small nonchalant shrug. "Does that answer your question?"

"You've kept things from me. You haven't been totally honest."

"Forgive me for not being forthcoming with my trauma," she

says, her voice reaching a morbid pitch. "Forgive me for thinking that I might spare you from hearing all the gruesome details."

She takes a breath, another slow sip of tea.

"Sophie," I say, "enough of this! Enough!"

Both teacups shoot off of the table and smash against the wall.

There's a beat. Then Sophie starts to clap. Slow applause.

"Don't you enjoy it, darling?" she asks. "Isn't it fun?"

"I don't want this," I say. My voice shakes. I can't tell if I'm crying because I'm angry or crying because I'm scared or if this is my default reaction to everything. Tears. "I don't want any of this. I didn't ask for this. I'm in a creepy mansion in the middle of the fucking forest! There are ghosts in the basement! There's a giant spider right there!"

I point to Ralph, who remains in front of the door, eating what appears to be a raw bird.

"Well, you upset him," she says.

"This isn't natural!" I yell. "This isn't cool!"

"Annie."

"And you poisoned me, didn't you? You poisoned me with that mushroom tea!"

"That wasn't poison," she says. "It was intended to awaken your mind. Perhaps it was a little strong. I should have warned you. Honest mistake."

"No. An honest mistake is accidentally picking up someone else's drink at Starbucks. Drugging someone isn't an honest mistake. It's crazy!"

"Please, pet."

"I'm not your pet!"

This particular outburst surprises both of us. I was completely unaware this term of endearment bothered me until this moment. Suddenly, I realize how patronizing it is. How it implies ownership and reinforces an unfair power dynamic. This resentment must have been simmering in my subconscious for months.

Sophie's face registers shock and, unless I'm mistaken, glee.

"I'm an adult. I'm my own person. I can make my own decisions. Even if they're bad decisions, Sophie. They're mine to make. Not yours."

She raises an eyebrow. She reaches back and snaps her fingers at Ralph, who begins to shrink down to his former, more reasonable size. He doesn't look too pleased about the whole ordeal.

"You're absolutely right," she says, smiling at me with what I think might be pride. "I won't call you that anymore."

"Thank you," I say.

"You have to understand, Annie, I do adore you. I only want what's best for you. Truly."

Does she? I don't know what to believe anymore.

"I don't want you to leave," she says. "You're my dear friend. I don't want to lose you. I've already lost so many friends. Friends like me. Like us. We should stay together. Protect each other. Enjoy each other's company."

"I can't stay," I say, my fear wearied. "I need to see what will happen with Sam. I need to know, or I'll spend the rest of my life wondering. I deserve certainty."

She looks away from me. She gets up, takes another cup from the cabinet, sets it down and pours herself more tea.

"Very well," she says. "You said yourself you can make your own decisions. If you want to leave, leave."

It's a relief like I've never felt before. Blissful.

"But," she says, "if you leave, you cannot come back."

"What?" I say.

"I'm not punishing you. I support your right to choose whichever path you most desire," she says, seating herself across from me at the table. "But I will lose all respect for you if you leave. And I don't believe I will ever get it back."

It might be the most hurtful thing anyone has ever said to me. The very definition of brutal honesty. Absolutely savage.

It stirs in me the urge for petty defensiveness. I stave it off. *Just leave,* I tell myself. *Just go.*

Why is it so hard? Ralph is small again and no longer blocking the door; he's busy gnawing on a bone. There's nothing in my way. It should be easy. I have the chance to extricate myself from all of this. This twisted fairy-tale horror-show bullshit.

I look at Sophie, who is sitting there casually sipping her tea. And up comes the resentment; up comes the pettiness, up with torches and pitchforks.

"You want to know why people are afraid of you, Sophie? I can solve that mystery for you. Save you the trouble," I say. "It's because you're a fucking witch!"

The word hovers between us like dust in the ether.

My resentment chips away, and underneath it are guilt and sadness and fear. I want to apologize, to take it back, snatch the word out of the air, chew it up, swallow it down. But of all the impossible, unimaginable things transpiring in my reality lately, I know this won't be one. Magic has its limits.

I know she's hurt. It's obvious to me in her erratic movements, in the oscillation of her eyes, the trembling of her hands. She seems aware of this. Maybe even embarrassed by it. Her cheeks glow exceptionally red.

She smacks her hands down on the table.

"Is that how you think of me?" she asks. "After everything, is that how you see me?"

She stands, and as she does, she begins to transform.

She lifts her hands, bending bony, haggard fingers. Her nails, usually artfully manicured, clean and well maintained, are a horrible yellow. They split as they curl under, and around, and around.

Her skin greens. Her veins seethe under her skin like hungry snakes. Her nose grows, breaking in multiple places as it extends out each foul inch. Her chin elongates with a loud, unrelenting crunch. Warts appear on her face, her hands. Sores rip open; they bubble and fester. Her lips shrivel. Her eyes expand to the approximate size, shape and color of undercooked eggs. She opens her mouth, a dark abyss punctured by pointy teeth.

She erupts in a fit of cackles. "Is this how you see me?"

A broomstick materializes in her left hand. Her dress is now puritan.

"Like this?" she says, lunging toward me.

I run for the door. I tear it open, topple outside. She follows, cackling louder and louder. I take off up the hill, into the woods.

"An-nnieee," she sings. "An-nnieee."

The rustling of the trees lets me know she's not behind me. She's above me. She's flying above me.

Flying on her broomstick.

I think I'd laugh if I weren't so terrified.

I keep my eyes down, focused on the ground in front of me, as I dodge rocks and branches, navigate the uneven terrain. The hut comes into view, and I notice the door is open. I can see inside. There's a fire burning in a small cauldron in the center of the room, thick smoke billowing.

And Sophie. She's here. She emerges from the smoke. She stands in the doorway clutching her broom.

"If this is how you see me, go on. Go on, then. Go running back to your old life."

The shock of the scene has glued me in place. I'm incapable of movement.

"Go," Sophie says, her voice breaking. The green of her skin begins to fade. Her nose recedes. Her chin returns to its normal shape. She leans against the frame of the door, her always-perfect posture failing for the first time. Her shoulders hunch. Her neck hooks forward.

"Go," she says. "And don't come back."

She steps back into the hut, and the door slams.

Now it's just me. Alone in the woods.

HAPPILY EVER AFTER

When I get back to my apartment, I stand in front of the mirror analyzing how traumatized I look versus how traumatized I feel. I decide my physical appearance is an accurate reflection of my internal distress.

I don't have time for another shower. Sam is almost here. I throw my hair up and attempt to redo my eyeliner, which comes out tragically uneven.

I walk into the kitchen and drink a glass of cold water.

"No, this is good," I say to myself. "This is really good. Sophie is obviously an unstable person. I don't need her in my life. Who needs a domineering friend who lives in a scary house with ghosts and hangs out with spiders and curses people? Plus, she's over four hundred years old. I need friends my own age."

When I first moved here, I tried not to get into the habit of talking to myself out loud, but it's actually doing a great job of calming me down. I was dangling over the edge, and the sound of my own voice is the thrown rope.

"You're okay," I say. "You're okay. Sam is going to be here any minute. You're about to see Sam. Everything is going to work out."

I go on babbling to myself until Sam calls to tell me that he's outside.

I take another sip of water and shake out my arms and legs, which are sore from all of the running I did earlier, which I'm officially not going to think about anymore. In the past.

When I get to the bottom of the steps, I pause before I open the door.

I wonder if he'll kiss me.

I open the door.

There he is.

"I'm selling encyclopedias," he says.

"Yeah?" I say.

"Yeah," he says. "I've got J, W and, I think, U? I'll have to check on that."

"Please. I'm most interested in you."

"See what I did there?" he asks, grinning. He has a dimple. I forgot about the dimple.

How could I forget about the dimple? I want to stick my finger in it. Have I ever done that before? How could I not?

Was it always there? Is it new?

He looks different. I don't know if he's changed or if he was altered in my memory.

"Did you spend the whole drive coming up with the setup for that line?" I ask.

"Just the last hour," he says.

"Come in," I tell him, moving aside so he can step into the stairway. He begins to climb, and I follow behind him, examining his butt on the way up.

It's a good butt. The butt I remember.

"It's nice up here," he says. "Quaint."

"You mean upstate?"

He opens the door to my apartment and steps inside. It's strange to see him in this space. Two lives colliding. He looks around, nodding.

"Yeah," he says, setting his backpack down on the coffee table. "Upstate. Your apartment. Very nice."

"You want something to drink?" I ask him. "Water?"

"Yeah, I'll have some water. Bathroom?"

"That door right there," I say, pointing.

I leave him to it, heading into the kitchen to get him some water. As I'm reaching for a glass, I notice there's a spider on the shelf. It's a small one, much smaller than Ralph, even at his normal size. The spider stays perfectly still.

"Don't worry," I tell it. "You can stay here."

It doesn't acknowledge my presence.

I'm suddenly stricken with a profound devastation over Ralph's absence. I miss him. The thought of never seeing him again, it weakens my knees. Literally weakens them. I have to lean against the counter to keep myself standing.

"You okay?" Sam asks. He's behind me.

"Yeah," I say. "I went running this morning. My legs are sore."

"Remember when we used to go running?"

"Yeah," I say, "I remember."

I fill the glass and hand it to him. He drinks it down, then puts the empty glass in the sink.

"So," he says, "this is where you've been."

"This is where I've been," I repeat. Somehow, I didn't anticipate reuniting with my ex being so awkward.

I'm amazed by my own mind. What it's able to accept. What it's able to overlook.

I stare at the empty glass in the sink. I hate myself.

"I'm tired," Sam says, yawning.

"You want some coffee? There's a place nearby." I realize as soon as the words leave my mouth that I can't just go waltzing back into town, into the Good Mug. Oskar might try to stone me in the street.

The thought yields a surge of empathy for Sophie. I mean, didn't she say she was thrown down the well? That couldn't have been fun. And she's alluded to worse. Attempted drownings, watching her friends get burned at the stake. What must it have been like to be ostracized and attacked, harassed, villainized?

I realize I don't know what she's been through. So much of her past is unknown to me. I think back to all the times I caught her staring off into the distance, all the times she went quiet, lost in thought.

I've been so preoccupied by my own pain; not once did I ever stop to consider hers.

"Nah," Sam says, sauntering over to the window, perusing the yard. "Just got here. I want to stay here."

"Okay," I say. I should be relishing the sweet relief that Sam doesn't want to leave the apartment, but I'm still thinking about Sophie.

Am I being hypocritical? I made Dan spit bones when he was being a jerk to me at dinner. I didn't mean to, but I did it. What would I do if someone seriously tried to hurt me?

Is it really so wrong to stand up for yourself? To punish those who deserve it, maybe take a little revenge?

"You got any food?"

"Oh, yeah," I say, trying to shake Sophie out of my head. "Sorry."

"What you got?"

"I could make you a sandwich," I say.

"Tell me more about this sandwich."

We end up eating chicken-and-tomato sandwiches while sitting at the table in total silence. I give him my crusts, and he eats them.

The only thing worse than the excruciating lack of conversation is the fact that now instead of thinking about Sophie, I'm back to thinking about Ralph. I can't stop picturing his cute, fuzzy little face. His delightful smile.

"So," Sam says, wiping a crumb from his bottom lip, "this is weird."

"Yeah," I say, "just a bit."

He laughs. It's dull and polite.

I need to get my head in the game. If this is a test, I'm failing. I need to do something to show him that I'm worth loving.

"I think we could make it work," I say. "I think we should give it another shot. I'll try harder. I'll be better. Tell me what I need to fix, and I'll do it."

He laughs that laugh again. It's a sterile laugh.

"What?" I ask.

"Nothing. It's just . . . I've been thinking a lot about us. Our relationship. When anyone asked me, when I told my parents, I always said that we broke up because we were more like friends than like a couple. But lately, I wonder why that was a bad thing, you know?"

"I know."

My anxiety begins to evaporate, to fizz away like an Alka-Seltzer tablet dissolving into fine grains of nothing.

He sighs. "I should have said something sooner. We could have talked about it."

"Yeah," I say. I should leave it at that, a simple agreement. But my time with Sophie has encouraged both confidence and the desire to seek what I believe I deserve. And I have a question that I want answered. So I ask it. "Why didn't you?"

"Why didn't I what? Talk to you about it sooner? I don't know. It's a hard subject. How was I supposed to bring it up? Just out of the blue say, 'Hey, can we not wear our pajamas all the time?'"

This disrupts the ascent of hope.

"Yeah," I say, "I get it."

"Obviously that's not the best way to put it. But you wore pajamas a lot," he says.

"I did," I say.

It's true. I wore pajamas a lot. I didn't realize. I didn't know.

"I wanted to ask you not to, but it felt like a dick thing to say," he says. "It's hard to be attracted to someone in pajamas."

"They make sexy pajamas," I say, looking down at my lap. I turn my fingers into the itsy-bitsy spider, climbing, climbing. I really miss Ralph. "I guess I should have invested in sexy pajamas. Would have saved me a lot of trouble in the long run. If you'd asked, I would have gotten them."

"Please don't take it the wrong way. I'm not saying it's all on you. I did things, too. Or didn't do them. I didn't make time for you. I didn't take you out on dates. I could have taken you out on dates. Had a date night or something. That just seemed like—I don't know—an old-person thing to do. To have a designated date night. I don't know. I don't want you to think I'm blaming you."

"No, no," I say. "I don't."

Why do I work so hard to appease him? It's exhausting. I'm so quick to kowtow to his every need. Was it always like this?

"It happens, I guess. You get comfortable, stop putting in that effort. If we could work out that part of it. Be *with* each other again, like we were at the beginning. I think it'd help us figure out if we should get back together."

"You want to get back together?" I ask, and I hear it in the pitch of my voice. A flimsy, pathetic hope.

I know if he says yes, it's a done deal. I'll pack my shit, quit my job. I'll go back to the city with him. I'll stay with him as long as he'll have me.

A few months ago, I would have been able to do that without any doubts, without any modicum of shame. But now, turns out the idea of abandoning my new life just because he asks me to completely vandalizes the sense of self I've been slowly and painstakingly assembling.

"If," Sam says, and I feel like Wile E. Coyote looking up to see the anvil about to fall on his head. "If we're able to be with each other again. Get back to how it was."

"Right," I say. "Can you be more specific?"

"Let's just hang out for a while," he says. "Remember when we'd lie in bed for hours and just hang out?"

"Yeah," I say, "I remember everything."

"Everything?"

"Yep."

"What'd we do on our third date?"

"We got dollar slices, then went to Sly Fox and split a pitcher of beer."

"They should study you," he says. "Let's sit on the couch."

It's strange to be near him again. I imagine it's like returning to your childhood home as an adult. The comfort and nostalgia eclipsed by the distortion of the dimensions. You remember it being bigger than it is. Because you're bigger than you were.

"This really is a nice place," he says. "You like it here?"

I shrug. If he'd asked me, say, eight days ago, my answer would have been yes. I would have said the people are nice, a little strange, quirky but endearing. My apartment is great; maybe I wish the bathroom were a little bigger, but it's otherwise perfect. I'm minutes away from amazing coffee, and when the weather is warm, there's a farmers market every Saturday. And I have a caring, smart, funny friend. A friend who saw something in me that no one else ever did. *Not even you.*

But . . . a lot can change in a matter of days.

"How's work?" he asks.

I tell him about my job, about how the pushy vice principal set me up on a blind double date. I tell him because I want to see how he'll react. If he'll get jealous.

"How'd it go?" he asks.

I consider sugarcoating, but instead I say, "Bad."

I tell him about Pascal, whom I describe as having the personality and general vibe of a ventriloquist's dummy sans ventriloquist.

"He barely said a word the entire night."

"Was he a creep?"

"If he had any defining personality traits, maybe, but he didn't. It was pretty incredible."

I tell him about Dan, about how he was rude and obnoxious. I say he choked on his food and someone had to come perform the Heimlich. I don't know how I invent this alternate history so easily. I guess when telling the truth isn't an option, lies will always be there. They're opportunists. They're dandelions.

"It was this awful German-themed restaurant," I say.

"No," Sam says, "I don't believe you."

"I swear," I say. "Beer steins everywhere. Everywhere."

"Yodeling?" he asks.

"No yodeling. Is yodeling German?"

We ask the Internet. We fall down weird rabbit holes. Soon we're looking up conspiracy theories about the Dyatlov Pass incident.

"Yeti," he says. "All evidence points to yeti."

I'd laugh him off, but . . . who's to say what's real and what isn't? Certainly not me.

"This is it," he says. "This is what I missed."

"Discussing the mysterious deaths of Russian hikers?" I ask.

"No," he says. "Discussing the mysterious deaths of Russian hikers with *you*."

I feel a swell of affection for him. When we were together, everything was simple. I knew who I was, what I wanted. I ache for that sense of certainty. With Sam, I know exactly what my future looks like. There's nothing scary about it. Nothing unknown.

I lean across the couch and kiss him.

I forgot what it is like to kiss. I forget how. My tongue remains limp in my mouth, suddenly heavy and inert, like a walrus on a rock. He prods at it with his. He has a very warm tongue. Very agile. I wait for some kind of rhythm, an implicit understanding of what should go where when, but it doesn't come. It's a clumsy exchange.

I pull away, wiping my bottom lip.

"You smell different," he says into my neck.

"Do you like it?" I ask.

"I liked your old perfume."

"Oh," I say. It bothers me probably more than it should. I know he doesn't mean anything by it, but I like this scent. I chose it myself.

"You smell good," he says. "Don't worry."

I wasn't worried.

"Here, I brought you something," he says, opening his backpack and gifting me a license plate key chain with my name on it.

It's a goofy gift, but I like goofy gifts.

"I'm going to ask you something," I say. "And I don't want you to be offended. But did you get this on the way here?"

"I'm offended," he says. "I'm so offended."

He kisses me.

Is this what I've been missing?

Is this what I've spent so much time mourning the loss of?

I wait for a sensation to travel through me, something warm and effervescent. I wait and wait, but I don't feel it. I don't feel anything. Except his wet tongue as it slips in and out of my mouth.

No, I tell myself. *Stop. Focus. You want this. This is what you want, what you've always wanted.*

"I made cookies," I say, breaking out of the kiss.

"Did you?" he asks.

"Yep, let me get them," I say, absconding into the kitchen.

I arrange the cookies on a plate and pour two glasses of milk.

I shoo my doubt. I tell myself repeatedly, *You want this. This is what you want. You want him. A life with him.*

When I bring the cookies out, he says, "Be honest. Did you really make these, or did you buy them and put them on a plate?"

"I made them," I say, annoyed.

"Was just a joke," he says, putting his hands up. "Relax."

"I made them for you," I say in disbelief. I spent my time—time I could have spent doing anything else—measuring flour, sugar, vanilla, cracking eggs, watching the oven to make sure the cookies didn't burn. And just now I got up. I brought them to him with milk. And he doesn't even care. He's eating one like it's nothing. Like they just magically appeared. Not so much as a thank-you.

Has he ever thanked me?

"I'm really happy," he says, licking some chocolate from the corner of his mouth. "This is what was missing. Us being together. Being present with each other. Paying attention. Gestures."

He helps himself to another cookie.

What he missed was me revolving my entire world around him. He broke up with me, and I took fucking turns with him sleeping on the futon.

I was always present. I was always paying attention, always making gestures. I never stopped. He just started taking it for granted.

And maybe I wasn't in lingerie every night; maybe I did spend some weekends sleeping in and binge-watching TV in sweats and no makeup, my hair a mess. Maybe I had the audacity to be human.

Only I'm not human.

Not really.

"These are amazing," he says. "You're amazing."

He slips his hand onto my thigh, and I study his face. I realize now he hasn't changed. Nothing about him has changed. He doesn't look any different, but I see him differently.

Because he hurt me, and I'll never look at him the same.

"I still love you," he says. "I never stopped. I want you back in my life."

Before I can process, before I can form thoughts or words, he kisses me.

Suddenly, he's on top of me. His hands are quick and busy.

"I've missed you so much," he breathes into my ear.

I take a deep inhale to calm myself and clear my mind, but Sam interprets this as an indicator of pleasure and grabs a fistful of my hair.

"Stop."

"What?" he asks.

The old me would have just gone with it, done whatever he wanted. Endured, hoped for enjoyment or, if that didn't come, for it to end quickly.

I wonder how much of a woman's life is spent this way. Enduring. Waiting for enjoyment or, fuck it, death.

"Stop," I say. He lets go of my hair, not quite understanding my demand. I pull my arms out from under him and push him back. "Stop. I don't want this. It's not what I want."

He gets off of me. His hair is messy, his eyes stark. It's an alarmingly similar feeling to that of staring directly into the sunken eyes of a ghost.

Sophie was right. It's too late now.

I know what it's like not to have to endure. I know what it's like to manifest things through sheer force of will. I've smashed teacups, broken glass, forced bones into someone's mouth. I've made these things happen with my mind. Manipulated the physical world with my thoughts, with my desires.

There's no going back to Sam. To sitting at the kitchen table in the morning eating eggs and joking around, all the while wondering what he wants from me, how I can make him happy.

"I'm sorry," I tell him.

"I don't understand," he says, literally scratching his head.

I stand up.

There's something new pulsing through me. Or not new. Awakened. An electricity. A vibrance. There's glitter in my veins.

"I don't want this," I tell him. "I don't want you anymore."

The look on his face is so delicious I could eat it. I could eat it in one bite.

"I think you should go," I say. "I'll give you a minute."

I walk into the bathroom, closing the door behind me so I can take a moment to admire myself. I linger in a reciprocal gaze with my reflection.

We're smiling.

"Tell me the truth," I say to her.

She does.

You must surrender everything for everything.

"I'm ready now," I tell her. "I surrender."

I surrender, she says back.

It's transcendent. An injection of straight sunshine. Pure fucking gold. It binds bone and sinew. It's in me; it's of me. It's me, it's me, it's me, it's me.

I don't know how much time passes, but when I open the bathroom door, Sam's no longer on the couch. I don't see him, but I hear him.

He's talking to someone.

"Just guy stuff . . . Yeah . . . Yeah . . . Miss you, too. Tomorrow night? Yeah, but make reservations. They're always crowded. . . . Okay . . . Me, too. Bye."

"Who was that?" I ask. But I already know.

He's standing in the kitchen with his phone in his hand. Guilty.

"Annie," he says, "are you all right?"

"I'm fine," I say. "Actually, I'm feeling pretty incredible."

For the first time in our relationship, I'm in control. And what makes it extra sweet is that he knows it. He's squirming in the corner.

"Ow," he says. "What's happening?"

His legs give out from underneath him, and he falls to the floor.

"You're still with her, huh?" I say "Shannon."

"Annie, what's happening?"

I ease up, and he stops his wriggling.

"You didn't break up with her before coming to see me, did you? Tell me the truth," I say, reaching out my hand and pinching the air.

He screams, clutching his kneecap.

I release my fingers.

"No," he cries. "I'm sorry."

"Insurance," I say. "Smart. In case things didn't work out with us, you wouldn't end up alone."

"I wanted you," he says. "I wanted things to work out between us— *Ahhh!*"

This, this I'm not doing intentionally.

He's writhing around on the floor, his limbs twitching madly, his face gravely distorted. There's blood coming out of his eyes. Not in neat drops, not in tears, but in a steady stream.

"Annie!" he screams. Blood begins to spray from his mouth now, too.

I close my eyes and take deep, unhurried breaths. If I can calm down, maybe I can make it stop. But . . . it's hard to let go of my animosity at the moment. It's hard not to torture him when it's so easy. When I can.

I open my eyes, and he's turning a pale blue color. I admire it for a second, the color, before realizing he might be dying. I might be killing him.

With that, he scrambles to his hands and knees, wheezing.

I allow him to catch his breath. He manages to pull himself up and prop himself against the fridge.

"What the fuck?" he keeps saying. "What the fuck?"

"I gave you so much of myself," I say, "and you wasted me."

His face. Such pure, exquisite horror. Such fear.

I don't mind. He fears me because he is small. I will not meet him there. I will not shrink myself down to his size, or anyone else's, for their comfort. For their appeasement.

I actually find it kind of amusing, his fear. Kind of funny. It's making me laugh.

I laugh.

No.

I cackle.

"I believe we're done here," I tell him. "Leave."

He rushes, tripping over himself as he grabs his backpack.

"Sam," I say.

He turns to me, a nervous glance over his shoulder.

"You never told me if you liked my hair."

I go on cackling, though he doesn't seem to find it too humorous. I guess that's fair.

"Good-bye," I tell him. "And thank you."

With that, he's gone.

"Well," I say to myself, listening to the sound of his car speeding out of the driveway, "there goes my dark fate."

And I know now. I'm finally free of doubt. I'm so glad I'm not with him in that car. I'm exactly where I'm meant to be.

Exactly who I'm meant to be.

What I'm meant to be.

LET'S PRETEND IT NEVER HAPPENED

The night sky is smeared with stars, glowing vigorously from far, far away. I count them with the eyes on top of my head. I walk these familiar woods buoyed by the thrill of my transformation. Otherwise, I might be too afraid.

There's a decent chance she'll refuse to see me. Or worse. But . . . I think it's worth the risk.

She's a good friend to me, and I could be a good friend to her, though I don't need her. I know that now. I understand. I don't *need* anyone. I never did.

I spent so much time searching outside of myself.

It's so funny to me now.

Sophie opens the door before I can knock. She's wearing a black velvet robe. Her hair is in loose, delicate curls. Her arms are crossed over her chest and Ralph is on her shoulder. He waves at me, but then Sophie shoots him a look and he promptly restrains himself.

"Did I not tell you never to come back?" she asks.

"You did," I say. "But I came back anyway."

She lifts her chin. "Yes. I can see that."

"I want to apologize," I say. "I also want to tell you that you were wrong. It was wrong for you to try to stop me and to give me an ultimatum. I needed to see him. I needed to make the decision for myself."

"And what decision is that, Annie?"

"I've evolved past him," I say.

She uncrosses her arms and begins to inspect her manicure. Her nails are now restored to their typical state of perfection.

"Go on," she says.

"Can I come in?"

She pauses to consider.

"You said you wanted to apologize," she says. "But you didn't."

"I'm sorry, Sophie. I really am."

"All right, then," she says, moving out of the way so I can enter. "Would you like some tea?"

IT'S MY PARTY

There are yellow roses. Hundreds of yellow roses all around my room. Ralph is on my nightstand in a stripy conical hat. He's got a tiny party horn in his mouth.

"Good morning, Ralph."

He blows the party horn and wiggles his little legs.

"I know, I know," I tell him. "Thank you."

There's a large box at the foot of my bed. It's tied with yellow satin ribbon. I yawn, flop over and pull it toward me.

"Is this from you?" I ask Ralph.

He deflates, shakes his head no.

"That's okay," I tell him. "Your presence is my present."

He holds his cheeks.

I tug gently at the ribbon and undo the neat bow. I set the satin aside, folding it up and placing it behind me on my pillow.

I open the box. Inside is a new dress. A birthday dress. It's a pale yellowy gold, with lacy sleeves and a corset back.

I put it on immediately. I admire myself in the full-length mirror. I run my hands over the fabric, over my body, over my skin. My face. My brilliant nose. My pretty eyes. My ample cheeks.

I get my hairbrush. It has a thin silver handle engraved with flowers.

I carefully lower myself to my knees, making sure the dress doesn't wrinkle. I fan it out around me. Then I brush my hair.

I never used to take the time to brush my hair, but it really makes all the difference.

Ralph is still blowing his party horn.

"You don't have to keep doing that," I tell him. "Save some energy for the party."

He gets in one more blow before letting the horn fall from his mouth. He then crawls into bed and takes a quick nap.

I check the time, and it's disappointingly early. I change out of my dress and back into my pajamas. I make myself toast and a mimosa. I watch a reality TV show marathon about women trying on wedding dresses.

"They're so excited for one day in a pretty dress," I say. "Someone really should tell them. They can wear a pretty dress whenever they want."

Ralph grunts. He's annoyed that I've woken him with my bullshit.

"Women are out there tethering themselves to mediocre men just so they can wear a ball gown. It's a shame."

He grunts again.

"Okay, sorry, sorry," I say. "I'll shut up."

Ever reliable, the TV has eaten away the hours. I thank it and blink to turn it off. I leave my dirty dishes in the sink.

I'm not going to do dishes on my birthday.

And besides, they can take care of themselves.

I put my dress back on. My shadow laces the corset. Ralph helps, too. He doesn't contribute much, but he's a good boy; he tries.

I feed him dead flies out of the palm of my hand.

"Few more minutes," I tell him as I step into the bathroom to put on some makeup. Lately, I don't wear much, because I've come to realize that I don't need much, but it's a special occasion. And it's fun to wear lipstick.

As I lean in close to the mirror, dragging the tube across my bottom lip, I'm afflicted with a very specific memory of putting on lipstick before a dinner date with Sam. It was maybe four years ago. We were just going to our usual place around the corner from our apartment, but I decided to put on lipstick. When I emerged from the bathroom, he smiled and said, "Look at you."

I haven't thought of him much since his grand exit from my life, but occasionally I'll experience an echo, the phantom sensation of an emotion that I know is expired. Sometimes it'll trick me, and I'll think that I miss him, that I still love him, that I'll never fully amputate him from me. Usually then I count to eight, because I remember once reading about how, after people were beheaded by guillotines, their severed heads could blink and twitch for up to eight seconds.

By the eighth second, I'll have regained my composure and reunited with the truth.

I'm glad to be rid of him.

"Look at you," he said, and I didn't hear it then, but replaying it now, I recognize the hint of condescension.

Condescension, the quiet destroyer. The spot on the lung discovered too late.

"Look at me," I say, marveling at my reflection. "Look at me."

I put Ralph in the front pocket of my dress.

"Ready?" I ask him.

He's got his party hat, his horn. He's so excited he can't stop dancing. I shouldn't have fed him the flies. He'll go crazy for another half an hour and then pass out cold.

I don't bother to lock my apartment anymore. I come and go as I please. Lynn has agreed to let me have the downstairs as well, and soon I'll be able to remodel. I have some ideas. Sophie will help, of course.

The sun is generous in June. It's high and bright despite the hour. It winks at me.

"Stay up as late as you like," I tell it. Ralph thinks I'm talking to him. He does a flip inside my pocket.

"Hi, Annie! Happy birthday!" My neighbors all wait for me at the ends of their driveways, waving as I pass by, wishing me a happy birthday. Some of them hold sparklers.

"Thank you," I tell them. "Thank you so much."

Strange to think that a year ago I was in some random bar in the city taking tequila shots with Nadia, making a wish on a tea light candle.

What did I wish for?

I wished for happiness.

At the time, I thought that meant I was wishing for Sam. It's best not to be specific with wishes. Otherwise, you end up getting what you think you want instead of what you really need. How dangerous.

When I get to Main Street, I pass the Good Mug first. Oskar and Erik stand out front. Erik hands me a bag of coffee beans.

"Happy birthday," he says, smiling. He's a very handsome kid. He's going to cause real misery with that face. Obliterate fragile young hearts.

Oskar says nothing. He stands in the shadow of a streetlamp, half of his face in darkness. The visible half is stern.

I stare at him. If I focus for long enough, he'll be forced to do something.

"Oskar," I say.

He bows his head slightly. Maybe of his own free will or maybe not.

I wait for him to meet my eye. I wait to see if he looks at me the same way he looks at Sophie. But then Rose begins to sing "Happy Birthday," and Deirdre is walking toward me with a giant cupcake.

Everyone on the street joins in except for Oskar, and Tom, who is hiding behind a bottle of syrup with a bow on top, which I assume is my present.

The crowd harmonizes in a big finale and then erupts in applause.

"Here you are," Deirdre says, bestowing me with the cupcake.

"Thank you," I say. "I don't want it right now but thank you."

"I'll save it for you," she says. She backs away from me, vaguely flustered. "I'm sorry."

"That's all right," I tell her. "It was really nice of you to make it for me. I just don't want to eat it right now."

There was a time when I would have eaten it anyway, because it seemed the polite thing to do, because I was too afraid of hurting someone's feelings.

Imagine.

I receive more gifts. The syrup. A book. A necklace. A bottle of wine. A jar of jam. A basket to carry all of my presents.

The crowd continues to clap for me as I make my way to the gazebo.

I cut through the field, which is crowded with empty tents. I follow the sidewalk, pass the playground.

"Annie," Sophie says, "happy birthday!"

She has decorated the gazebo with thousands of flowers. Roses and peonies and lilacs. Snapdragons and spiral eucalyptus and carnations and thistle. Ranunculus. There are candles and sparkly lights. And she stands in the center of it all, wearing a dress that matches mine. Only hers is dark purple.

"You look beautiful," she says. "You like the dress?"

"I love it," I tell her. "Thank you."

"Come sit. I've set us up a little birthday picnic. Bread and cheese and figs and roast chicken and wine. Lots of wine."

She's put a table in the middle of the gazebo. It's covered with a black lace tablecloth. The food is beautifully arranged, and she's brought glass goblets for the wine. I climb the steps, and she greets me with an embrace.

"It's fun to celebrate birthdays," she says. "Make sure you write it down. Otherwise, you'll forget it eventually."

"That's good advice," I tell her.

I sit on a stool and let Ralph climb out of my pocket and onto my lap.

I try to feed him a bit of chicken, but he's not hungry. He's overexcited; he can't stop fidgeting. I close my hand and summon a compact mirror. I prop it open on the table and lift him up so he can admire himself in his party hat. This should occupy him for a while.

Sophie pours the wine and begins to scoop pomegranate seeds onto her plate, adding slices of bread and cheese.

"Go on, Annie," she says. "Birthday banquet."

I tear off a piece of bread and begin to nibble. I don't have much of an appetite. Maybe I'm overexcited, too. Something tumbles in my gut.

"What a special year it's been," Sophie says. "We met. Became friends. We fought. We made up. It's been such a privilege to witness your transformation, Annie. So wonderful to be your friend."

She raises her goblet to me.

"Thank you, Sophie," I say, clinking her glass with mine. I sip my wine.

There's a small crystal bowl filled with blackberries. I take a few and eat them out of my hand.

"It's such a rare thing," she says. She's staring off into the distance somewhere beyond me.

I turn around. There are only woods there. Only twilight.

"What?" I ask her.

"This. Our friendship. You."

I nod. "I don't know where I'd be without you, Soph. I owe it all to you. Honestly, I do."

"Nonsense," she says.

"It's true," I say. "If it weren't for you, I'd be somewhere feeling sorry for myself. Feeling powerless, hopeless. Or worse. I'd be in a relationship with someone who was slowly sucking the life out of me without me even realizing, thinking it was what I wanted."

I take another sip of wine. I hold my goblet. I like the way the cool etched glass feels in my hand.

"When I was young, I used to pick out my cereal based on the prizes advertised on the box. I'd eat all the cereal, and then I'd get to the prize, and it'd never be as good as how it looked on the box. And I would have eaten all this cereal I didn't even like just to get this disappointing, dinky little toy or whatever. I've been thinking about it a lot lately. About how that could have been my whole life. I would have been an old woman somewhere, wrinkled as a raisin, realizing I'd spent all my good years eating shitty cereal for an unsatisfactory prize."

"Mm," Sophie says. "I've never had cereal."

I laugh. "Really?"

"I'm glad you see now," she says, "what I'd been trying to tell you all along."

"I do," I say. "I'm so happy. The happiest."

"Oh, Annie, to think! We'll be able to celebrate so many more of your birthdays together. So many you'll lose count."

She reaches across the table and wraps her hand around my wrist, her fingers stroking the soft valley of veins, feeling the gentle surf of my pulse. Her amber eyes drip with affection.

I lift my glass. "Another toast!"

She raises hers. Ralph perks up and begins to parade around the table.

"To the years ahead," I say. "To the future."

And what a thing it is to know.

My future is my own.

EPILOGUE

I don't leave the house now without flowers in my hair. Today, the first day of October, of a year I don't know, I wear a crown of yellow freesia. I amble through the farmers market, eating an apple. It's crisp and pink and delicious. There's another one in my pocket for later. When I'm done, I'll save the seeds. They have many uses.

"Hello, Annie," I hear as I pass by the tents. "Good morning!"

I smile and nod. If I like the person who says it, I'll say "Good morning" back. If I don't, I'll say nothing at all.

"Miss Crane?" A woman dressed in overalls waves at me. She calls me by a name I haven't heard in a long time. "Miss Crane?"

I almost say, *No, I'm not Miss Crane. You're mistaken.* Instead, I say, "Yes."

"It's Madison Thorpe," the woman says. "I was in your class. You wrote me a recommendation letter for college. You let me eat lunch with you sometimes. You were one of my favorite teachers."

I remember her now. The palest blue eyes. She still wears excessive black eyeliner. It settles into her crow's-feet. I wonder how old she is.

"God," she says. "You haven't aged a day."

"Oh, thank you," I tell her. I'm now interested in this conversation. "It's good to see you. How have you been?"

"Eh," she says, shrugging. "Got my bachelor's at Sarah Lawrence, as planned. Then I moved to California. I was out there for a long time. I wanted to get my PhD, but I'm massively in debt and my partner and I recently separated, so . . . I'm back in Aster living with my parents. Which is great, because they're horrified that I'm forty-two and unmarried."

She rolls her eyes, and I remember. She used to have pins on her backpack. She stood up for me once. When they were chirping at me.

"Sorry. I'm vomiting all my problems. Oversharing. Anyway. It's funny. Back then I was convinced we'd be friends if I were a little older. I thought I was so deep, so wise. That I understood life and all its intricacies. I look back and laugh. I must have been insufferable."

"You weren't," I say.

"You were a really great teacher."

I wasn't a great teacher. I was okay at best. But I appreciate the compliment.

I look at her. Her overalls are dirty, paint spattered. Her hair is dark and parted straight down the middle. She's flushed. There's something doll-like about her. An innocence.

She's in pain, of course. She burns with it. It's in the air around her, billowing up past the treetops, up toward the bright morning sun.

"Would you like an apple?" I take it out of my pocket and offer it to her.

She accepts.

"Thanks," she says, and takes a bite. "Would you want to get coffee sometime? I kind of hate everyone else who lives here. I mean, in Aster. Rowan is pretty nice."

"Yes," I say, "I would like that."

She smiles at me, her cheeks fat with apple, her shoulders rising in the posture of a moment's joy.

"Do you mind if I bring a friend?" I ask. "There's someone I'd like you to meet."

ACKNOWLEDGMENTS

Thank you to my stellar agent, Lucy Carson, for absolutely everything. To my brilliant editor, Jessica Wade, for helping me spin my straw. To my publicist, Alexis Nixon, for her savvy and exceptional style. Thank you to the entire dream team at Berkley; you're all so smart and talented and I appreciate the hard work you put into this book so much. All of my gratitude. Thank you, thank you.

Thank you to my mom for sewing me all of those Halloween costumes, and for always encouraging me. Thank you to Maria for the trips to Salem, and to Courtney for the cackles. Thank you to my family and friends for their support; forgive the cliché but it really means the world to me. And thank you to Nic; "Witchy Woman" could still be our song. Love you all.

DISCUSSION QUESTIONS

1. How do you think the novel's title—*Cackle*—is important to the story?
2. What role do you think Annie's early encounter with the fortune-teller serves in the narrative?
3. Do you identify with Annie? Do you think she is a reliable narrator? Does she remind you of anyone in your life?
4. In addition to the magic she learns, how does Annie's relationship with Sophie help her grow as a person? Do you think there are any ways in which the relationship holds her back?
5. How does Sophie's portrayal as a witch in this book compare with other depictions of famous witches in TV, film, and literature? What do you think the author would say about the notion of "good witches" and "bad witches" and why powerful women have been persecuted for so long?
6. When you think back on the book, what scene, description, or plot development stands out to you as the most memorable?
7. Sophie tells Annie that she doesn't believe in fate because it's one of the "myriad of ways we're conditioned to passivity. Women, especially." Does that idea resonate with you?
8. Were you surprised by the ending? Do you identify with Annie's choices? What do you think you would have done in her position?